SECOND MOON

KURT WINANS

BOOK TWO OF **THE NEW WORLD** SERIES

Livonia, Michigan

Story concept by Brian Schaber and Kurt Winans

SECOND MOON

Published by Indigo
an imprint of BHC Press

Library of Congress Control Number:
2017936686

ISBN-13: 978-1-946006-96-7
ISBN-10: 1-946006-96-3

Visit the author at:
www.kurtwinans.com &
www.bhcpress.com

ALSO BY KURT WINANS

THE NEW WORLD

Pilgrimage
(Book One)

Evolution Shift
(Book Three)

TO THE REPUBLIC

Fractured Nation
(Book One)

TRAVEL BOOKS

College Football's American Road Trip

ACKNOWLEDGEMENTS

With good cause, I mentioned a handful of people that were helpful with the prequel to this book. As *Pilgrimage* was the first segment of this ongoing saga, it is fitting that those same kindhearted souls assisted with *Second Moon*. I would therefore like to acknowledge them again for their efforts, and I can easily foresee their collective influence during preparation with the upcoming third segment and beyond.

First, there is my wife Cathy. As always, she provided the strength for me to carry on with this endeavor. Her faith and patience were an inspiration. Brian and I, as during work on the previous segment, discussed and shaped the content of the storyline. We met regularly with intent to escape the bonds of traditional thinking, and developed concepts that were both interesting and thought provoking. Good friends Karl and Ken once again read through rough drafts, and offered suggestions or asked questions if certain aspects were unclear. Renée was also involved with that same process, but she took it a step further. Her additional insight and observations were important aspects as polish to the finished product.

Thank you all for being there,
Kurt

SECOND MOON

CHAPTER ONE

FORWARD TO YESTERYEAR

Janet had never received such a greeting in her entire life. She was standing face to face with two people that were clearly much older than her current age of thirty-four, yet they were supposedly her children. Although the complexity of that possibility was fascinating, it was also shocking. The man, who claimed to be her son Ross, stood proud and tall a few inches over six feet in height. He was admittedly handsome, and his facial features and gray hair resembled those of an older version of her husband Robert. The elegant woman next to him, with the beautiful smile, claimed to be her daughter Jessica. Janet was pleased with the woman's appearance, because if she was her daughter, then she provided Janet with a glimpse of what she herself might look like many years from now. A glance downward then revealed a leg brace on the woman's right leg. Janet asked herself, could this truly be her precious little girl.

After all that Janet had been through, it was certainly not beyond the realm of possibility. Although the implication was daunting to mentally absorb during the first few minutes after being introduced,

Janet knew that if their claim were true, then this wasn't the first time she had met either of them.

Janet asked them each a few questions about their father, Robert, and then a few additional questions about their early childhood in an attempt to verify their supposed identity. Although it was true that most of the information about Robert could have been researched, it was unlikely that some of the minute details they were discussing would have become public knowledge. With each precise response to her inquiries, the unbelievable became more acceptable to Janet. These two people might actually be her children.

Janet's inquiries then turned to what they knew about her own disappearance, as she asked, "What were each of you told about what happened to me?"

Their responses, which included the shocking revelation that came from their father on his deathbed, made all doubts vanish as a warm-hearted feeling washed over Janet. With misty eyes she extended her arms, and Ross and Jessica stepped into her embrace.

A moment later that silent embrace was broken when Janet said, "I want to know everything that has happened to you since I've been away."

Ross assured her that he and Jessica would fill her in, and field all her questions in due time, but it could wait until after she told them her story.

It all began on a warm central Texas summer night in 1957 and Janet remembered every detail vividly. At the time, her abduction seemed beyond comprehension. One minute she was in the back seat of her family's white station wagon with the red stripe on each side fetching some extra blankets for the campsite. Suddenly an intensely bright light enveloped the area immediately surrounding the car, and she was unable to move anything below her neck as the car mysteriously began to levitate. She screamed for Robert to help her, and several seconds later distinctively heard him calling for her to jump out of the car. She tried with all her might to move her arms and legs, but it was no use. Somehow the bright light, or something else, had paralyzed her.

Then the area around her suddenly became completely dark when the station wagon had become engulfed within a hovering spacecraft. That was just the beginning of what Janet termed "a wild ride". She must have lost consciousness for a short time, because her next memory was that of lying flat on a table. She was still unable to move except for turning her head from side to side, and at that moment she began hearing voices in her head. Those voices informed her that she would not be harmed, but she found that information to be of little comfort. Although rapid and shallow due to the circumstances, breathing was not a problem. The air around her was comfortably warm and somewhat humid, almost matching the conditions of the campsite somewhere below. A bright cone shaped beam from directly overhead was the lone source of light within the room, and it only illuminated the area immediately surrounding the table.

Uncertain of exactly how much time had elapsed, she was startled to see four alien creatures suddenly emerge from the darkness and take positions near each corner of the table. Although she could not see any of their mouths move, she could hear and understand each of their thoughts clearly in her head. She thought the creatures looked familiar somehow, and then remembered the bodies she had caught a few brief glimpses of back at Roswell in 1947. To her it seemed likely that these alien beings were of the same species, but she couldn't be certain. In the midst of asking several questions of her own, she verbally responded to a few that she heard in her mind. After several minutes of moving her head from side to side in an attempt to study them, the creatures turned and moved away as quickly as they had appeared into the darkness that surrounded her.

At that moment she noticed an interesting feature on the back of one of the alien's heads before it disappeared from view, and her training as a former nurse made her wonder if it was a normal aspect of their anatomy. She was then once again left alone for an unknown amount of time to contemplate her destiny, while she remained hopelessly paralyzed on the table.

Janet stopped her story for a moment and asked, "Do the two of you really want to hear all of this?"

As Ross and Jessica nodded positively with anticipation, Ross said, "Yes. Please tell us everything."

She continued by stating that her next memory was of light suddenly pouring into the dark room, as a doorway opened along a portion of a distant wall. She once again heard a voice in her head instructing her to rise from the table, and use the doorway to exit. After testing her mobility by slowly raising her right arm, she quickly realized that she could stand from the low lying table of her own free will. Understanding that in her current situation she was completely powerless to resist the will of the alien species, she complied with the instructions given to her and moved toward the doorway. She emerged from the spacecraft to discover that she had somehow been transported to the inside area of a much larger alien vessel. Within that vessel, there were humans of multiple ethnic backgrounds from various locations on Earth living in peaceful captivity.

She assumed that she must have been the most recent of the abductees, for she was immediately approached by other humans who wanted to know what significant events had been taking place on Earth since the time of their own abductions. She met people from various times in recent Earth history, and began to realize that the alien species had been visiting and studying Earth for nearly two centuries. She tried to wrap her brain around everything that was happening, as she witnessed humans and alien creatures mingling about and communicating with one another.

Her series of questions toward them revealed that there had been no acts of mistreatment by the alien species toward humans, or heinous medical experiments performed, but the humans could not leave the vessel. The only glimpse that she, or the other abductees, would ever have of the outside world was through a series of viewing windows much like the one that was currently behind Ross and Jessica. Unfortunately that view consisted only of pitch black water. She learned from the alien species that the giant vessel she was held captive on was, at the time, resting on the floor of what was known on Earth as the deep southern Atlantic Ocean.

When she had been lying on the table unable to move her arms and legs during transport to the vessel, she had lots of time to think. She had initially wondered if she was chosen because of accidentally seeing the bodies of similar looking aliens a few times at Roswell in 1947. She knew that she had nothing to do with those three dead pilots or the supposed crash of their spaceship, so that line of reasoning seemed rather sketchy. It appeared unlikely now that she had been grouped with what she guessed to be a few hundred other abductees.

As for her human counterparts, each new encounter seemed to always begin with their question to her of, "What year was it when you were taken?" That was usually followed by a discouraging realization of just how long each of them had been held in captivity. Some abductees, whose clothing style suggested they had been held captive for close to, or more than, a century, seemed to have a quiet peacefulness with regard to her response. That was probably due to accepting the likelihood that all of their friends and loved ones had passed away long ago.

Four very important facts about her new life on board the deep water vessel suddenly became apparent to her. First, she had been thrust into, at least until some new abductee came along, the role of the teacher. She, like those before her, would need to fill in the gaps of Earth history for those who hadn't been around to see, hear, or read about it as it unfolded. Second, it appeared that she would now age very slowly. She had already met a few people that had been aboard the alien vessel for over one hundred years, and they looked to be younger than she was. Third, there would be no escaping the captivity, as it was abundantly clear to her that the alien species was far more technologically advanced than her own. If they had taken, and held, some of the people around her for well over a century, then she would be one of their captives for as long as they wanted to keep her. That led to the fourth fact, which was perhaps the most unsettling. She realized she would probably never see her husband Robert or their two children Ross and Jessica ever again.

In retrospect, she realized that the supposed quiet peacefulness associated with some of the humans she had recently met, was in reality a complete numbness of the senses and a resignation to their plight. She vowed at that moment to become not just a teacher, but a student as well. She had the rare opportunity to learn from people who had actually lived some of the history that she had read about throughout the years, while informing those same people of the more current events. In time, the process would be reversed as she would converse with future abductees. She felt that could be a useful way to become more educated and to occupy her time, while also attempting to avoid the resignation that others displayed. It would be challenging, but she was determined to keep a hopeful and positive attitude that the alien species would someday allow her to be reunited with her family.

Another realization for her was that each day on the alien ship was significantly longer in Earth time. What seemed to be only hours or days to her and the rest of the abductees, was in reality years. Although the exact ratio was still unknown to her, she did have a rough estimate. A series of discussions with more recent abductees from various years had proven her thesis. She knew that the millennium of 2000 had come and gone, and was also aware that she had passed her personal fifty year mark as a guest of the alien species. That was verified when she met a young woman, with extremely low fitting blue jeans, who was abducted in the fall of 2007. She had counted seventy-nine days since her abduction when the vessel rose from the deep ocean floor to the surface and took flight, but was unaware of the actual year and date. There was one factor that could have altered her count of captive days significantly. She did not know how much time had passed when she was on the flat table aboard the first alien spaceship that had abducted her. She knew that she had not remained conscious during that entire timeframe, but how long had she been asleep?

Janet once again paused to ask her captive audience, "Shall I continue?"

Without waiting to hear Jessica's response, Ross said, "Of course. You can't possibly stop now!"

Janet looked at Jessica, who nodded in agreement with her brother's sentiment, and resumed her story.

If that amount of time aboard the alien vessel hadn't been enough to endure, then her wild ride would continue as she was taken into outer space. The vessel landed for a brief time on the Moon in a position where the Earth could not be seen. She later learned that was done so the spacecraft could gather personnel and equipment. Then the vessel took off again, and moved into a higher orbital position above the Earth. During that most unbelievable ride, and subsequent time of hovering, it became almost impossible for her to do anything other than gaze out the observation windows. In her opinion, the view of both the Earth and the Moon were far beyond anything that she had ever imagined during her lifetime on the planet surface. She had attempted to calculate the passage of time on Earth as opposed to what ticked by on her own wristwatch, but couldn't do so. The Earth below was spinning quickly like a record on a turntable, and the relative position of the orbiting Moon was visibly changing as well.

To continue the mind altering view of just how small Earth was in the truly big picture of the galaxy, she and many other abductees at the viewing windows could then see twelve large alien transport vessels pull into formation alongside their own vessel. Those ships remained at their station in high Earth orbit for a very brief time before heading toward the planet, while the Moon moved more than half way around the Earth since their arrival. None of the abductees had a clue as to why the other ships had come, but there was speculation that the spaceships were headed toward the planet surface to abduct a large quantity of human specimens. She then heard, like many times before, a voice in her head assuring her that was not the case. The next aspect to the wild ride was when she was singled out by the aliens to be transferred onto a small three seated scout ship. Once on board and en route to this vessel, she learned that she was to meet two other humans, who had supposedly volunteered to come with the aliens into outer space.

Janet concluded her recollection of the events since her abduction by pointing toward Ross and Jessica while saying, "The two of you are those so called volunteers, and imagine my surprise to discover that you could be my children!"

There seemed to be a reasonable amount of evidence to show that Janet was indeed their mother, but it had not yet been proven. Before either Ross or Jessica could verbally respond, the alien projected his thoughts into their minds as well as Janet's. They learned that the alien species advanced computer system had already verified that Janet was indeed the mother of the other two humans. As an abductee, Janet had been fully scanned for DNA without ever knowing it when she was motionless on the table. Ross and Jessica, along with all the other humans on the transport vessels, had been scanned as they passed through the multiple doorways when they first came aboard. The computers had run a series of compatibility tests with the samples, and found that Ross and Jessica were the offspring of a long term abductee aboard the deep water vessel. They also learned that there were a few other unlikely cases of family DNA aboard the transport vessels that had been discovered during the compatibility tests. Those humans were currently being reunited in the same way that Janet, Ross, and Jessica had been.

The three of them stared at the alien in bewilderment for a long silent moment, and then Janet said, "Your species has the ability to map DNA that easily?"

Ross quickly responded, "So does ours."

He informed the woman who had now been proven to be his missing mother that, "A tremendous amount of medical advancements have taken place on Earth since your days of working as a nurse, and the ability to correctly map DNA was considered one of the most significant."

She looked at Ross and Jessica with a smile, and then said, "Well kids, please pardon me for asking, but what year was it on Earth when we left, and how old are you?"

Ross smiled and replied, "It was late August of 2022 on Earth when we departed, and I turned seventy-two last month."

Jessica hugged Janet again and said, "Mom, I celebrated my sixty-seventh birthday this past January."

Janet held the embrace of her daughter for several seconds, before Ross wrapped his arms around both of them. Then she took a deep breath after quickly calculating the math and said, "Well, since we all celebrated Ross' seventh birthday just a few days before I was abducted, that means slightly more than sixty-five years have passed since I went missing!"

In near perfect harmony Ross and Jessica responded. "Sixty-five years too long."

Janet then added, "So how do I look for a woman that will be one hundred years old in six months?"

CHAPTER TWO

TALES OF DECADES

With a multitude of topics that the three of them needed and wanted to discuss, they all knew it would be time consuming.

Hardly knowing where to begin, Janet finally broke the ice by asking Ross and Jessica, "Can you tell me what happened to all of you after my abduction? Start with Robert please, and then we can get to each of you."

Just then, they once again all heard the thoughts of their host, as the alien was suggesting the four of them could go to a more secluded area of the ship for some privacy. The alien believed he could help answer some questions that Ross and Jessica might have about their mother's experience, and he also wanted to learn more about the complete life of this human family.

After relocating to the same room where he and the alien had discussed the ramifications of the asteroid impact, Ross began to tell the story of his father. Janet learned that Robert never remarried, and her children seemed quite sure that he had also never slept with another woman. Grandpa Hank had come to live with the three of them soon after Janet had supposedly died, and his primary responsibility was to help Robert with the daily challenges that lay ahead. That included the establishment of routines for raising two young children, while also maintaining the cleanliness of the house.

In some regard Janet was pleased to hear that her husband had never found a replacement for her. At the same time, she also realized that Robert's life could have been made easier by having another female influence in his life. It was probably also true that Ross and Jessica had suffered by not having a mother figure, or any other woman, around during their developmental years. They agreed with her assessment that those times had been difficult for them, but Grandpa Hank had been a wonderful and supportive role model for nearly four years before he passed away. Their neighbor, Elizabeth Wright, had also been helpful at times, especially after Hank's death.

Ross and Jessica knew that it would serve no purpose to inform their mother about the darker and less appealing side of Robert's personality during the post 1957 years, so they left it unsaid. Although he had never raised a hand against them or been verbally abusive, he had also never been much of a father figure with the exception of providing food and shelter. They told her he had remained in the Army until the winter of 1973, but had never attained the rank of General. He had actually fallen two steps short of that personal goal, by retiring from the service as a Lieutenant Colonel. Janet also learned that her husband had lived until November of 1985. He had seen both of their children accomplish many things in their respective lives that they would inform her of in due course.

Janet then listened intently to her children as they told her the story of her own demise. They, and the entire town of Rumley, had always assumed that she had been killed in an automobile accident during the summer of 1957. There was never an opportunity to view the body, because the authorities that handled the case claimed she had been burned beyond all recognition. With that in mind, it seemed logical that the car had been completely burned as well. It wasn't until the day before his death in 1985 that Robert revealed to only the two of them the story of her supposed abduction. At that time, Robert reminded them both that his wife had been "taken away from them", but he had never in all the years referred to her as dead.

Jessica reached for Janet's hand and said, "Mom, dad fully believed in his heart until his dying breath that you were still alive somewhere, and that was why he never remarried."

Feeling temporarily satisfied by the account of her husband's life, and her own disappearance, Janet then wanted to hear all about the adventures in each of her children's lives.

Grandpa Hank had taught Ross early on that ladies should go first, so he said, "Jessica, you start, and I'll finish."

There had always been a very strong bond between the two of them, and they sometimes knew what each other was thinking. Jessica knew it would be necessary for her to leave out certain details of her own life experience, or risk revealing some surprises that Ross surely had in store for their mother as he filled in the blanks.

She said, "Alright Ross. Thanks."

Jessica began by putting her mother's mind at ease when she informed Janet that the problem with her right leg had not been too much of an inconvenience throughout her life. As was evident, Jessica still wore a brace to give her leg some added support, but had maintained complete mobility for many years. Ross had been very helpful when they were kids by teaching her how to put the brace on properly. He had then worked with her over the years with various exercises to strengthen the leg.

Jessica then recounted her youthful years and the close sisterly friendship that she had developed with a girl named Patty Wright, before moving on to tales of her college years at Rice University in Houston. As the story continued, Janet was overjoyed to hear that her daughter had attended a prestigious university, then been accepted to law school and subsequently enjoyed a successful career. The next aspect of her daughter's life was even better, as Janet learned that Jessica had parlayed that legal career into a position on the staff of a United States Senator in Washington D.C. After that, she had even worked on staff in the White House. As a mother Janet was very proud, but what she didn't know yet, was who Jessica had worked for.

Unfortunately Janet felt there was also a sad side to her daughter's life, as she learned that the wonderful career had been more important to Jessica than raising a family. Her beautiful little girl had never known the joy of getting married and becoming a mother, so there were no grandchildren.

Jessica turned to Ross and said, "Your turn."

Janet didn't notice Ross wink at his sister as he replied, "Thank you Jessica."

Ross began his story by pointing out that both he and Jessica had been the valedictorian of their respective Rumley High School classes of 1968 & 1972, and the girl Patty that Jessica mentioned had done the same in 1969. Ross then informed his mother that he had attended the United States Naval Academy in Annapolis, Maryland, so that he could pursue his dream of flying jet planes. He had then become a Navy pilot, and fought in a foreign war like his father and grandfather had done in the Army. He also told his mother that before going off to war, he had married that same Patty in June of 1973.

Janet was very excited to hear all that good news, and immediately asked, "Do I have any grandchildren?"

Ross told her she would find out as his story unfolded, and Jessica smiled as she knew their mother would be blown away by what was to come. He continued by adding that shortly after the war he had been accepted into NASA, but then realized it was doubtful his mother would know what that was. He explained to Janet that the National Aeronautics and Space Administration had been founded in 1959. Among many other accomplishments, NASA had landed on the surface of the Moon, and safely returned, six different pairs of astronauts by the close of 1972.

Janet interrupted Ross briefly, and revealed, "I heard a story that mankind had landed on the Moon from a more recent abductee aboard the deep water vessel. The man who told me the story had not provided any specifics other than the fact it had been accomplished. I was unaware when the event took place, or that there had been multiple successful missions."

Continuing on, Ross informed her that he hadn't joined NASA until 1975. He had then enjoyed a seventeen year career with them as a still active member of the Navy before moving on to other things.

He smiled at Jessica and said, "Should I tell her now, or drag it out a little while longer?"

Jessica shrugged her shoulders and said, "It's your story, so tell it the way you want to."

Ross nodded with agreement, then looked back at his mother, and said, "This current journey is actually my fourth venture into space, as I rode aboard a rocket vehicle on three separate occasions during my NASA years."

Janet was amazed that her son had done such a thing, but she hadn't heard the most interesting aspect of his story.

He continued by adding, "On the last of those missions, in November of 1985, I became the thirteenth human to set foot on the surface of the Moon."

Ross then took a few steps to his right. He placed his hand on the shoulder of his old alien friend, and said, "That was just a few weeks before dad passed away, and it was also when I first met this very alien!"

Janet staggered, and her mouth fell wide open from shock for several seconds before she regained her poise. She looked directly at Ross, and then briefly glanced in Jessica's direction for some sign of verification. A few seconds later, she looked over and down at the alien. She heard a voice in her head from the alien's thought projection that was confirming Ross' claim.

Ross would fill his mother in on more of the details surrounding his friendship with this specific alien at a later time, but he wanted to complete the tale of how he had lived the second half of his life on Earth. First, he informed Janet that she indeed had two grandchildren. He and Patty were the proud parents of two women named Aurora and Rachel. After their daughters had grown into adulthood, he and Patty had become the grandparents of two children from Rachel. Janet smiled broadly at the news.

She then wept with joy when Ross said, "There's a boy named Luke, and then a little girl Janet, who was named after you mom."

While drying her eyes, Janet listened carefully as Ross continued. She learned that he had worked in Austin for twelve years after leaving NASA in 1992, but he had been non-specific about his job. Ross and Patty had then moved the entire family, including Jessica, to Washington D.C. in 2004. That was done so that he could take on the responsibilities of a new job. They had remained there for nearly eighteen years until volunteering to climb aboard this alien transport vessel.

Janet put a few pieces of the puzzle together, and asked Jessica, "Is that when you started working for a United States Senator?"

"Yes mom, I did start working on Capitol Hill about the same time that Ross moved the family to the east coast."

Janet looked back at her son and said, "Ross, you still haven't told me where you were working in Washington D.C."

"Actually mom, I was working very closely with Jessica, because I was the United States Senator she spoke of!"

Her mouth fell wide open again in disbelief, and then Janet looked over at her daughter.

Jessica nodded her head positively and said, "It's true. Ross was a United States Senator representing Texas for twelve years, and I proudly served on his staff for the entire time."

Janet gave Ross a hug, before cupping his face in her hands as she told him how proud she was of him.

Looking into her eyes he said, "There's more to the story than that mom."

Janet waited through several long seconds of silence before briskly asking, "Well, are you going to tell me or not?"

Ross clasped both of her hands fearing that she might faint after hearing his next statement. He said, "Jessica was also on my staff in the White House, because until I resigned from office a few days ago, I was the President of the United States!"

⨎

CHAPTER THREE

THE UNVEILING

Ross quickly wrapped his arms around his mother to keep her from falling to the ground. She had nearly fainted, and Jessica stepped in to lend a helping hand. Janet was fine after a moment or two, but had definitely been overwhelmed by the discovery of what her son and daughter had become.

Jessica looked at Ross and said, "I think I should go retrieve a few things from our sleeping quarters that mom should see, and I'll come back as soon as possible."

He nodded in agreement as he said, "That's a good idea, and we really need to show her everything."

A few moments later Aurora, who had been sleeping rather soundly, groaned as her Aunt Jessica continued to shake her into consciousness. Rubbing the sleep from her eyes, she looked at her aunt and said, "What's the matter with you, and why are you so insistent on waking me up?"

With a huge smile on her face, Jessica said, "There's something going on that you will want to be part of. Take a quick moment to get yourself together, because your father and I would like you to meet someone."

Jessica turned to retrieve a few photographs that she had brought along in her backpack, and added, "You should probably brush your hair before we go."

Meanwhile Ross had heard a voice in his head again, as the alien asked if there was anything that could be done to help the situation. Ross seized that opportunity to request a few things of his old friend. First, he asked if the alien could become more involved with questions and answers that might arise during the group discussion. Up to that point Janet, Ross, and Jessica had been revealing aspects of their life adventures, but the alien had remained mostly silent. Ross also wanted the alien to be more informative about some of the characteristics of his own species. There was a certain physical feature that was present on some members of the alien species, and Ross couldn't have been the only human on board the transport vessels that was curious about it.

Jessica returned, while clutching two significant photos in her hand, and Aurora was just a few steps behind her. She presented the old black and white picture of the family that was taken when she was a little girl to Janet, and informed her that Robert had kept it on his nightstand until the day he died. She had then kept the photo in good condition for memory sake until this very moment, and planned on cherishing it for the rest of her days.

Janet smiled as it showed the four of them on the front porch steps of the family home in Rumley, and said, "I vividly remember the day this photo was taken."

Ross interrupted as he brought Aurora to within a few feet of Janet and said, "Aurora, I would like to introduce you to your grandmother Janet, and Mom, this is my oldest daughter Aurora."

Janet had already become somewhat numb from all the amazing information that her two grown children had recently provided, but the same could not be said for Aurora. It was her turn to gasp in disbelief after hearing what her father had said. She reached out her hand in ladylike fashion while uttering, "It's very nice to meet you Janet."

Janet returned the pleasantries as she took the woman into a loving embrace, and said, "This has all been quite a shock to me as well dear."

Not knowing what else to do, Jessica showed her niece the old black and white photo. Aurora had seen a copy of the photo at some point during her life, and knew that the young boy in the group was her father. She also was aware that the little girl was her Aunt Jessica, and the man was her grandpa. She had only seen him a few times when she was very young before he had passed away, but she still had the flag from his funeral. Now she took a closer look at the woman in the photograph, and realized that it was indeed the same woman who was standing in front of her.

Jessica thought it was a good time to show Janet the other photograph she had brought with her. That way her mother could have a visual account of what the rest of the family looked like. Jessica identified who everyone was in the color photo that was taken when Ross was the President, and Janet smiled with delight.

She asked the obvious question of, "When do I get to meet Patty and the rest of our family in person?"

To which Ross responded, "You won't mom, because the three of us are the only ones who came on this pilgrimage."

He and the ladies could provide Janet with more of the details later, but Ross informed her that only they believed in this endeavor strongly enough to partake in the journey.

Suddenly they all heard the thought projections of the alien in their heads, and learned that another of his species would arrive soon. Why another alien would be joining the group discussion was unknown, but it soon became perfectly clear. The same physical feature that they had all been curious about was clearly visible on the back of the second alien's head.

While pointing toward the second alien, Ross looked at his old friend and asked the obvious question, "Can you please explain why the back of your head doesn't have four tentacles like his?"

Ross and the others waited patiently for a responsive thought from the alien, but nothing came. Ross decided to compound his question with, "Does that physical trait grow or shrink with relation to how your species ages?"

With that Janet offered that she had seen several aliens, both with and without the four tentacles, during her captivity on the deep water vessel. She had always believed they were somehow related to gender as opposed to age.

After several seconds of awkward silence, Jessica shook her head negatively from side to side and responded to the alien's thoughts by saying, "No, I thought they had something to do with gender as well."

Aurora then added, "I was thinking that they might be reproductive organs of some sort."

Ross realized that the alien's thought question must have been directed at only the two of them, because he had not heard it in his own mind. Janet had been silent after her initial comment, which suggested the same was true for her.

Suddenly a thought projection came through that all four of them must have heard, as the alien was informing them it was time to reveal his entire anatomy. They all continued to hear his thoughts of explanation as the alien turned away from them. He reached up toward the back of his head to pull part of his scalp away. Two long slits in the skin that resembled the shape of a large "X" began to open up slightly, and four tentacles roughly six inches long unfolded from the smooth surface of the skin. Ross moved closer to get a better look, and the three ladies followed suit. There was no apparent need to fear the appendages, but Ross was denied permission when he asked if he could touch one.

The tip of each tentacle, from near where the two slits had crossed over each other, was thin and moved about both independently and somewhat wildly. As each tentacle became wider and thicker further from the tip, they also became less flexible. There was a thin layer of skin or flesh below the now open area on the back of the alien's head, so there seemed to be no direct exposure to the brain area.

Ross spoke first by asking, "What purpose do these serve you?"

He then heard that the tentacles were a normal aspect of the alien's anatomy, and they had nothing to do with age, gender, or reproduction. Their purpose was that of a pleasure center, because the tentacles enhanced sensory awareness. Having them exposed to the atmosphere was simply relaxing for the mind and body. Many of the alien species enjoyed moving about freely with the tentacles exposed, while others preferred to keep them covered except during private meditation.

Unfortunately the down side to exposing the tentacles was that the area around them was very susceptible to disease if dirt or other pollutants were present. In that regard, they were similar to some of their major organs. That was why the alien had been wearing the protective covering on the Moon and subsequent visits with Ross on Earth. Ross remembered learning many years before that the alien clothing was used primarily as a filter for the same reason, so the skin like covering on the back of their heads made perfect sense.

The alien's thoughts must have been transmitted to all present, because the ladies were nodding as if they understood what Ross had heard. Wanting to provide additional insight about his species, the alien then removed his clothing so his entire body could be viewed. From the back, a few major organs could be seen close to the surface of the skin, but the real surprise was a series of slits on each side that were almost directly under the alien's arms. Upon close inspection, the slits were roughly four inches in length, and the alien's thoughts informed his human observers that they were in fact gills used for breathing. There were three on each side that moved very little during normal breathing, but the alien flared them out for a moment to showcase their maximum potential. He turned to face them all as he informed them that the gills were an aspect of their anatomy that they were born with just like a heart or lungs. Much like the tentacles, they too could be susceptible to contaminants.

From that new angle, or orientation, additional organs could be seen through the thin and somewhat transparent skin, but there didn't appear to be any dominant feature that would distinguish male from female. The alien informed them that he was a male of his species, as the other alien disrobed. He identified the subtle difference between himself and the body of the second alien. That alien was a female, but unlike most humans, it would have been impossible to notice the difference if had not been pointed out. In simple terms, the height of roughly four feet and body shape of both male and female aliens was nearly identical.

At that moment Ross, and the others, were prepared to answer any questions with regard to their own human anatomy. Luckily, disrobing probably wouldn't be necessary in order to showcase male or female specifics. After all, it was probable that the alien species had long ago studied and discovered the answers to such questions of human gender and functions of reproduction. Still, there might be other questions.

The alien put his uniform and scalp covering back on, and the female exited the room. Janet prepared herself to ask him a few troubling questions.

At what she felt was the appropriate moment, she asked her host, "Why was I abducted, and then held with the group of other abductees for such a lengthy period of Earth time?"

The alien's thought projections reminded them all that even though many years had passed on the planet since the time of her abduction, her actual ageing process had only been measured in days or weeks. They learned that her selection for abduction was actually a random act performed by a stealthy scout ship, and it had been a common occurrence for many Earth years. Depending on the point of view, Janet was simply in the right or wrong place at the right or wrong time. The reason she had been held for so long was actually flattering, if she could accept that way of thinking.

Thousands of humans had been abducted and briefly studied over the most current few Earth centuries, but the vast majority had been returned within a very short time due to their lack of development. Only a select few, like Janet, who passed initial mental and physical testing, were then taken to the larger deep water vessel for prolonged observation. The first mental test given to an abductee by the aliens was to deliver a thought, and wait for a response. The power to form the message that had been sent rested within the individual recipients mind. If the abductee responded verbally to the aliens thoughts, then they had passed that first mental test.

To that end, Janet, like the other humans she had met during her captivity, was a special case. They each represented a very thin slice of the human population that was deemed by the alien species to be somewhat advanced. During the time of certain revolutions around the host star, many specimens from the planet were kept in captivity, while other cycles produced no viable candidates. Janet learned that in her case, she was the only specimen who warranted additional observation of those taken during 1957.

Her next question was even more direct, and carried a slight tone of aggression as she asked, "Are the four of us, along with all the other human specimens as you call them, destined to provide slave labor for your species?"

The alien became somewhat direct as well when his thoughts asked them all just how many times they needed to hear that was not the case.

Ross pulled his mother back a few feet to help defuse the situation, and asked his old friend, "Can you try to see this entire situation from her point of view?"

He then heard a voice in his head asking to explain, and Ross said, "Most of us on your transport vessels became a new breed of pilgrims when we volunteered to travel to a new world. It's simply not the same for the abductees like my mother, because they never had that same chance to exercise their free will."

His point was that Janet, like many of the others that had been held captive, missed a large portion of their lives just to appease the curiosity of the alien species. Janet also realized that she was probably unconscious aboard the alien scout ship longer than she originally thought. It must have taken some time to administer all the mental and physical testing the alien had spoken of.

The alien nodded in acknowledgement of Ross' opinion when he realized how difficult captivity could be on any species.

Janet heard his apologetic thoughts along with an additional question. She replied, "It's true that we were never mistreated or used for breeding experiments, at least as far as we could tell, but we were also never given the opportunity to return to our lives on Earth if we wished."

Once again the alien nodded in acknowledgement of Janet's statement, and then informed them all that her captivity had only been for observational purposes. Their species wanted to learn if the specially selected humans could mingle with other life forms. That observation was an important aspect of determining how far the human evolution had come from a philosophical point of view during the previous few centuries of Earth time. The conclusions drawn from those experiments would play a major role in determining if the species was ready for non-secretive public contact. The observations may have gone on for as long as another Earth century, but the discovery of the asteroid altered the plan. It was then determined that the abductees could be used for an additional purpose. Because Janet and the others had experienced lengthy exposure to the aliens', it seemed they would be perfect to assist with the integration of the two species during the flight.

As Janet listened carefully to the thoughts of the alien, it occurred to her that she, along with the other long term abductees, had just been thrust back into the role of teachers. Only time would tell how much she would be called upon by any of the voluntary pilgrims for her insight, and she decided that she would help them whenever she could. After all, it wasn't their fault that she had been living among the aliens for an extended period of time.

To that end, she used a more relaxed and civil tone toward their host when she asked her final question of, "How long will it take us to complete the journey to this new world you keep telling us about?"

ℒ

CHAPTER FOUR

MARBLES IN THE DARKNESS

The gathering of people near the observation windows was larger than in recent memory. They were well aware that the time all of them had been waiting for was drawing near. According to the information provided by their hosts, the fleet of transport vessels would be arriving at the new world very soon. It was therefore understandable that almost everyone wanted to gaze upon it during final approach.

As far as Ross was concerned, the timing couldn't have been better. Six weeks had been a long time for many of these people to be crowded into cramped spaces, but then again it was preferable to what they had all left behind. Ross figured it was sometime around 2057 back on Earth, or year 35 if a post-apocalyptic calendar had been implemented. He, like many others to be sure, wondered if anyone had survived the multiple impacts created by huge chunks of the asteroid and the Moon.

During the late stages of their present journey, several people had come to Ross with complaints about the dimensions of their sleeping and living quarters. Although Ross had nothing to do with how they had all been accommodated, he needed to remind them that the transport vessels had been built by the alien species. It was only logical that the specifications of the sleeping quarters would be more fitting to the alien species own size and body type. Ross couldn't fathom why some people were complaining to him about what couldn't possibly be altered, but his own height of six foot-two had certainly made him well aware of the discomfort they spoke of. He also realized it was just one of the means by which the passengers blew off some steam. He couldn't blame them really. After all, there was a huge level of uncertainty of what was to come.

Janet on the other hand had really enjoyed the six week journey. She had used the time to become acquainted with every detail she could about the lives of her two children and one granddaughter. Throughout the exchange of information about her children's respective lives, Janet had also been able to fill in knowledge gaps by entertaining them with several stories of her own youthful years.

During one such conversation, Janet discovered that neither one of her children had ever been told the origin of their names. Shocked and somewhat miffed at Robert for neglecting such an important task, she immediately asked, "Would the two of you like to be enlightened as to how you were named?"

Jessica spoke for them both, "Of course we would."

Ross had been born on July 7, 1950, which was almost exactly three years to the date after Robert and Janet had met during the cleanup and investigation of a crash site near Roswell, New Mexico. It seemed only fitting to make good use of the coincidence, so Ross was named for Roswell.

Jessica was born on January 20, 1955, and Robert and Janet once again used an aspect of their introduction to assist with the naming of their new baby girl. The lead intelligence officer at the Roswell site throughout those several days when Robert and his men were cleaning up the debris from the alien spacecraft was Major Jesse Marcel. Jessica became the obvious choice as a female derivative of his name.

It was instantly obvious that both Ross and Jessica were surprised to learn of the commonality in their naming, as they had always thought that their parents had simply picked names for each of them that began with the same initials as their own. Their choice of names had also become another interesting connection between the Martin family and the alien species. Janet was then equally surprised to learn that the alien Ross had become such good friends with had been the flight leader of that mission when the 1947 crash had occurred.

Ross decided the current conversation provided a great opportunity for him to divulge exactly how he had arrived at the choice of names for his two daughters. There was incentive to do so, because a coincidental parallel to how he and his sister Jessica were named now existed.

Ross looked at Aurora, and said, "I never really thought it was important to inform you of how both you and your sister were named, but your grandmother's recent story has changed my mind."

He began with the naming of Aurora, and she, along with Jessica and Janet, listened intently as the story unfolded. Although Janet had no previous knowledge of the article, Ross reminded the other two ladies of the necklace and emblem that he had cherished until recently since the days of his youth. He continued by adding that Grandpa Hank had originally received the emblem from his father in 1897 when he was four, and had kept it until his death when it had been bequeathed to Ross. Between the two of them, the necklace and emblem had remained in the family for one hundred and twenty-five years before Ross returned it to his alien friend. It had come from the debris at a crash site of what was an alien spacecraft, and Ross had discovered that the craft had been piloted by the father of the alien that they all knew so well.

Both Aurora and Jessica nodded. They remembered seeing the necklace countless times, and hearing the story of the origin on several occasions as well.

Aurora then asked, "What does all that have to do with my name?"

Ross reached for her hand and said, "I'll get to that."

They all continued to listen as Ross told Aurora about how he and his grandfather would speak at length about space and extraterrestrials. Those conversations were what sparked his interest in venturing into space someday. Grandpa Hank had also told him all about the small dusty town where the crash of 1897 had taken place, and that town was the genesis of this entire family odyssey. Ross then took a deep breath, and with a smile on his face said, "The location of that crash was north of Fort Worth, in Aurora, Texas. I named you in honor of the small town that my Grandpa Hank grew up in."

All three ladies gasped in response to their new found knowledge, and Jessica said, "I'm surprised that you never told me the story behind Aurora's naming."

Ross replied, "I'm sorry Jessica, but I never told anyone, including Patty, that story. She loved the sound of the name, but she would have never agreed to use it if she had known where the idea had come from."

The story continued, as Ross told of how Rachel's name was chosen. They learned that Ross had spent a portion of his early days with NASA, before Aurora was born, training in southern Nevada. It was another aspect of his life that neither Patty nor Jessica had known about, because it was a top secret location. Ross had done some flight testing, and desert survival training, at an airbase next to Groom Lake in what most civilians now commonly refer to as Area 51. He decided to call upon his experience during that time in the Nevada desert when it came to choosing a name for his second child.

On rare occasions, his survival task would be to hike several miles to a very small town known as Rachel that was located outside the northern perimeter of the airbase along state highway 375. He learned later that one aspect of each mission, or test, was to determine if he would inform anyone he encountered of his point of origin. Would he crack, while faced with the fatigue and delirium that can be associated with dehydration and exposure to extreme desert heat? He had always passed the test, without ever realizing that the people he encountered on each occasion were undercover government operatives. In spite of the extreme conditions, Ross thought Rachel would be a fitting name for a girl. He recommended it to Patty, and she also liked the name.

Once again without ever knowing the true origin, their child had been given a name that Patty would have otherwise balked at. From Ross' perspective is was a wonderful secret, because she just thought he was very good at picking names. It was pure coincidence that the town of Rachel would later become a major point of interest for UFO enthusiasts. Due to the numerous sightings of strange aircraft in the area, highway 375 became known as the "Extraterrestrial Highway". No one could ever be sure if the aircraft were secret military projects from nearby Area 51, or alien scout ships. It really didn't matter what the origin of the flights were, but to Ross, he found the naming of the highway to be somewhat humorous.

Aurora bluntly exclaimed, "You're kidding me. All these years of not knowing, and now I find out that we were named in honor of a couple of old dusty towns in the desert!"

Ross laughed aloud and said, "Yes, but look at the bright side. At least the one you were named after is in honor of Grandpa Hank, and in our home state of Texas!"

Throughout much of the long journey, the observation windows had become a favorite area of the transport vessel for Ross. Although there was rarely anything new to view in the vast darkness that lay beyond, it offered him some comfort in that the ceiling was higher near the windows than in his living quarters. At least he could stand fully upright in any of the accompanying wide corridors, as opposed to crouching down in most other areas of the vessel. There was something to look at on a few occasions though, as the transport fleet would pass in close proximity to a pulsating star, or some type of distant massive colorful nebula. When he asked his alien friend about an intensely bright white star that seemed to be very close, Ross learned that the star was in fact a tremendous distance from their current position. It gave off the appearance of proximity, because it measured more than a thousand times the diameter of the star that hosted Earth. The star was used as a navigation point by the alien species, but was void of orbiting planets. It became another humbling example to Ross of how small Earth was in the big picture.

When the transport closed in on the solar system that would be their new home, Ross was contacted once again by his old friend. There was some information he needed to relay to Ross, and then it would be communicated to all those aboard the other vessels. The system contained five planets that varied greatly in both size and atmospheric conditions, yet it was one of the few systems his species had charted that contained life of some sort on the majority of the spheres. Ross was free to ask any questions he wished about the system, and did so as the vessel slowed for final approach.

The first few questions were rather obvious, as Ross asked, "How have you identified the system, and which planet will we be on."

Ross heard that the system is known as ₹-593, and he would be shown the location of his new home world when it came into view. Soon a large vibrant blue planet could be seen as the fleet entered the outer edge of the solar system, and Ross thought it looked very similar to Earth.

Forgetting the thought projection of his old friend just a moment before, Ross asked, "Is that our new home?"

It seemed rational to assume that the planet would be their new home, but the alien's thoughts quickly informed him otherwise. Although that planet looked appealing, Ross learned that nearly the entire surface consisted of deep water in excess of sixty degrees Celsius. Volcanic activity had been recorded on a somewhat regular basis, as the planet was still in its cooling phase. There were many species of aquatic life on the planet that thrived in the very hot water. A few of them were even beginning to morph into amphibians similar to the ancient alligators of Earth. The temperature was far too extreme for extended human exposure, and there were no substantial land masses so that the water could be avoided. Besides that, it would probably be thousands of Earth type years before any life indigenous to that planet could stand fully upright.

The second planet to come into view was dark green in color. It appeared to be a little larger than the first, but scale was difficult to measure. Ross had no idea how the size related to that of Earth, because six weeks had passed since he gazed out the window for a final glimpse of his home world fading into the distance. His instinct told him that both of these planets were much larger, not that it really mattered, but he had no verification at the present time.

The alien informed Ross that the planet contained vast amounts of thick forest. Very few areas of the surface offered large enough clearings to land a vessel the size of the one they were on, let alone thirteen of them. The atmosphere produced an almost constant rain, and the species that lived on the planet remained aloft within the giant trees to escape the mud and water below. Ross learned they closely resembled humanoids, but were dozens of centuries behind his own species level of development.

Next in line was a smaller planet of dull gray. The alien informed Ross that the dominant species of that world simply wished to be left alone. They had been contacted, as the humans of Earth had been, and were evolved enough in a technological sense to venture into space if they so desired. In spite of an offer to mingle with another species, that civilization had respectfully declined to do so. The alien pointed out the fantastic example of how his own species had respected the wishes of the species that was indigenous to the planet below. As requested, they had left them alone for centuries.

Gray was also the color of the fourth planet to come into view, as the fleet of transports moved closer to the host star. It was roughly the same size as the one they had just observed, but Ross soon discovered it was quite different. According to the alien it contained no measurable life because of a poisonous atmosphere, but unlike the previous three, this planet did have orbital spheres of its own. Two small moons were now visible as the transport slowed more noticeably and moved around the planet. Ross was then informed that the human population would be living on the second moon.

He instantly asked, "You mean the one over there that is pale green in color?"

A verifying thought response popped into his head, so Ross began to take a closer look as they approached the green marble. The sphere contained huge land masses and a few bodies of water that could easily be seen. Ross learned that the moon had been selected for the human pilgrims because the atmospheric conditions were similar to that of Earth. The size was considerably different however, with a diameter slightly over half that of their former home. Human life could thrive on the surface of this moon with the indigenous life forms, but it would not be easy. The moon was similar, but definitely not the same as Earth. The lifestyle that most everyone had enjoyed while on the modern

Earth would need significant alteration, and only the strong willed could make a successful transition.

Ross asked, "Can that critical information be conveyed to the entire population?"

His education continued as he was informed that the other moon also contained life, but every species found on it was winged. The inhabitants ranged in size from a few inches that lived low among the small trees and bushes, to those with a thirty or forty foot wing span that ruled the sky high above. Unfortunately, there had been a few instances when an observer from the alien home world had become an unwilling food source for one of the giant birds. In each case his alien brethren had not been focused enough on his surroundings while on a scouting mission. They had all paid the price for that lapse by being plucked from the ground by a set of unrelenting talons. Ross thought that specific plight was not much different than what his mother and countless others had experienced at the hands of this alien species, but at least the humans had not become a food source.

Before landing, the fifth, and closest, planet to the host star was discussed as Ross asked, "Is there life on that planet?"

It was dull orange, and it, along with two of the four orbiting moons, contained life. The alien informed Ross that the life discovered on each of those worlds was in the early stages of biologic development. His species considered it doubtful that they would ever evolve.

Ross ran the numbers. Solar system ₹-593 consisted of eleven orbiting spheres, with biologic life of some type present on eight of them. The diverse life forms throughout the system had found a way to survive within a wide range of climate and atmospheric conditions. Ross hoped that he and the human contingent of pilgrims could do the same, as he braced himself for the conditions that they would all encounter on their new home world.

꡷

CHAPTER FIVE

ONE GIANT LEAP

A slight bump of the transport vessel could be felt by all those present as it touched down on the surface of the pale green moon. The movement was less than any of these humans may have experienced on a typical airplane flight back on Earth, but it seemed significant after six long weeks of perfectly smooth travel through the vacuum of space.

Before the hatch to the outside world was opened, Jessica handed Ross a scrap of paper. With help from the alien, she had been able to determine the exact number of humans that had made this pilgrimage. That base number would be important for tracking the rate of growth, or decline, of the population in the future, and she wanted Ross to have it. The alien had also verified that the people aboard the various transport vessels had received a briefing. They had now been informed about the diverse forms of life on the planets and other moons within this solar system. That would help prepare them for what they might expect to encounter on this moon.

Ross unfolded the paper to glance at what she had written down, and said, "Thanks Jessica, but how did you get this information?"

He flashed back to his days in public office when she responded with a familiar, "I have my ways."

Although thankful for the information, it raised another important question. The topic had nothing to do with the outcome of the asteroid and subsequent moon impact upon the Earth, because it would serve no purpose to dwell on such matters. His question centered on something that had actually been puzzling to Ross since before the fleet had left Earth.

Straightforward and simple, he asked the alien, "With the many different languages spoken by the people aboard these transport vessels, how did you ever deliver the necessary information about this new world to all of them?"

The alien informed him it was done in the usual way. That response was somewhat frustrating to Ross, because it didn't really answer the question.

Ross added, "I have always heard your thoughts in the language that I speak, but many among our population don't use the same language to communicate."

To that the alien responded more specifically, and informed Ross that the process was really quite simple. The same thought projection used as the initial mental test is transmitted and then received in the human brain to whatever form of language the individual feels most comfortable with. Some of the pilgrims, like all of the long term abductees, could hear the information clearly within their minds. Others, who were unable to receive the transmission, were informed via word of mouth from those who did. Ross then learned that the vast majority of the human population aboard the transports had not formed the message within their minds. Had they been abducted on Earth instead of volunteering for the flight, most would have been returned immediately due to being unworthy of further study.

That was important information for Ross to digest. He had never considered that an individual recipient would be responsible for translating the alien thought messages. He now understood why there had been, at least in the United States, so many documented claims of normal everyday citizens being abducted by an alien species throughout the past century.

Ross reflected back to a time during his first term as President, when he had used his temporary power to access all the top secret reports that dealt with supposed alien activity. Being part of a rare group of people that actually had insight to the subject at hand, Ross found most of the reports to be both vague and wildly incorrect in their assumptions. It was almost unbelievable how imaginative the government officials of the time had been. They went to great lengths to develop as many different fabrications as possible for explanations of what had now been proven to be true accounts of alien encounters. That was especially true for the events of the 1947 Roswell incident. Ross remembered having laughed out loud in the oval office when he flipped through that particular file.

The official accounting released to the public of those few days in New Mexico claimed that the wreckage was from a high altitude weather balloon. Ross wondered how many of the people living in the surrounding area had actually believed that load of bull. That story was in sharp contrast to the actual truth, and the top secret file contained several very interesting photographs to prove it. On the extreme edge of one picture, taken from roughly twenty feet away, the white sleeve of a nurse's uniform could be seen between the camera and the body of an alien species. Nothing more of the woman could be seen, but based on what Robert revealed on his death bed about the event, Ross wondered if that arm in the photograph belonged to his mother.

Janet and Aurora approached, and Jessica poked Ross in the ribs to bring him back to the present moment. She looked toward their alien host and said, "I think the time has come to tell Ross about the big surprise."

He nodded toward the three ladies, while sending them a confirming thought that the other transport vessels were standing by. A tremendous honor had been bestowed upon Ross by the majority of the other humans who had made the voyage, and the time for him to receive that honor was now at hand. Each of the twelve transports had carried their full allotment of eight hundred passengers. The deep water vessel had another two hundred twelve abductees, as well as various species of plant and animal life that had been gathered from earth prior to departure. There had been some minor shifting of the passengers as abductees, such as Janet, had been brought together with family members or their descendants, but the total count of nine thousand eight hundred and twelve people had been confirmed.

In a ballot measure brought forth by Jessica that Ross had known nothing about, it had been decided by a landslide vote that he should be the first human to set foot on the new world. As the man who spearheaded this effort to save a small fraction of the human race, Jessica felt Ross deserved such recognition. Because he was also the only former astronaut in the population, and one of only fourteen humans to walk upon Earths now destroyed moon, the choice was obvious as many people agreed with her assessment.

Ross smiled broadly as the large hatch to the transport vessel hissed open, and said loudly to all those nearby, "I want to thank you all for this tremendous honor."

A blast of hot dry air rushed into the viewing corridor, and Ross drew in a deep breath to fill his lungs. Before making the historic descent, he asked his old alien friend to join him for the walk down the ramp.

Ross asked, "Can you please make sure through thought projection, or other available means, that what I'm about to say is heard by everyone on the transports."

He could see hundreds of people pressed against the observation windows of the transports that had landed in a circular pattern. Ross knew his next action needed to be quick, and gave them all a wave as he reached the bottom of the ramp.

After a brief pause, Ross loudly proclaimed, "All of us have made a journey that could not have been possible without our alien friends. We must all thank them for their concern, and work together to insure that the voyage to save a portion of our species was not made in vain." Intending no disrespect toward the memory of Neil Armstrong, Ross added to the powerful message by saying, "Nine thousand eight hundred and twelve of us have now made a truly giant leap for mankind!"

Stepping off the ramp onto the ground of the new world known as ₹-593-૩π-2-2, Ross turned to shake the hand of his old alien friend. He said, "It's difficult for me to believe that I'm actually standing on the surface of a second moon with you during my lifetime. This moment is even more special to me because I'm the first human to set foot on this moon!"

The alien reached out and clasped Ross' hand in congratulations for completing the journey, but his thoughts informed him that there was more for them to discuss. Ross learned that although he was the first of this group to walk on the surface, this was not the first group of humans that had been brought to this moon.

With no real time to adequately digest that most recent and alarming news, Ross suddenly found himself surrounded by several people. An instant after he stepped off the ramp, the anxious throngs began to disembark from the transport vessels. Many of those in his immediate vicinity were seeking guidance from Ross about what to do now that they had arrived. He found himself ill prepared to provide what they desired. Jessica, Aurora, and Janet were attempting to screen some of the many questions, but the task soon became impossible as the crowd continued to swell. Ultimately Ross needed to retreat several steps to a location part way back up the ramp, so that he could confer with his alien friend more privately. With a mass of people still descending from that particular vessel, the task became somewhat like swimming upstream.

Ross didn't want anyone to hear what he was about to ask his old friend, so he leaned toward the alien and quietly said, "What do you mean this is not the first group of humans to be brought here?"

ᘦ

CHAPTER SIX

BASE CAMP

Within an hour after Ross supposedly became the first human to set foot on this moon, the entire population of slightly over ninety-eight hundred had made their way down the ramps of the thirteen different vessels.Ross had just learned that there was a mostly aquatic assortment of plant and animal life from Earth aboard the deep water vessel.He was assured that those other species of life from Earth would be placed near or within the body of water that could be seen on the distant horizon.They could provide additional food sources to compliment some of the indigenous animal species of this moon, but they could also become extinct if the human pilgrims became overzealous in their hunting and fishing habits.

Ross had also been informed of a few other important things about his new home from his alien friend throughout the previous hour.Certain aspects of that knowledge could lead to tremendous challenges for him and the rest of the population.For that reason, Ross had requested that the most incredible piece of information that they had discussed remain a secret for the time being, and the alien agreed.

Although aspects of natural beauty such as distant mountains and forested lands could be viewed from their current location, the area around the landing zone was barren and dry. There were no apparent sources of water in close proximity to the arid landscape, or fertile land to harvest crops. With that in mind, it seemed only logical to find more suitable locations for any permanent settlements. That would become a top priority, but moving everyone on this day was not an option. They would need to wait until the entire group became more organized.

According to the alien, the large body of water in the distance was safe for human consumption, so they could move in that direction when ready to do so. Ross had no idea how pure the water was as opposed to certain areas on Earth, so some people might wish to boil the water before consumption. The breathable atmosphere could also be a concern, but it was compatible with human needs. The alien had informed him this moons atmosphere was equivalent to twelve thousand feet of elevation. Ross knew that those who had come from certain regions of Earth with higher elevations might handle the thin atmosphere with the most ease, as for the remainder of the population, only time would tell.

There was also the potential danger associated with some of the indigenous animal species. Ross had learned that a few of the larger predators could easily take down a human if they so desired. The history of this pale green moon also had that interesting human element to it, but was not a concern for the moment. With all of those factors to consider, and others that had surely not yet been thought of, Ross moved toward the top of a nearby small rock outcropping. The time had come to address his fellow human contingent about what needed to be done in order to survive.

The first order of business would be to set up some sort of base camp. The population had been informed via thought projection and word of mouth that the now empty transport vessels would soon depart for the trip back to the alien home world. They had also learned that the alien species had no intention of helping the humans survive on this new world. The alien had informed Ross that they would return from time to time to check on the progress of the humans, but that was all.Nothing more should be expected, and Ross knew that would be a scary thought for many among the population.

Back on Earth, the aliens' had made it quite clear to all of the pilgrims that they could only bring a minimal amount of personal belongings on the voyage.In spite of the advance knowledge, many passengers had obviously decided to ignore the warning.Instead, many had arrived at the Washington D.C. departure site on the National Mall loaded with much more than the one allotted suitcase or backpack.As a consequence, Ross and his group had seen a large mound of abandoned suitcases and bags near the bottom of the loading ramp.It was fair to assume that scenario had been duplicated at each of the other departure sites as well.Ross was proud that everyone in his group had heeded his advice and brought backpacks, as that choice had now become even more practical.Not only could they hold more useful gear for frontier life, but they would be easier to carry when the population moved to a new location.His camping experience during his more youthful years seemed to be paying off an immediate dividend, and although he didn't have much faith in the prospect, Ross hoped that many others had the same foresight to pack wisely.

As for the present moment, Ross had no idea of how long the current daylight would last.The speed with which the sun was moving across the sky implied that it wouldn't be long, so he began his speech. Ross spoke loudly so that many in close proximity could hear what he had to say, and requested that some of them help spread the word to those who were too far away.First, he was searching for any of those among the population who spoke more than one language.Translators would be of significant importance not only for the present message, but also throughout the upcoming challenging days.Second, the entire population needed people who knew how to create fire that would provide the valuable commodity of heat and light when nightfall came.It made no difference if the fire was created via matches, a lighter, or by rubbing two sticks together, but it would be needed quickly.To that end, some type of fuel for the multiple fires would need to be located. Ross requested that people form scouting groups to search the nearby terrain for anything useful.He reminded them all of the potential danger of native predatory animals, and asked them to use caution while searching in groups of no less than eight or ten.Until more was known about what was out there, his request to remain in large groups was the prudent move.

Next was to get some idea of what food was available to the general population for immediate use.Ross knew that it could be several days until fishing or hunting could produce anything tangible.He requested that additional groups form up to check the surrounding area for any source of food, and both Janet and Aurora immediately offered to be part of such an effort.There would also be a need for small tools of any kind, and Jessica would speak with anyone who came forth with anything useful.Ross then requested to speak with any members of the engineering community.They could discuss plans about how to proceed with infrastructure.He did the same with the scientific community of astronomers from around the globe that had made the voyage. Ross knew that the diameter of this moon was slightly more than half the size of Earth, and the rotational speed was probably significantly different as well.He wanted to have some of the bright minds within the population figuring out how long a day was here as opposed to Earth.That would determine how many hours of sunlight they could expect on a daily basis.

Before thanking the population for their attention and future efforts, Ross made one final request.Not wanting to overstep his limited authority in anyway, he requested that a small group of representatives from each transport vessel be designated to come forth with any ideas, questions, or concerns.He wasn't sure if any type of structured government would be established on this new world, but Ross had no desire to be labeled as a dictator if there were.

While climbing down from the rock outcropping, Ross noticed many people were already forming search groups and heading off in multiple directions.Before making the final jump to the ground, a hand reached out to offer some assistance.It was Colt Jensen, the lone member of his secret service detail to have come along on the voyage to the new world.They had spoken many times during the six week trip, and had become much closer because of it.Ross had learned that the thirty-six year old man had been born and raised in Spring Creek, Nevada, but had opted many years ago not to follow in the ranching footsteps of his grandfather, father, or uncles before him. He knew at a young age that his destiny was for something grander. Colt had come on the voyage because he had been a believer in the alien species since before Ross informed the world about the asteroid. Ross didn't know it at the time, but Colt had witnessed the Presidents' encounter with the alien from a distance while patrolling the woods of Camp David.

That encounter had served as proof to something that Colt had believed in strongly since the days of his youth. While he and the rest of his family were visiting friends for several days in the Phoenix area during the spring of 1997, Colt had witnessed an event. They, like many other people, had gone to a location in the desert where there was considerably less light interference from the city in order to view the Hale-Bopp comet. What he witnessed on the night of March 13th changed the eleven year old boy's life forever. Several strange lights could be seen flying in a perfect "V" shaped formation over the area for a few hours. Colt was not alone, as literally hundreds of people from several locations in Arizona had reported seeing that same formation of UFO's. The subsequent investigation revealed that the control towers at Sky Harbor International Airport in Phoenix had no verbal contact with any of the craft. There was also no identification of any intended flight plan from passenger airliners or privately owned aircraft. The nearby Luke Air Force Base had no reasonable explanation either. They had no scheduled flight exercises taking place, or even a single plane in the air during the time of the sighting. In short, the lights could never be explained away by anyone. Colt had believed in the existence of extra-terrestrials ever since that night, but he couldn't reveal such a belief publicly. Having done so would have seriously jeopardized his intended career with the United States Secret Service.

It had come as quite a surprise to Ross when he learned that someone had actually witnessed his encounter with the alien at Camp David. He was honored that Colt had been so dedicated to his duty, and had the ability to remain silent about what he had seen.

Ross smiled at the former agent when Colt said, "Here Mr. President, let me help you down from that rock."

Ross was glad to accept, and replied, "Thanks Colt, but you don't have to call me Mr. President anymore."

After safely landing on his two feet, Ross heard, "As you wish sir, but it wouldn't surprise me at all if this group of people someday elected you as the President of this moon!"

A moment later, Ross made his way over to speak with Jessica. He whispered into her ear, "I have some very important information to share with you when we have a more private moment."

He knew their discussion would have to wait until later that night, because there were too many other things to tend to before darkness fell upon the population.

Jessica nodded with understanding while pointing toward a small group of people that had approached her. They were the first of many translators and engineers that Ross would meet within the coming hours. She said, "Ross, please allow me to introduce you to a few people who could be very helpful in the future."

CHAPTER SEVEN

A RESTLESS NIGHT

In spite of tremendous effort by several groups, little was found in the way of scrap wood or other materials that could be used as fuel for campfires. Unfortunately, the search for food had also produced a minimal yield, so the first night for the human population on their new world was somewhat less than comfortable.

Using everything that had been scrounged from the nearby terrain, six small campfires were lit in an extremely large circular pattern during the waning moments of daylight. Ross, and most everyone else, knew that the fires wouldn't come close to providing enough warmth or light for everyone, but it was better than nothing at all. They were spaced at a distance that enabled the people to gather around from all directions. If packed closely together, there was room enough for perhaps a few thousand to be situated within the circle itself. Ross and Jessica, with Colt at their side, spent several hours strolling from one fire to the next until they had made their way around the entire circle. They met with hundreds of people from various locations on Earth, and tried to offer whatever comfort they could through words of encouragement.

One such meeting, and subsequent conversation, was with a group of six astronomers that Ross had first met at Camp David to discuss the asteroid. They assured him that they were reasonably comfortable, and then provided Ross with some possible insight to his earlier request. Knowing that it would be important to determine how long both the day and nighttime hours of this moon were, the astronomers had begun a running time clock when twilight had faded away. They would chart the duration of darkness, and then reset the clock at first light. A log would then be maintained on a daily basis to determine if the timeframes of daylight and darkness remained constant. If no variations were evident in the daily time tests, then this moon was not tilted on its axis as the Earth was.

The astronomers continued by revealing that they had already discovered two important facts about this moon that were indisputable. The first was that the moon had a rotation of its own beyond revolving around the host planet. That was obvious since both daylight and darkness had already been observed during the short time they had been on the surface. That fact made it different from the rock that had previously orbited the Earth, as that moon always had the same side of it facing the planet. The second fact became apparent to Ross when the astronomers asked him to look at the multitude of stars overhead. A portion of the large gray planet was plainly visible, and it stretched across a significant section of the night sky. Most of what they could view of the planets outline was in darkness from their orientation point, but there was more to it than that. The completely black and void of stars area adjacent to the inner portion of the crescent provided the scope of how large their host planet was. It also meant that the planet was currently positioned in nearly a direct line between this moon and the host star. Ross was asked what he thought of the planets visible crescent, as opposed to the view of Earth he had seen from that planets moon many years before.

With a look of concern he uttered, "It appears to be massive in comparison."

Based on historical photographs they had all seen, the group of astronomers informed him that was their assessment as well.

Although it was impossible to determine at the present time when it would next occur, the size and close proximity of the planet would most probably create an occasional eclipse on this moon. If that happened, it would be much more significant than any that had ever been experienced on Earth.

Eventually Ross, Jessica, and Colt made their way back to the center of the six fires near the small rock outcropping. Janet, Aurora, Mrs. Patterson, and the remainder of their group of friends seemed to be resting comfortably. The temperature had dropped significantly since the sun had gone down, and Ross hoped everyone had some way to keep warm. Certain people had undoubtedly made better choices than others with regard to truly vital possessions, and he hoped those with a blanket or coat would share what they had with a neighbor.

Unable to sleep, Ross quietly passed the time by either looking out over the many people that were close by, or gazing upon all the stars in the sky. That temporary peacefulness was disrupted when distant shouts of panic could be heard. A few seconds later a multitude of screams amplified the disruption. Most of the people within close proximity to Ross were now awake, and like him, were looking in the same general direction. He surmised something awful had taken place along the outer perimeter of the population, but visibility was non-existent. The area was beyond any light cast by the dwindling campfires, and there was no hint of the coming dawn.

When daylight finally arrived, an investigation was begun. What Ross, Colt, and a few others found was disturbing. There were blood trails that led off into the distance, and a few small body parts were found. Eight people were reported missing, and witnesses claimed that a pack of large fury animals had dragged them away.

One woman said to Ross, "I heard heavy footsteps and growling noises, and then something as large as a rhinoceros came out of the darkness about thirty feet away from me!"

Her opinionated description was that the creature was agile, and looked similar to a wolf. It was also powerful enough to toss a full grown man around like some type of chew toy.

The timetable for relocating the population toward the distant shoreline had just been moved up. The recent events of the predawn attack had seen to that. Ross had hoped to be more organized before the move, and perhaps send out a large advance group to scout for a suitable location. That plan would need to be altered, because the large wolf like animals had found an easy source of food in mass numbers. If they behaved with a true pack like mentality, then they would most definitely return for more food every night until it no longer existed.

Ross spoke plainly as he moved through the frightened crowd toward the small rock outcropping. "Anyone who wants to stay here is welcome to do so, but I don't recommend it."

He knew that the lack of food, water, and firewood, coupled with the now present threat of the animals, made that a less than desirable option. He requested that anyone who could speak multiple languages begin a search for people who possessed any weapons such as a knife or small hatchet. Ross couldn't guarantee anything, but he felt the entire population stood a better chance of survival near the distant shoreline.

ƒ

CHAPTER EIGHT

THE VALLEY OF FATIGUE

Within an hour, the restless population began their trek toward the distant shoreline. They were filled with an eager, yet cautious, optimism of what was to come. As long as the slightly downhill terrain would allow for it, the plan was for the group to move forward in a wide column with the women and children positioned in the center of the mass. Some of the men creating the outer perimeter carried whatever knives, hatchets, or other items such as fist sized rocks that could be used for defense in case of another animal attack.

Moving such a large group in unison would surely be a difficult task, but it needed to be done. In spite of their early morning start, Ross continued to urge a livelier pace. Their intended destination appeared to be only a few miles away, but it was difficult to be fully confident of that assessment. If they could somehow make it to the water's edge before nightfall, then in theory they would not need to defend a three hundred and sixty degree perimeter. The water itself could potentially provide one defensible side from the wolf like animals.

Descending from the arid and rocky plain where the alien transport ships had deposited them, the population was making good progress. The sun had reached its zenith, when the surrounding terrain began to give way to a more hospitable landscape. In spite of their pace, Ross realized that they would never reach the intended shoreline before dark. The group of astronomers whom he had met with the previous evening had informed Ross that the darkness had lasted slightly more than eight and a half hours. The running clock, combined with the suns current position, suggested the daylight hours would be roughly the same. Faced with that realization, Ross asked if a few hundred young and physically fit people could advance ahead of the main body. There appeared to be an area of small trees and foliage a short distance away, and he thought it might provide some useful cover during the upcoming night. If the grove of trees were thick enough, perhaps the large wolf like animals would have a difficult time moving through them.

Within minutes the advance scouting party was on their way, and began jogging toward the wooded area. Upon their arrival, they discovered that the surrounding area wasn't as thickly overgrown with vegetation as had been hoped. There was however a bright side. None of the trees stood much taller than fifteen feet in height, but their proximity to the arid and exposed slope had made many along the leading edge dry and brittle. With that, many of the branches could be snapped off and used for much needed firewood. Additionally, some of the more sturdy limbs could possibly be fashioned into clubs or spears to help defend the people from the animals.

Word was sent back to Ross via a group of ten strong runners who had boarded their transport vessel in Nazca, Peru. They were virtually unaffected by the thin air, because they had lived high in the Andes Mountains back on Earth. Their message to Ross was that more people were needed within the advance party to help gather and position stacks of branches for several dozen fires. Seeing immediate hope, Ross thanked the young men and women for delivering the news. He then spoke loudly when requesting that a few hundred more able bodied people move ahead with the Peruvian runners.

Turning back to the runners, Ross said, "Could I ask all of you to do me, and the rest of the population, a favor?"

He had realized that their skill of quick and seemingly tireless movement could be useful, so he wanted them to act as messengers again if the need ever arose.

Sometime later, when the leading edge of the main column reached the first of the trees, they could see piles of branches for several intended campfires ready to be lit. The advance working group instructed them all to keep moving deep into the cover of the trees. That way everyone behind them had room to follow. Before long Ross reached the site as well, but did not enter.

He asked, "Is the grove large enough to provide some level of protection for everyone, and are these nearby trees indicative of the size and spacing throughout the area?"

Much to his dismay, he was informed that the spacing varied greatly. Although it was certainly more cover than if they had remained on the open plain, it was also doubtful that the grove was large enough to adequately protect the population from animal attacks.

There was also the danger that some people wouldn't complete the required distance to the outer ring of campfires before nightfall. The sun was getting very low on the horizon, and the column had stretched into a much thinner line during the past few hours. That was a normal reaction to a segment of the group jogging ahead for scouting purposes, because some of the stronger walkers had then instinctively set a quicker pace. Ross knew that those who were in the back of the main body might need some assistance, so he and Colt left their backpacks with the ladies. They each grabbed a few sturdy branches and borrowed a hunting knife. Their intent was to bolster the defense perimeter of men that were protecting any stragglers, and get them safely delivered into the grove of trees.

Making their way back along the column, Ross provided encouragement as he said both loudly and often, "You are all doing great so far, just keep moving as best as you can."

Colt looked over his shoulder to gauge how far they had traveled from the relative safety of the trees, and reported, "Sir, I can see that a few fires have already been lit."

Dusk was close at hand as the sun was dipping behind the mountains when they reached the last of the column, and they immediately handed a tree branch to two of the younger men nearby. Colt guessed they were more than half a mile from the now more distinct line of welcoming campfires. He honestly didn't know if everyone in the group of stragglers could cover the distance. They probably numbered at least two hundred, and had become separated from the main column by a gap of at least one hundred yards. That coupled with the crawl of their current pace made them all extremely vulnerable.

Within a few moments, the initial attack came. For the first time, Ross saw one of the huge beasts. The description provided earlier that day had been correct with regard to overall size. The beast was as large as an adult rhinoceros, and it did resemble a wolf with short fur. On the positive side, it seemed to lack the overall agility that the woman had claimed. Perhaps that would be an exploitable trait.

As the animal approached, the people began to panic. Some broke formation by dropping their belongings and moving at a quicker pace toward the wooded area ahead. Others scattered as they ran directly away from the incoming direction of the attacker. Ross' concern that the animals behaved with a pack like mentality was then confirmed when he turned around. He could see four other predators waiting for those who had broken from the column. The first animal had driven some of the intended prey toward the pack, and those few people were probably not savable.

The chase began, and it wouldn't be pretty. Each of the four large animals had selected a target. Suddenly it occurred to Ross that the beasts were intelligent, because they only chased after those who were older and slower. He also noticed that they did not deviate from their original targets, even when another source of food ran close by in a panic. Ross and others yelled for the non-targeted people to return to the group, but their current state of emotion made comprehension difficult.

Spinning in the opposite direction, Ross noticed that the initial attacking animal was now very close to the column of people. It would have a choice of targets, as the people were simply grouped too tightly together to attempt an escape. A young man swung a tree branch at the hind quarter of the animal just as it lunged toward an elderly woman. She was pinned down instantly by the force of the animal's momentum, and screamed with pain as it sunk its teeth into her leg. The man continued to swing his tree branch at the animal, but it was having little effect. From the other side of the beast, two men began an attack of their own. One was relentlessly pounding away at the head and shoulder area of the huge wolf with a grapefruit sized rock. The other repeatedly plunged a knife into the thick hindquarters of the animal. Attempting to spin around toward the persistent and pesky attackers, the animal raised its head as the old woman's screams fell silent. Suddenly another man jumped into the fray. He began slashing away at a front leg of the beast with a small hatchet, and was rewarded for his efforts. Deep growls of pain could be heard from the animal, as it attempted to move away from the motionless body below. The old woman was probably already dead, but the group of men continued their attack on the animal in a fit of rage.

Ross turned quickly to insure that none of the other animals were advancing from his side of the column. Each of those four animals had caught up with their prey, and screams of pain could be heard.

He yelled instructions for those people nearby, "Stay together and run toward the fires as fast as you can."

Fortunately they didn't hesitate, but the animals were all too busy with their respective prizes to care about chasing anything else. Ross also noticed a weakness in the animals pack like structure, as they didn't seem to care that one of their own was under attack. Soon there were very few people left in the vicinity of the initial attack, and that animal was now in obvious distress. With severe damage to the left front leg, right hind quarter, and head, the wolf attempted a retreat. The four attacking men would not yield, and Colt leapt onto the back of the beast to finish it off. With one swift move, he plunged a knife deep into the back of the animal's neck and twisted. With a horrific yelp of pain and then sudden silence, the beast fell to the ground with a mighty thud while exhaling its final gasp of life. Colt was in no mood to take any chances, so he drew his blade across the throat of the wolf in a manner that nearly caused decapitation. Those that had taken part in the effort of the kill now stood triumphantly over the dead beast, but there was little time to celebrate.

Roughly fifty yards away, three more of the creatures moved about in slow circles. Positioned on the initial attacking side, they were intended to be the second wave. Surprisingly, they did not advance during the next few anxious moments. Having seen one of their own die at the hands of their intended prey had perhaps scared them into brief passivity, but no one could be sure. Ross spun around to locate the other four beasts. They were all dragging their kills into the distance, so he reversed his pivot. He realized that the previous night had been easy for the animals. Motionless and totally exposed, their intended prey had no defense during that surprise attack. It seemed logical that each of the eight beasts had made a single kill and then dragged it away into the night. They had now discovered that it would no longer be quite so easy.

Meanwhile, the attention of the triumphant men had turned to the old woman. As was feared, she had been killed by the now dead beast. The young man who had bravely taken the first swing at the beast was now crying over his dead mother's body. Two other men picked up the limp woman and carried her body toward the safety of the trees.

Taking up a position next to Colt at the tail end of the stragglers, Ross asked, "Where did you learn to use a knife with such expertise?"

He knew that Colt had been superbly trained in hand to hand combat and the proper use of small firearms as a secret service agent, but the knife was something different.

Colt replied, "I did a great deal of hunting and fishing with my father and others while growing up in northeastern Nevada. The Ruby Mountains near my home town of Spring Creek were like a playground for me when I was a young man. Learning to skin and dress out a deer with a large blade after it had been shot was just part of the program."

He also admitted to Ross that the Wolf like creature was significantly larger than any other animal he had ever shot or worked on with a knife, but had learned from his grandfather that the back of the neck was vulnerable for most animals.

Ross nodded and replied, "I learned several important things from my grandfather as well."

Nearly a dozen men emerged from the trees with lit branches to assist with the last of the column, as dusk had now completely turned to darkness. Once all were safely within the wooded area and ring of campfires, Ross asked that the word be spread to quiet down as soon as possible. The people along the outer edge with weapons who were manning the fires would need to be able to hear if more animals were coming. In that regard, silence was vital. Five more lives had been lost during the late stages of the days march, and that was tragic, but he hoped no more would be lost before daybreak.

Everyone huddled closely together within the grove of trees in fear of what the coming night would bring. Ross felt the close proximity would create a measure of warmth and security for many, but it would also make sleeping difficult. Those who wished to lay flat quickly learned that they would need to do so along the outer perimeter, as many were beginning to defend their small patch of ground with determination. Ross wondered how those people who had complained about their sleeping and living quarters aboard the transport vessels felt now.

Ross located Jessica and the rest of his group along the outer edge near one of the fires, and informed the man placing wood on the fire that he would relieve him in an hour. He then asked if he could do anything for those around him, but Janet and Aurora informed him that they would tend to those needs.

Aurora said, "We are perfectly capable of relieving the man tending to the fire when the time comes."

Janet added, "Ross, you have already done more than your share of the work throughout the day."

As a former nurse she knew that it was imperative he get some sleep. The entire population would be much better served in the coming days and weeks if Ross didn't collapse from exhaustion.

CHAPTER NINE

DIVIDED PROCESSION

Ross opened his eyes and bolted upright to see the first hint of dawn casting its light over the tired and scared human population. Still somewhat groggy from his lengthy slumber, he spun around to locate Jessica. She motioned to the ground around him so that he could see his entire group was resting, and quietly informed him that he had slept through the night.

Jessica told Ross that there had been no further attacks throughout the long silence of the night, and regardless of the reason, that came as a welcome relief. For Ross, the reason for no attacks was less important at the moment than the fact that there had been no attacks. The men and women who had been guarding the outer perimeter and tending to the fires were also beginning to breathe a sigh of relief. It seemed unlikely that the wolf like beasts would never return, and they could now see if one was actually approaching.

After walking the entire perimeter to thank those who had stood as sentinels of defense, Ross met with some of the representatives who had been chosen to voice the interests of the main population. The consensus was that many could not take another day like the previous one without some additional rest, but Ross wasn't sure if that was the best course of action. He was reminded that the majority of the population had not slept well the previous two nights. Additionally, the column had walked a distance of roughly six miles from the unprotected elevated plain, and it looked as if a nearly equal distance would need to be covered in order to reach the intended shoreline. Those factors, added to the fatigue associated with the thin air and lack of substantial amounts of food or water, could create a problem. A large portion of the population wouldn't be able to advance at the same quick pace that had been set the previous day. Many needed to rest for an entire day before moving on. Otherwise, there was a risk that the column would become divided more significantly than it had been the previous day.

There were other factors to consider as well. A small percentage of the people would need to backtrack a short distance in order to collect their personal belongings. Left behind out of necessity during the dusk attacks of the animal pack, they could now be safely retrieved. Additionally, a few people wanted to provide a funeral service for the thirteen victims of the wolf like beasts, and bury the body of the dead woman that had been carried into camp.

Ross considered those factors, and a few others. He realized that he had been lucky to actually sleep for several hours, and agreed that more rest might be needed by many within the general population. The tasks that had been mentioned were both necessary and time consuming, which would delay their advancement during the short daylight hours significantly.

With that in mind, he asked the representatives, "How do you feel about splitting up the column?"

He knew that perhaps a few thousand were strong enough to push forward, and they would move much faster than the main column. They could probably reach the water's edge before nightfall, set up a new camp, and begin foraging for food and firewood. A separate smaller group of people would be needed to provide some protection for those who were backtracking in order to retrieve their personal belongings. There were two benefits to that. First, it would undoubtedly provide safety during the return to the site of the most recent attack. Second, there would be an opportunity to get a closer look at the dead animal. If the huge carcass had not already been eaten by other predators, then perhaps it could be carved into small enough sections to be carried back to this camp as a much needed food source. That would provide a wonderful psychological boost, because the rhinoceros sized body could provide a scrap of meat for a great many people to munch on. Unfortunately, the funeral service for the fallen was a different matter. Ross believed that would have a negative psychological effect, and was probably not the most efficient use of energy at the present time. A service would eventually be an appropriate measure without a doubt, but the overall safety and relocation of the entire surviving population took precedence.

The representative group of men and women agreed that Ross' plan made sense for the greater good. They were also glad to hear that he planned on remaining in the current camp with the larger segment of the population. Word of the multi-faceted plan spread quickly, and those who felt they could venture forward began to muster. Ross and Colt were part of the small group that would backtrack the necessary distance to inspect the wolf carcass. They would determine if carving it up was feasible, while others retrieved their belongings.

Within a few hours, they had safely returned to the confines of the trees. Most of the people who had remained at the camp were either sleeping or resting quietly. Jessica and Aurora reported that they, along with a few other women, had attempted to get an accurate count of those who had moved on ahead. Each woman counted a line of people as they exited the grove of trees, and the total was slightly less than twenty-three hundred.

Jessica said, "If our count is close to accurate, roughly seventy-five hundred people have remained at this campsite for another night. It's probably a good idea to gather whatever provisions we can find."

Ross replied, "Please give my thanks to the ladies for their help with the count, and your right about the provisions."

Meanwhile, well hidden on a high ridge top a few miles away, several pairs of eyes were watching the actions of the population quite intently. A hunting party had been working an area on the far side of the ridge the previous night, and had noticed something rather peculiar. Against the clear star filled night sky, the cumulative glow created by several dozen raging campfires was visible to the naked eye along the ridge top.

Thinking that the glow in the sky was a message from the Gods, the hunters quickly climbed the last few feet toward the summit in order to pay respectful homage. They soon realized that the commotion in the valley below was not caused by the Gods at all. It was something entirely different, so they hid themselves in order to study the actions of the people they had discovered.

They observed minimal movement throughout the camp during the remainder of the night, and that movement had been mostly near the ring of fires. The daylight hours however, were a different story. A large group had emerged from the trees that housed the ring of fires, and moved toward the distant water. They also noticed a much smaller group had moved in the opposite direction. Among other things, the hunters could inform their King that this new group of people possessed the skills needed to hunt animals, because they had returned to the trees with the remains of a large kill.

The distance to the shoreline from the grove of trees was slightly shorter than the previous days trek, and the group that had gone ahead of the main body reached their intended destination shortly after midday. Spreading out along an ever increasing line at the shore, the mass of people began to wade in and drink the refreshingly cold water. They all needed to cool down from the long march in the hot sun, and fight back the symptoms of dehydration and exhaustion. What they had all endured had still not fully sunk in, but eventually some would need to begin the all-important search for food and firewood. That in turn would hopefully prompt the remainder of the group to get busy as well. There was limited hours of daylight at their disposal, and much needed to be done before nightfall.

At the camp of the main column, meat from the carcass had been cleaned, cooked, and carved into bite sized chunks. Although the portions were small, the supply provided a large percentage of the population with a much needed shot of protein. The women, and any children, were the first to eat. They formed single file lines leading to various campfires, and they each received a precious scrap of meat. When those lines were taken care of, the men followed suit. Considering how long it had been since their last substantial meal aboard the alien transports, Ross was amazed at how smoothly the process had gone. With the lingering aroma wafting through the grove, he noticed that the spirits of many had visibly been lifted.

Word was passed that the people now had an option to consider. They could work now, or later, but the remainder of their time in camp couldn't be treated like a holiday. Additional sources of food needed to be foraged, and firewood collected, before the coming nightfall.

Ross spoke in plain terms again when he said, "We all need additional wood and food if we can find any. Whoever doesn't help with collecting those valuable resources now, will be responsible for manning the perimeter fires and defensive positions throughout the night."

CHAPTER TEN

REUNITED

Not long after first light, Ross led the large column of people from the grove of trees toward the distant shoreline. The general mood of the group was better than the previous morning, and Ross realized that the additional rest and a scrap of food had indeed served them well. He also knew that the advance group had successfully made it to the shoreline the previous day. That confirmation had come courtesy of a young man who had climbed the sturdiest of the short trees the previous evening. He reported seeing a line of flickering small fires in the distance. It was unknown if the body of water had provided protection as one aspect of a required defensible perimeter, but the fires would have been in a circular pattern if the group had fallen short of their intended goal.

Jessica provided some much needed inspiration before the column departed from the cover of the trees. Although most were ready to forge ahead, her message was intended for those who still seemed unwilling or unable. She removed the leg brace from her right leg, and raised it high overhead.

Speaking loudly enough so that hundreds of people could hear, she said, "I have been wearing this leg brace, or one similar to it, since I was two years old. Because of the brace, I was able to pursue certain goals in life that otherwise would have been much more difficult to obtain. They have provided tremendous comfort in helping me to overcome a physical disability, and increased my belief that all things are possible." Jessica then looked around in all directions while shaking the large titanium object, and added, "I'm so confident in our collective ability to reach the shoreline, that I will walk the entire distance without wearing this leg brace!"

Ross was proud of his sister for finally realizing that she no longer needed the leg brace. The act in itself was a hugely significant moment for her, and she had done so at the most appropriate of times. Many people within close proximity were nodding their heads in a positive manner. They were each discovering an inner strength to tap into, and Jessica had aided in that accomplishment.

The grove of trees opened up onto an area of rocky soil and ground shrubs as the column continued their slow decent. Approximately three miles later the terrain suddenly changed. Steep mountains on both sides of the valley had been slowly pinching in on the column since the beginning of the hike, and had effectively funneled them into a narrow exit area. Roughly three hundred yards in width, the opening led down a soft dirt embankment onto a massive field of tall grass and other vegetation. The drop was no more than thirty feet, and held back the encroaching wispy veil of fog that hung peacefully within the grass. Stretching for perhaps a mile, the seemingly tranquil field would need to be crossed in order to reach the shoreline.

Ross led the descent into the field, and the tall grass reached well above his waist. The ground was much softer than what the column had experienced to that point, which was a welcome relief. Several minutes later, Ross paused long enough for at least one-third of the population to walk beyond his position. It was obvious that the column had begun to slow considerably. Many were still in a weakened state, and were fading fast. As he witnessed the last of the column descend the embankment, Ross and others urged a quicker pace. Jessica moved among the people speaking words of encouragement, and was eventually told to mind her own business. The column was thinning as it had during the first long march, and many people in front of Ross were showing signs of not caring about the slower members of the group. He realized that the hike had just become one of survival of the fittest. That was not good news, as his present position appeared to be only slightly more than halfway through the grass field.

A moment later, Ross was startled by the sound of a distant scream. Panic quickly spread throughout the column as a man had suddenly disappeared from view. Within seconds several more bodies were lost in the tall swaying grass, and shouts of horror could be heard from all directions. Ross didn't know what the problem was yet, but it had caused a human stampede. Those who were capable began running very quickly toward the distant shoreline.

Initially Ross thought the Wolf creatures had returned, but soon dismissed that possibility. They were simply too large and tall to effectively hide in the long grass. Even if the pack of animals had been lying flat on the ground, their bodies would have created large openings in the waves of grass. Perhaps that was a new tactic though. A natural instinct for most people would be to walk through an area of foliage or vegetation with the least resistance, so those who had disappeared may have simply walked directly into the clutches of the waiting beasts. Still that entire scenario seemed unlikely, as they had not attacked during the heat of the midday before. Whatever the case, Ross knew that standing in his current position was probably not the smartest idea. While running the best that he could for a man of seventy-two, Ross called out while visually scanning the surrounding area. He needed to locate his family and others within his close circle, but that could be a daunting task. As the mass of bodies moved ever closer to escaping the seemingly endless acres of tall grass, several people continued to suddenly disappear from his view. Although he didn't have an exact count, Ross guessed that he had personally seen thirty to forty people vanish. He couldn't possibly have noticed every person to go down in the sea of waving grass, so he knew that represented only a portion of those taken.

Through the deep breaths caused by running in the thin air, Ross said, "What the hell is going on?"

In what could only be described as pure luck, Ross noticed a familiar figure roughly fifty yards in front of him. His mother Janet was moving with great efficiency. That was good news, and an instant reminder that the woman was a physically fit thirty-four year old. He had also found another of the family, as Jessica was close by her side. Neither Aurora nor Mrs. Patterson were in eyesight, and Ross almost fell when he looked behind in a vain search for them. That was when he noticed Colt, who had dutifully remained close behind him.

Colt yelled out, "Sir, do you need any help?"

Ross looked back again and said, "I'm alright thanks, but have you seen Aurora or Mrs. Patterson?"

Colt quickened his pace slightly to move up beside Ross and replied, "No sir I haven't, but I see Janet and Jessica in front of us."

Ross noticed that his sister was beginning to labor somewhat. Her right leg had never been worked so strenuously without having the brace on it. Janet's motherly instincts kicked in instantly, and she visibly slowed to assist her daughter.

Ross turned to Colt and said, "They need help, and you can get there faster than I can."

Colt nodded and took off toward the ladies. Ross was also closing in due to their ever slowing pace, but he never caught up to his sister. When Colt arrived at Jessica's side, he took charge immediately.

Removing his backpack, he shouted, "Climb on now!" She instantly wrapped her arms around his shoulders and rode "piggyback" the remaining distance to safety, as he clutched her outer thighs with his powerful hands.

Janet looked back briefly to see Ross approaching as she picked up Colt's backpack.

Ross yelled out, "Keep moving."

She heeded her son's advice, and the two of them ran in tandem as they each held onto one end of Colt's backpack. Trailing him by no more than thirty yards, they kept Colt in sight until the fog and tall grass gave way to sandy soil. Colt moved at least fifty yards clear of the grass field before stopping so that Jessica could dismount.

He fell to his knees while gasping for breath, as Jessica removed her backpack and said, "Thank you Colt. Thank you!"

Jessica had remained a slender woman of good physical fitness for her entire life, but she knew that lugging her body weight for well over a quarter of a mile could not have been easy. Add to that the weight of her gear, and she had probably become very cumbersome and heavy. Jessica knew that it must have been pure adrenalin that had kept Colt going, and she would be forever thankful.

Within a few seconds, Ross and Janet arrived at Colt and Jessica's side. They set down his backpack and removed their own, as Colt continued to heave for more oxygen. Janet's motherly instincts were still evident as she quickly hugged Jessica, and then leaned in to give Colt a kiss on the cheek for his heroic deed.

Smiling with obvious pleasure, he nodded when Ross said, "Thanks Colt. I'll never forget what you just did for my sister!"

Ross and Jessica then turned their collective attention back toward the tall grass, and moved closer to the boundary. They could see the upper torsos of perhaps a few thousand people still within the confines of the tall grass. Most of them were moving in their direction in anticipation of surviving the ordeal, but some had stopped to search for their respective friends or loved ones.

Ross and many others shouted out, "Keep moving this way", as a few more stragglers disappeared from view.

Looking back over his shoulder, Ross could see that Janet was tending to Colt. He felt confident that the man was in good hands, and just needed a few more minutes of recovery time to catch his breath.

Ross could also see that the campsite of the advance group was now less than a mile away. The terrain was sandy soil, with clear visibility in all directions, and those who had already emerged from the tall grass were making a beeline for it without a thought of looking back.

The column was definitely becoming more divided, and not just with regard to the pace of physical movement. Ross realized that a new philosophy within the population had evolved. Most people would no longer risk their own safety while waiting for others to catch up.

Returning his gaze to the vast sea of tall grass, Ross felt a different level of concern. There was still no sign of Aurora or Mrs. Patterson. He knew they would not have continued on with the others toward the advance camp. There was no sense in even considering that option. They were either already safe somewhere near his current position, still attempting to move through the tall grass, or had been two of the many that had vanished within it.

Jessica said, "If you want to search to our left, I'll go to the right."

Ross nodded and replied, "That's a good idea. We can cover more ground that way."

Just then, a woman, along with several men in military flight suits, jogged past them to safety. Janet noticed them, and motioned for the group to stop so she could say hello. Their outdated clothing made it obvious to Ross and Jessica that they had been some of the long term abductees held with their mother on the deep water vessel. Ross had a suspicion as to the identities of each member of the group, and made a mental note to confirm those thoughts with his mother at a more appropriate moment.

Ross repeatedly yelled out, "Aurora" as he continued moving to his left.

Jessica echoed the gesture while fanning out to their right. In spite of her recent need for assistance, she had not put the leg brace back on. Her bold statement to walk the full distance to the shoreline without it had been derailed due to the current threat the column had encountered, but she still intended to finish the trek as it had begun. It was doubtful if anyone would really care one way or the other, but it was important for Jessica to be true to herself.

Within an hour, the last of the column had cleared the danger zone of the tall grass. Throughout that time, many more people had been lost. Ross had asked several people if they had actually seen what type of creature had attacked the column, and there were varied reports. The common thread was that they were some type of lizard creature. Larger than an adult alligator, they were supposedly very quick as they sprung for their victims from holes in the ground. They were also strong enough to drag a body back into their burrows, and the victim had virtually no chance to escape their clutches. Ross thought that the huge Wolf creatures of the previous few days had been a difficult challenge, but this new animal had already proved to be significantly more dangerous to the safety of the population. He also realized there must be several hundred of them living beneath the vast field of grass in order to inflict that much damage in so short a time.

Ross continued to search and called out, "Aurora. Mrs. Patterson."

Several other people were scanning the high grass for their loved ones in similar fashion. He wanted to urge them to move on toward the advance camp, but couldn't ask them to give up hope unless he was willing to do the same. Eventually, he took the lead in the hope that others would follow. Resigned to the grim belief that both Aurora and Mrs. Patterson had been lost to the lizard creatures, Ross began to walk back toward where he had left Janet and Colt.

A trembling voice off to his right said, "Daddy?"

Aurora was only twenty feet away, and he rushed to her side. She had not called him daddy since his days at NASA, so he knew something was terribly wrong.

While sobbing on his shoulder, she said, "She saved me daddy, and now she's gone."

Ross looked into her eyes and asked, "Who saved you honey?"

"Mrs. Patterson."

Ross didn't want to believe what she had said, but it was true. While fighting back the tears, Aurora explained how the two of them were making their way through the grass when it suddenly happened. More concerned with searching for the family as opposed to watching where she was going, Aurora had walked directly toward the burrow of one of the creatures. Without ever seeing it coming, the creature suddenly sprang. In an instant Aurora was falling forward to the ground, as Mrs. Patterson had pushed her forward with all her strength. By the time Aurora rolled over to stand up, Mrs. Patterson was in the clutches of the creature and being pulled hopelessly back into the deep burrow.

The tears began to flow again as Aurora said, "She looked right at me as she was being pulled underground by that awful creature. I'm so sorry daddy, but there was nothing that I could do to help her."

For the first time since being deposited on this new world, Ross truly felt loss. He had known Wendy Patterson for many years, and she was a trusted and loyal assistant for that entire time. In essence she was almost like a member of the family, and had proved her loyalty to that family even in her last moment of life.

Ross and Aurora began a solemn walk back toward where he had left Janet, Colt, and all the backpacks. They spotted Jessica who was still in search mode, and he wondered how he was going to break the news to her that Mrs. Patterson had been killed. The women had known each other since the days of working together at the law firm back in Houston, and it was Jessica who had introduced her to Ross when he was searching for a new executive assistant. With just one look at her brother, Jessica instantly knew the sad truth. Although overjoyed to see that her niece was safe, she was saddened by the loss of her dear friend Wendy Patterson.

After a momentary embrace, they reunited with Janet and Colt. Ross then asked his mother, "Where did your group of friends go?"

She pointed toward the shoreline and said, "The same place everyone else is going."

Ross looked in that direction while adding, "I don't blame them, but it would have been nice to meet them."

He could see that some members of the column had already reached the site of the advance camp, and there was a steady stream of others following. Ross couldn't wait to speak with several members of the advance column. He wondered how many of them had fallen prey to the lizard creatures when passing through the same killing zone the previous day.

Before moving forward with the group of those around him, Ross said, "Hey everybody, look over there."

Off to their distant left, on the farthest edge of where the small mountain range approached the large body of water, a small waterfall was barely visible. Their current vantage point had just enough altitude above the water's edge, that they could also see a peninsula of fairly flat ground in the same area. The two geographic features would have been more obviously visible from the top of the dirt embankment, but Ross had been singularly focused on the large grassy field at that juncture. The fact of spotting the waterfall at this now lower elevation had just been pure luck.

Ross pointed as he exclaimed, "That could be a great location for a permanent settlement. The almost flat land area looks as if it could be large enough for everyone, and there's a fresh water supply close at hand."

The group of those still within ear shot mumbled and nodded with agreement. Unsure if anyone else had noticed the waterfall, he intended to discuss it with the representatives at the advance camp.

The sun was getting low again, so Ross slipped on his backpack and said, "We should get to the advance camp as quickly as we can." With affirmative nods from everyone he added, "It will feel good to take a swim."

He took one last look at the killing field of tall grass, and saluted those who had fallen. Then Ross said a silent farewell to his old friend Wendy.

CHAPTER ELEVEN
LONG THIN LINES

Emotions were mixed within the population of pilgrims during their fourth night on the new world. The advance group had done an outstanding job of setting up a temporary camp, and seemingly everyone had been in the water to bathe, cool off, and rehydrate. One hugely significant problem facing the population had been addressed, as a vast supply of fresh water was now close at hand. There was also a new source of food. Several people who had arrived the previous day were able to catch some fish for the collective good. Those factors lifted the spirits of many, but others still seemed defeated. For the less physically fit, the recent sprint through the tall grass in the thin atmosphere had sapped what little energy they had left. That coupled with the sorrow of losing friends or loved ones to the attacks of the wolf or lizard creatures had put a damper on the euphoria of the moment. Ross knew that many were on the verge of giving up. It would take courage for each of them to reach deep within, and fight for their survival.

In spite of the recently improved conditions, Ross was aware that the now exhausted population faced other major concerns. Over the past three days, everyone endured two full days of high altitude hiking, while living on limited water, scraps of food, and insufficient sleep. A steady supply of nutrition would be needed very soon if the majority of the population were to survive. Besides that, adequate shelter was the top priority. Very soon, prolonged exposure to the elements would most definitely impact the abilities of most people.

While meeting with representatives to discuss the pulse of the people, Ross mentioned the distant waterfall he had seen. Several others had noticed it as well before their final descent to the beach, and agreed with Ross. Although their current location was definitely better than where they had camped during previous nights, the lack of shelter made it unsuitable for a lengthy stay.

Ross said, "I believe the entire column should make one final push toward the waterfall at first light. Once we arrive, work can begin on whatever is needed to establish a permanent settlement."

During that same meeting he learned that the number of dead must now number in the hundreds. An exact count of the carnage was not yet known, but the advance group had lost forty-eight while crossing the field of tall grass the previous day. That group had been less than one-third the size of the column that Ross had been with, and much more agile and fleet of foot. It seemed obvious to Ross that the lizard creatures had probably claimed as many as two hundred more victims from the slower mass. He couldn't imagine another time when the creatures would have had such easy pickings.

There had been no additional attacks on the advance or main group after leaving the field of grass, so the consensus was that the creatures only dug their burrows and lived within that specific camouflaged area. That thought seemed presumptuous to Ross, but he had no desire to point that out at the present time. Increasing the level of fear that already existed within the population would not help their current situation. He had been correct about one thing though; the water had provided a defensible perimeter.

Word spread quickly of the intended plan for the next morning, and people began to spread themselves thinly along a vast section of beach. Thousands were now located outside the protective semi-circle of fires, but it was obvious that most of them felt safer sleeping near the water's edge.

When Ross and his group joined the two seemingly endless long thin lines of those trudging toward the waterfall, the fresh water of the enormous lake was slightly more than twenty feet to their right. They also had no idea of what was happening roughly two miles to their left.

* * * * *

Throughout the entirety of the previous three nights and two days, the hunting party had tracked the actions of the new human arrivals. Moving stealthily along the ridge top, they had kept a distant watchful eye on the divided column as it slogged its way down the valley. Now they were faced with a lengthy trek of their own. In order to return to their city, the hunting party must cross two valleys and two mountain ranges. The journey would take nearly two full days at a quick pace, and the King would be very interested in what they had to report.

They would inform him that while moving through the valley the large group of newcomers had become divided and then reunited. They had been hunted by animals, become the hunters themselves, and then ran in terror when hunted again. Some had shown signs of being strong and agile, while others were weak and lethargic. Although they had been viewed from a great distance, the new arrivals appeared to be both male and female. There were young and old, and their skin appeared to be many different shades ranging from pale to dark. Most importantly, the direction of their travel was bringing them closer to the Kings domain.

* * * * *

After walking for over an hour, Ross laughed out loud and said, "This is like traveling on an interstate highway in the United States."

Several of the younger and more physically fit had been passing on the left as if Ross was standing still. The two lines had become some-what like traffic lanes with the faster walkers on the left, and the slower ones to the right. People stopped for a water break when they needed to, and the column was already thinning out considerably. Ross knew that his group was doing well, but they needed to maintain a sane and comfortable pace. He didn't want to get caught up in the most current version of the "rat race" that had become such a stable of the human endeavor throughout the previous century.

With the sun moving higher into the sky, Jessica said, "Maybe we should all stop for a water break."

Aurora replied, "I'll second that motion."

As their group rested at the water's edge for a few minutes, Ross looked back to see that one line was thinning to the point of having gaps form. The other was steady and true, and hundreds more would probably pass them long before reaching their intended destination. Others would undoubtedly fall further behind, and Ross felt bad for them. If they could eventually make it to the permanent settlement, then of course they would be welcome. Unfortunately, he knew some of them wouldn't. It was uncertain what other forms of peril might be waiting in the near future, but Ross realized it was unfair for the many to sacrifice their best chance for the sake of the few.

Suddenly Janet recognized a group of people that were approaching, and waived for them to come over. When they recognized her intent, she tugged on Ross' sleeve. Then she said, "Ross, can I interrupt you for a moment? I would like for you to meet some friends of mine."

He turned to see a group of men in military flight suits, and they fired off a salute. Ross could think of no reason why they would do such a thing, unless they somehow knew who he had been back on Earth.

The lone woman in the group gave Janet a hug, and said, "Is this your son Janet?"

Ross returned the salute of the men so they could stand easy. He then turned his attention toward the two ladies.

Janet said, "Yes it is, and I want him to meet you."

Ross looked at the group, and said, "I recognize you from yesterday afternoon. You all jogged past me when you emerged from the tall grass, and I'm sorry that I didn't get a chance to meet you then."

He then moved closer to the woman standing next to Janet. Smiling, he reached out his hand while saying, "I have seen many photographs of you, and it is indeed a great pleasure to meet you Ms. Earhart."

She clasped his hand, and said, "It's a pleasure to meet you as well Mr. President, and please, call me Amelia."

Ross suddenly realized that his mother must have informed her friends of his former title while he searched for Aurora and Mrs. Patterson the previous day.

Jessica rose with an expression of astonishment, and inquired, "You're Amelia Earhart?"

Spinning from Ross she replied, "In the flesh!"

Throughout the next several minutes, Ross and Amelia became better acquainted. He was saddened to learn that she had also lost a close friend the previous day. Fred Noonan, who was the navigator for Amelia Earhart during the attempt to fly around the globe, had disappeared with her while flying over the Southern Pacific Ocean in 1937. He had, like far too many others, become one of the victims of the lizard creatures in the tall grass. That created a common cause to mourn for both Amelia and Ross, as Ross had considered Wendy Patterson to be one of his navigators.

The world had believed that Amelia and Fred had crashed into the ocean, and multiple conspiracy theories had circulated for decades. As far as he knew, alien abduction had never been part of the discussion. Their disappearance was ten years before the Roswell incident, so the thought of such things had not yet become well known. Those theories could now be dismissed for anyone who still might care one way or the other. Amelia and Fred, like Janet, had been quietly abducted by the alien species that had been observing Earth.

Ross flashed back to a time when Amelia's name had once again become big news. It was during 2013, more than seventy-five years after her disappearance, when Ross was still a member of the United States Senate. Resting in the shallow waters just off shore from an atoll, the remains of a plane that was supposedly hers had been discovered. As intriguing as that prospect had been for some people, it remained, like most things, in the news cycle for only a limited time.

As for the collection of fourteen military men that were currently with Amelia, Ross shook the hand of each one before the now combined groups moved onward. Ross learned that they, like him, had served as pilots in the military. Their group disappearance on December 5, 1945 had been cause for other conspiracy theories. Their mission, Flight 19, consisted of five airplanes that suddenly vanished near the southeast coast of Florida. A subsequent rescue plane was lost a few hours later, and so it began. Reports claimed that the rescue plane may have exploded, but no trace of Flight 19 was ever located. An area known as the Bermuda Triangle was tabbed as the culprit for that particular mystery and for many years became the supposed cause of other strange events that took place within that section of ocean. Although the myth of the triangle itself could not be completely put to rest, Ross now understood that it had nothing to do with the disappearance of Flight 19. The pilots and crews of that mission had been abducted and held captive as a group for nearly seventy-seven years. Collectively they claimed to have met no other people aboard the alien deep water vessel that had been abducted in the area of the Bermuda Triangle. Accordingly, they believed their case to be an isolated incident. Ross realized that they, Amelia and Fred, and his mother must have gravitated toward one another after their respective abductions. A logical assumption considering they had all come from a similar time in the big picture.

Several hours later, the now larger group of friends and family climbed up and over an embankment to a large plateau. The embankment was similar in height and composition to the one near the killing field of the lizard creatures, and could be used as a defensible position. That would be a topic to discuss with the representative council, but first Ross wanted to survey the area where the new colony would reside. He could see the waterfall at the far end of the plateau. It looked to be roughly a mile from his current position, which would provide plenty of room for the population. To his right, the midsection of the plateau led to a flat peninsula. That extra land would increase the amount of waterfront access for the colony, as it gently sloped toward the beach on all three sides. To the left, the plateau bumped up against a fairly steep wall of rock. Several of the early arrivals were scaling the surface, and exploring a series of small pothole shaped caves scattered throughout.

Gazing back at those still marching toward him, and then the angle of the sun, Ross knew they wouldn't all make it. He wished them well, but his most pressing task was the safety of those who had completed the journey.

Looking at his family and friends, he said, "Everyone sleep well tonight, at daybreak we start building a permanent home for the colony!"

CHAPTER TWELVE

ORBITAL MECHANICS

Having already crossed the width of the plateau, Ross and Jessica walked down the gentle slope that led out onto the peninsula. They had stopped on several occasions to converse briefly with several members of the colony, and would do so again if the need arose. Throughout the previous twenty-three days since reaching the plateau, that action had been repeated more times than Ross could possibly remember. Fortunately, those conversations had become more positive with each passing day. Cause for that new found enthusiasm within the colony was due largely to establishing routines, as the entire population had settled into their chosen living spots. The majority were now located on the plateau, but others could be found living on the peninsula or in small mountainside caves. In general, most had also been working diligently to help establish the permanent settlement. Many intended projects were taking shape, and Ross was proud of the collective effort.

The first order of business for the colony had been the creation of shelter. That included using whatever was available to build something simple, yet suitable. Thousands of sturdy tree limbs from a nearby forested area had provided usable material, and the bulk of them had been transported to the plateau strapped on the backs of several hundred colonists. Used as the basic framework for the construction of a lean-to, hundreds upon hundreds of the small shelters now graced the landscape. The challenge of creating the stable covers for each and every lean-to had proved to be more difficult. Surprisingly, a lucky few had actually packed a useable tarp in their gear. For most however, the use of small branches or bushes scrounged from the forested area were needed to provide a less than waterproof roof. On the rarest of occasions, flags depicting the national origin of an inhabitant had even been used. To Ross, the ingenuity to put a solid piece of cloth to such a practical use was a good idea, so he followed suit. The two American flags that once covered the coffins of his father and grandfather were now providing a portion of the shelter for his immediate group of family and friends.

Ross hoped he was not alone in his understanding that the colony still faced a multitude of tremendous challenges. Each night had been difficult for the majority of the population. Faced with the cold and fear of more animal attacks, it was obvious that many had not slept well. Sadly, there was no solid indication that the colony was becoming accustomed to the conditions. Adequate food stores were another major concern. Massive foraging efforts in the area between the former advance beach camp and the plateau had yielded some positive results. There were a few species of plants and small animals similar to squirrels that were edible, but nowhere near the amount needed to feed everyone consistently. Consequently, one hundred fifty-five more of the population had died due to starvation or exposure. Those who had lived their lives on Earth in an overly sanitized bubble initially found the food options to be unpalatable, but had adapted. Luckily, at least in the short term, an abundance of fish was available. That was helpful, and kept the population going. In time, the bushels of seeds that had been brought from Earth would help ease the pressure. A variety of crops would eventually sprout, but it was not known exactly when a yield would be available. Without a doubt there were other factors that required additional consideration, but Ross needed to remain as an optimistic presence. In spite of the many challenges that the colony had, and would, face, it was beginning to look as if the worst of times were in the past.

On the flats of the peninsula, the team of astronomers eagerly awaited the arrival of Ross and Jessica. Their research related to length of daylight and darkness on this moon had revealed some interesting conclusions.

After greeting each of the men with a handshake, Ross said, "Well gentlemen, it's a beautiful day to enlighten us about what you have discovered."

An Australian began the briefing confidently. "We have measured the duration of darkness for each of the twenty-eight nights we have been on this moon, and that duration has not ever varied a single minute."

Another voice added, "As we were dropped off on this moon at midday, we didn't begin tracking the daylight hours until the following morning. The lengths of those twenty-seven have also remained constant."

Ross glanced over toward Jessica, then looked at the group of astronomers and said, "Alright, so as you suggested sometime ago, this moon is not tilted on its axis like Earth is, or was. We can set our watch by the constant length of each of those daily events. That is useful information to be sure, but what does it all add up to?"

The bold Australian announced, "Both daylight and total darkness are five hundred nineteen minutes, or eight hours and thirty-nine minutes, in length. Dawn and dusk, although very brief, have both been included within that count."

Ross ran the simple math through his head before responding with. "So that totals seventeen hours and eighteen minutes of the Earth clock for one full day on this moon. My alien friend informed me that this moon was slightly over half the size of Earth. If the length of a complete day is roughly seventy-two percent of what they were on Earth, then the rotational velocity must be significantly different as well."

The group nodded to confirm his calculations, but were somewhat taken aback by his statement. They had collectively forgotten that this particular man had actually been an engineer and an astronaut before becoming a career politician.

Ross added, "I believe this information presents us with an interesting opportunity. We could explore the development of a new time keeping method that will be easier for everyone to follow?"

An American astronomer addressed Ross more formally by saying, "That is an interesting thought Mr. President, but we have more pressing information about our findings that must be discussed first."

Looking studiously at the rather short heavyset man, Ross said, "Fair enough professor, would you please be kind enough to provide some details about your concerns?"

Gulping at suddenly having been put on the spot, the man replied, "Mr. President, our first additional item creates more of a question than a concern. During the first few days it was difficult to pinpoint because our collective position in the valley continued to change, but we now have no doubts."

"Get to the point please."

"Yes sir Mr. President. Although the length of daylight remains constant, the sun has set over a different location along the mountain range every evening. We have been tracking the progression, and it is undeniable."

"So what does that mean?"

"Sir, this moon has a second rotational pattern as it orbits the planet, and none of us, in all our limited observations of planets, has ever encountered one like it. On paper, multiple rotations would cause a wild tumbling effect that would make the length of each day a random mystery. Those laws of physics and mathematics don't seem to apply on this moon though, as the rotations are seemingly working in perfect synchronicity to maintain a constant length of daylight and darkness."

"That sounds very interesting professor, but you don't seem to be too concerned about the effect it may have on us."

"I'm not Mr. President, because, at least for the present time, our other discovery could be much more significant."

The length of silence that followed gave Ross more than enough time to brace for the potentially bad news. He said, "Go ahead professor, I need to know what's going on."

"Pardon me for asking Mr. President, but do you recall our discussion during the first night on the surface about this moons host planet?"

"Yes I do, and please don't call me Mr. President. There is no reason for you, or anyone else for that matter, to address me that way ever again."

"Sorry sir, it won't happen again."

Knowing that he needed to ease the discomfort he had obviously created, Ross smiled as he placed his hand on the astronomers shoulder. After drawing in a deep relaxing breath, he added, "I have gazed upon the visible slivers of the planet and the inner moon every night since our arrival. They both grew larger until the planet became full. On that one night I was unable to see the inner moon, but it became visible again when the planet began to wane."

Jessica suddenly asked no one in particular, "Do you still believe our host planet will cause an eclipse?"

She was then taught a quick lesson in orbital mechanics when one of the previously silent astronomers said, "Without a doubt. All spheres orbiting a star, be they planets or moons, cast a shadow. Those shadows are what cause an eclipse. That is why the inner moon couldn't be seen on the one night when the planet appeared full."

Ross attempted to deflect the attention away from Jessica to protect what remained of her self-esteem by asking for further explanation. Her question had been both intelligent and relevant, but he could tell that the smug response of the astronomer had made his sister feel as if it were neither.

The American sensed her discomfort as well, and while looking at Ross said, "Sir, our position that night was in direct alignment between the host star and both the planet and inner moon. Our shadow blocked the moon from view, but wasn't large or intense enough to be visible on the planet surface. What's even more interesting though, is the orbit of that moon. Its visible portion grew at the same rate as the planet every night, and is now waning at the same rate."

Ross put the pieces together and said, "That evidence would suggest that both moons stay in perfect alignment as they orbit the planet. If that's true, then the inner moon will always be directly between this moon and the planet."

Another previously unheard astronomer said, "That's our collective assessment as well sir. Now that we all agree about the synchronized orbital path, the only really important question to ponder is if both moons will pass through the much larger shadow created by our host planet!"

Ross thought about that for a moment as he looked over at Jessica. He could tell that she had already shaken off the temporary effects created by the demeaning tone of the one astronomer. She was a secure enough person to know that there was always something else for her to learn. Even so, that man would be wise to understand that she would not be bullied by him in the future.

The question of what to do about the altered length of day still existed, so Ross returned to that subject. He asked the group, "Do you, as scientists, believe that the colony would be better served by continuing to use the old Earth system of time measurement, or should we attempt to develop a new system?"

Perhaps the question was ridiculous, but he wanted to hear what everyone in the group thought about the concept. Unfortunately, there was no response from the astronomers or Jessica that suggested support of a new system, so Ross let it go. He would ask the representative council their thoughts at the next meeting, but doubted they would be interested in such an undertaking.

Before he and Jessica could begin their return to the plateau, the confident Australian stated, "Sir, about the eclipse. I'm sorry, but we can't be sure if, or how often, this moon will pass through the shadow of the planet. If it does, the extent or duration of such an eclipse is also unknown at this time."

"I understand, and I appreciate your collective efforts of both observation and discovery up to this point."

CHAPTER THIRTEEN

CORNERSTONES

When Ross and Jessica reached the plateau, they took a detour to their left. The construction of a perimeter project was nearing completion, and Ross had been asked if he would come take a look at what had been accomplished. At the top of the steep embankment that he and everyone else had climbed to reach the plateau, stood a new line of defense. Ross and Jessica were instantly impressed as the group of engineers proudly explained how they had tackled the challenge by employing an ancient method of moving heavy objects. The same forested land that had provided vast amounts of sturdy tree limbs for shelters had been used for this particular endeavor as well. The entire grove of thirty foot tall barren trees was painstakingly cut down using nothing more than the hatchets and other small tools that the colony possessed.

Lifted by teams of strong men and women to an area of clear and level ground outside the confines of the grove, the two foot diameter trees were then rolled by other teams for more than half a mile to the base of the embankment. Along the lip at the top of the embankment, a long deep trench had been dug at close to a forty-five degree angle by additional teams. After removing roughly ten feet from the base end of the trees, the tops were shaved and sharpened to a point using rocks or knives. Then they were carried up the embankment, and the blunt ends were inserted into the trench. Several of the sections that had been removed from the trees were then placed horizontally within the trench for added stability. Finally, the trench was backfilled and compacted. The leading edge of the embankment now had a long row of sharpened treetops protruding at an outward angle from the ground. They ran almost the entire length from the base of the steep cliff to the large rock outcropping that plunged into the water. Roughly fifteen feet from ground to tip, they had been placed together tightly enough so that no animal much larger than a squirrel could fit between them.

Ross shook the hand of each engineer and worker that was in close proximity, and said, "This is fantastic. I want to personally thank everyone who has worked so hard on building this protective fence line."

One engineer responded by saying, "Thank you sir. We should have the last of it, including a small gate, completed by late tomorrow afternoon."

Usable firewood had also been foraged from the area, and what were once several acres of forested land was now nothing but barren ground. Ross thought it was sad that the entire area had been flattened beyond recognition, but it was necessary to help the colony survive. On the positive side of the destruction, no part of the wooded area had been wasted and no one had been lost to further animal attacks.

Ross and Jessica began the next day by taking a trip to the opposite end of the plateau. There, a project of even more significance was nearing completion. A slew of shallow trenches had been dug throughout the flat landscape on the far side of the stream that led from the waterfall to the shore. Various types of crop seeds brought from Earth had recently been planted in the area, and the trenches would provide them with a regulated supply of water. The main trench, designed as the gravity feed from the stream, had been lined with flat rocks to help maximize the flow. Additional flat rocks, turned on edge, would then act as rudimentary gates. They could be lifted or lowered from their positions between stakes to direct water into different sections of the field. Ross had been informed the previous evening that on this day, a similar gate would be positioned at the edge of the stream as the last phase of construction. When completed, water could be completely shut off from the fields of crops when necessary. Overall, the concept was as old as farming itself. Variations of the same irrigation method had been used for perhaps thousands of years back on Earth.

Megan Crenshaw shouted out, "I didn't think you two were going to make it. We were just about to go ahead and cut out the last few feet of trench without you."

Ross and Jessica were surprised to hear the news. They had been making their way across the length of the plateau in no particular hurry, because they thought it would be several hours before the project would be this close to completion.

When Megan Crenshaw volunteered to lead a team of workers that would build the irrigation system, Ross was admittedly skeptical about her qualifications. That was before he knew anything about the woman, or her passion for taking on such a task. She had been born and raised in Blandinsville, Illinois, and had spent her entire life of fifty plus years involved within the agricultural industry. By definition that meant she was very familiar with physical labor, and would see a task through to its completion. Her extensive skill set also included the currently useless ability to operate any form of agricultural machinery known to man, but it was her vast knowledge of soil preparation and hydrodynamics that had made her the obvious choice. Now that the project was being completed ahead of her planned time table, that choice was further validated.

As they approached, Megan greeted Ross and Jessica from the opposite side of the stream and said, "What took you two so long to get here?"

Ross replied, "My apologies, but I was unaware that our presence was required for the event."

"It isn't sir, but we were waiting as a courtesy."

"Well, thank you for the thoughtfulness, but please don't let us delay you any longer."

"All right then. Let's get on with it."

Megan believed in being direct and to the point, which was a trait that Ross found to be refreshing. An agricultural life had toughened her over the years both physically and mentally. There was no nonsense in this woman, and she didn't believe in wasting time that shouldn't be wasted.

Pointing to her left, she said, "There's the final cut."

Ross noticed that two large flat rocks needed as the flow regulating gates had already been put in place. They were spaced roughly two feet apart along the prepared trench, and were each held in proper position by a series of stakes driven into the ground. No more than a foot of ground separated the first gate from a placid portion of the stream, while the last of the dirt was being removed from beyond the second gate to complete the trench. Within minutes, the lining of the "U" shaped trench was then completed with the fitting of a few more flat rocks.

A young man with a deeply southern drawl said, "All set here ma'am, anytime you're ready."

Megan nodded and said, "Thank you." She then looked across the stream at Ross and Jessica while asking, "Either of you want to make the last cut?"

"No thank you. This was your project, so you do it."

Without wasting any more precious time she replied, "All right then."

As soon as the section of ground had been removed, Ross understood why she had chosen that particular spot in the stream. The placid water gently lapped up against the flat rock, and there was only a small amount of leakage. That leakage was easily handled by the now explained second gate. Had a turbulent portion of the stream been used, that leakage could have been more significant and less controllable.

In what Ross now realized to be her favorite catch phrase, Megan said, "All right then. Let's see how well this whole thing works."

The two gates were gently lifted from their blocking positions, and within a few minutes water was flowing into a portion of the planted field.

She summoned Ross and Jessica by saying, "Use those stepping stones over there to cross the stream, and come take a look at the process."

A diagonal walking path along the gentle hillside had been carved out on the downhill side of the main trench. It would serve the purpose of those who maintained the trench system, as well as those who would labor to carry future yields of crops to the colony. Once down at the level of the crop fields Megan explained to them how everything worked. They walked through the many acres where seeds had, or would be, planted, and inspected the maze of trenches.

While resting in the shade of a nearby tree, Ross took the opportunity to say, "Megan, I'm truly impressed by what you, and your team, have been able to accomplish here."

Jessica added, "In the future this will be of tremendous help to the colony."

"Thank you both for the kind words. It would be good if you could personally thank as many of my team as possible for their hard work."

"I promise you that both Jessica and I will make a point of doing exactly that."

"All right then. Now we can discuss an area of concern. This irrigation system will work just fine, but I can't be sure how much yield we will get unless I can improve the quality of the soil."

"Do you have any ideas on how to do that?"

"I can only think of one way sir. With no chemicals or additives at our disposal, we may need to figure out a method of using human waste as a substitute."

The thought may have been revolting to some, but Ross had seen and heard enough evidence from Megan to know that she was serious.

She added, "We won't know if such a measure will even be necessary for quite some time. The first crop yield may be wonderful, but I don't want to risk all of our seeds in poor soil. I would like to find out if there are any other people in the colony who have a solid understanding of agronomy and consult with them."

"That is an excellent idea Megan, and we will help you locate those people. You are officially in charge of this project, so do whatever you and your team think is right."

"All right then. Thank you. It's nice to come across a career politician that doesn't take forever to make a decision. So many of you seem to just sit around and argue about things without ever getting anything resolved."

Jessica seemed shocked at her bluntness, and said, "I'm not sure that's an entirely fair statement Megan!"

Ross didn't say a word. He didn't mind the comment at all because he knew there was a measure of truth to it. He knew first hand that the government of the United States had become lethargic and mired in quicksand due to its own obesity long before he had become the chief executive.

During the walk back along the plateau, Ross and Jessica decided to take a look at how Janet was coming along with her pet project. She, along with several others of similar training, had decided to set up a clinic of sorts. Rudimentary in scope, the cluster of shelters were in no way equipped to handle major medical problems. Instead, the intent of the few doctors and nurses within the population was to provide those with minor issues some level of comfort. In the few months' time that Ross and Jessica had been around their mother, they had learned she was a woman of action. It came as no surprise to either of them that Janet had overseen the construction of a few rather large lean-tos for use as a now operational medical clinic.

With one more planned stop on their agenda, Ross and Jessica pressed on. As they made their way, Ross suddenly became strangely quiet. The conversations and observations of the past two days had showed him that certain aspects to insure the safety and wellbeing of the colony were coming together nicely. Before reaching the fence line to view the now completed structure and gate, he concluded that the time had come to explore more of the surrounding area. Ross knew it was important to determine if, and where, additional natural resources and food existed.

Turning to Jessica he said, "I think it's time for me to organize a small scouting party. We need to explore some of the vast terrain along the shoreline beyond the new crop field."

"Sounds like a good idea. When do you plan on doing this exploration and how many people make up your definition of a small scouting party?"

"I would definitely like to start early tomorrow morning if possible. I also believe that roughly a dozen of us can remain easily mobile."

CHAPTER FOURTEEN

THE SHADOW

With a mix of emotions that ranged from exhilaration of the discovery, to outright fear of walking toward their demise, Ross and his scouting party approached the outer edge of the city. Although they had not seen any posted sentries up to that point, the feeling of having been watched for several minutes was shared by the entire group. The path they had followed leading up the valley from the water's edge had become much more pronounced during the previous quarter mile, and all twelve of the inquisitive explorers could now easily walk side by side along it if they so desired.

As they reached a point roughly one hundred yards from the first small hut, four sentries emerged from within and stood side by side across the path. The feeling of having been previously watched was then instantly verified, as a glance to the rear revealed six others taking up similar positions. Ross' scouting party was now bracketed, and he knew their left and right sides would soon be flanked. Under the circumstances, the most logical course of action was for his group to remain as calm as possible. After requesting that they show no signs of aggressive behavior, Ross took the initiative by slowly moving forward roughly ten yards away from the group with his arms and palms open. He wanted to show the sentries that he had no weapons, and hoped they understood that his intent was peaceful.

Several members of the scouting party, including Colt, voiced their opinion that he was taking a risk by doing so, but Ross knew they could be killed by the sentries at any time if that was their desire. In that regard, it didn't really matter if he was standing alone, or with the group.

In most cases it would have been unbelievable for Ross and the others to think there could be another civilization living in the challenging environment that this moon provided, but the proof was standing directly in front of them. His old alien friend had informed Ross when they all disembarked the transport vessels that his group of pilgrims were not the first people of Earth to be brought to this world. Although that information was not generally known throughout the population, it had made this entire circumstance somewhat easier for Ross to fathom. Still, he hadn't known until very recently that another group had actually survived, and he wanted to learn more about them. Much to Ross' surprise, early indications were that this civilization had not only survived, but it appeared as if they had developed a complex infrastructure as well.

One of the four sentries blocking the path handed his spear to the man next to him, and began a confident advance toward Ross and the scouting party. Unlike his initial reaction of many years before when he encountered an alien species on Earths now extinct moon, Ross held his ground. The man was considerably younger than Ross with dark hair and complexion. Slightly shorter in stature, he looked to be physically fit, and most importantly, definitely human. He stopped a few feet in front of Ross, and began speaking in a language that Ross didn't comprehend.

Ross then responded with a greeting of his own. His words weren't as trite as "Take me to your leader", but the intent of the message was certainly close to that. The puzzled look upon the face of his counterpart informed Ross that his message was not understood, so he requested some help. Ross had a suspicion of what civilization on Earth these people had descended from, but he needed to gather more information in order for that suspicion to be either refuted or confirmed.

He called upon Gabriela Ignacio. A woman in her mid-fifties of Hispanic heritage, she was tall and slender with thick black hair cut just above the shoulder. Her formal education had been focused mainly on the ancient civilizations of Earth, and she spoke several languages fluently. Ross had met her for the first time after they had all been deposited on this moon, as Gabriela was one of many that answered the call for needed translators. Through several discussions, Ross learned that she had spent many years working in the field on expeditions to explore the historical ruins of those civilizations. She had also given lectures on the subject at many universities throughout the world. Her combination of mental skills, and the ability to handle an advanced level of physical challenges, made Gabriela a perfect choice as a member of a scout team. Ross was glad to have her along, and Colt had taught her some of the basics in how to handle a blade or spear in the event of animal attacks.

Ross said, "Gabriela, be cautious during the process, but would you please advance to my side. You might be able to translate what the sentry and I are trying to say to each other."

He couldn't be sure, but he thought the language of this newly discovered civilization was something close to Spanish. She was most definitely the best suited among the scouting party to determine if Ross was correct in that assessment.

After a respectful bow of the head toward the sentry, Gabriela began a dialogue that seemed to establish a delicate peace. Looking at Ross she said, "I believe that everything will be alright now sir, but it is proper that you bow slightly to him before he can escort you deeper into the city."

Ross was happy to comply, and thanked her for the help. He then asked the entire scouting party to join him in a respectful bow until Gabriela gave the word to discontinue.

Much of their walk over the next several minutes was spent looking at all the huts, rows upon rows of irrigated crops, and the people hard at work with their respective tasks. Ross and the others marveled at the infrastructure that had been developed by these people, and he asked Gabriela, "Do you have any idea who these people might be?"

She responded immediately by stating, "Without a doubt sir, but I would like to see if you and the rest of the group come to the same conclusion on your own."

Ross was then so busy looking around for verification of his suspicion, that he didn't notice the escorting sentry come to a halt. He literally almost walked right into him, before Colt arrested his advance. The scouting party was then handed over to a man wearing much more formal attire. Gabriela bowed her head, and Ross motioned for the rest of the group to join him in a similar show of respect. Their new escort then led them to the awaiting King. After watching the escort bow deeply at the feet of his King, Ross flashed back to his days as President of the United States. Some things were apparently universal. It didn't matter where in the cosmos a civilization resided, there would always be a measure of pomp associated with addressing the leader.

It made no difference where such a meeting took place; initial contact was always of tremendous significance. Ross thought this other civilization was probably just as surprised as his own to learn of the existence of other people on this moon. With that in mind, he offered a bow to the King as he rose from his chair. What Ross didn't expect was a return bow from the King. He quickly learned that Gabriela had informed the escort that Ross was the leader of the group of strangers to visit the city, and that many others resided back at their own village. She moved forward to Ross' side, and offered a deep bow to the King until she felt it was appropriate to rise. As with the sentry, Gabriela began a dialogue so that the leaders of two different civilizations could effectively communicate with each other.

A moment later she turned to Ross and said, "Sir. How would you like me to respond to the Kings belief that I am just one of your many wives, and that I am only here to speak on your behalf?"

Ross was puzzled by her question, but said, "That it's not true of course. You know you have just as much value in our society as I do."

Although pleased to hear how the ever humble Ross felt about gender equality, Gabriela cautioned him as she said, "Ancient civilizations of Earth, and frankly some of the modern ones, are not known for such enlightenment sir!"

Ross nodded while asking, "What do you suggest?"

"It might be best to let him believe I am one of your wives. Otherwise he might interpret it as a sign of weakness in your leadership. Worse than that, he could demand that you turn me over to him as a gesture of good will."

Ross looked surprised to hear that, but was aware that Gabriela was the expert in the customs of ancient civilizations. He said, "If you believe that it will help smooth the current situation, and are comfortable with playing that particular role while we are in their city, then go ahead and inform the King that you are my wife."

She nodded, and gave the message to the King.

What Ross and the scouting party didn't know, was that the King had been aware of their presence on the moon since shortly after their arrival. A hunting party had reported the actions of a large group of people moving through the valley that lay beyond three mountain ranges. Since that report, the King had sent out additional scouts to keep an eye on the new arrivals progress and intentions. He had been informed of how the strangers had chosen a site for a permanent settlement, and had completely destroyed a forested section of land. The King was also aware of the scouting party's approach to his city. He informed Gabriela that they had been tracked since not long after leaving the shoreline along the path to the city.

After roughly twenty minutes of questions and answers between the two leaders, the King offered to show Ross and his scouting party more of the city. Many citizens were busy with different tasks, but upon seeing their King among them, they gave a polite gentle bow. At that moment Ross realized that the second of their two escorts was nothing more than a "brown nose" toward the King. The overdone bow at his feet had been the proof. Another example of a universal constant, as Ross once again flashed back to the memory of a few people who had fawned over him during his presidential years.

While on the walking tour, they came upon a large open area. Located in what Ross assumed to be the center of the city, there were no buildings of any kind in close proximity. Within that vacant space, there was a large circular area that was defined by a series of markers. In spite of heavy foot traffic in the area, Ross never witnessed a citizen entering the circle. At first he thought the markers might be headstones, and the people didn't want to disrespect the dead by walking over their graves. It was a logical assumption, as each of the stones stood straight up about two feet in height. That thought was quickly proven to be incorrect, as the King strode directly toward the circular area. The entry point was between two large statue looking figures that faced toward the center, and the King motioned for Ross and his supposed wife Gabriela to follow. The remainder of the scouting party was halted by sentries, so they would have to wait outside the circle. Each statue stood almost equal to Ross' height of six foot-two. Magnificently detailed carvings of stone, they were apparently designed to resemble someone of significance to this civilization. They were identical in size and position, with their facial expressions being the only discernible difference between the two. One smiled broadly while the opposite statue frowned. At the foot of each statue there was a large flat stone imbedded into the ground, and Ross initially thought they resembled home plate on a baseball diamond. Further inspection revealed that the size of each was roughly the same as home plate, but their shape was closer to that of a pyramid with the top cropped off. In the center of each pyramid shaped rock, a carved etching of a much smaller pyramid was also visible.

While following the King to the obelisk in the center of the open area, Ross noticed that the flat stones formed a complete circle around them, and they seemed to be aligned inside the outer circle of the two foot high stones. The stone obelisk stood roughly twenty feet in height. It narrowed slightly throughout the upper reaches, but formed an arrowhead as opposed to the more familiar pyramid at the top. A mid-length shadow was currently being produced, and Ross suddenly realized that he was standing in the middle of a very large sundial. The dimensions were bigger than anything he had ever seen back on earth, as the diameter of this circular formation must have been at least fifty yards.

Through the translation process of Gabriela, Ross asked the King "Is there any location where they could all view the structure from above?"

The King nodded positively, and motioned for Ross and Gabriela to follow him back out between the statues. The remainder of the scouting party was allowed to re-join the group once the King had exited the sacred circle, and a moment later they had ascended a small bluff to a public viewing area.

From the low angle vantage point, the entire sundial could be easily viewed. That particular location placed the two statues directly behind the obelisk, which produced the illusion of them standing on either side of it. Ross and the remainder of the scouting party listened intently as Gabriela translated for the King. He began to tell the story of how the sundial came to be built and its overall function, and then pointed out the flat stones forming the inner circle. They were vital in that they each represented one day in the cycle. Each day, just moments before sunset, the shadow cast by the obelisk would attain its maximum length. The tip of that shadow would reach the center of the appropriate flat stone for a brief time, and then disappear when the sun faded from view.

Ross was already aware that the length of both daylight and darkness on this moon were equal. The timing experiment performed by the group of astronomers to prove that fact had been brought to his attention. That explained a lack of seasonal change that could alter the length of the shadow, but a quick look around raised another question.

Ross turned to Gabriela, and said, "Please ask the King how this magnificent sundial accounts for the differing height of the surrounding terrain just before sunset."

It seemed obvious to Ross, and now the others, that the sun would set earlier over the mountains, as opposed to the time during the cycle when it set over the open end of the valley. The King listened to Gabriela as she translated Ross' question, and pointed in various directions as he responded. The scouting party was then shocked to learn that various nearby buildings had been constructed in their locations with exacting height to create several false sunsets. That was done so that the time of sunset upon the obelisk became uniform throughout the cycle. As Ross scanned the surrounding area, it became obvious that many of the taller structures were located toward the low lying open end of the valley. It was engineering genius at its best, and he was immediately impressed.

As their education about the sundial continued, Ross noticed that the shadow from the obelisk was moving closer to one of the flat stones. He took that opportunity to finally count them all, as that would provide the information of how many days were in a complete cycle of this moon around the host planet. The easiest place for Ross to start was at the foot of one of the statues, and that's when he noticed some of them were a different color. The count was forty stones from the foot of one statue all the way around to the foot of the other, with four more stones placed between the two statues.

Another member of the scouting party leaned into Ross and whispered, "I counted it as a total of forty-four stones a little while ago, what was your count?"

"The same as you, forty-four."

Within the nearly complete circle of forty white stones, they had each noticed that two of them where a color more typical of a brick.

Ross once again asked Gabriela to translate his question of, "Is there a reason that those two stones within the circle are a different color than the rest?"

He soon learned that the first, located just one stone into the cycle from the foot of the first statue represented a day of planting certain crops. The second, two stones short of the other statue, signified a day of harvesting.

This civilization had a system of rotating their crops in the field. Every month they would plant a section, and thirty-six days later they would harvest a different section. Each crop that was harvested had been growing for nine stones, or days, less than three complete cycles of the sundial. Ross quickly did the math and realized that came to one hundred and twenty-three days from planting to harvest. Although there may not have been any cosmic significance to the ascending order of numbers associated with the count, he felt the information could be useful to Megan Crenshaw.

The final aspect of the sundial that caught Ross' attention were the four black stones placed between the two statues. He remembered seeing the different facial expressions of the two statues as he walked past them and it suddenly became very clear as to why. Gabriela had a concerned look when Ross asked her to present his next question to the King, but she translated anyway. The King confirmed Ross' suspicion that the four black stones between the statues represented the time of total darkness. It was the time of the eclipse caused by the very large host planet that the astronomers had warned Ross about. He now had an answer to their unsolved question. Complete darkness would last a total of four days. The shadow cast on the current day had not yet reached its maximum length, but it was closing in on the stone marker very quickly. Soon the scouting party would know exactly how many days remained until their first eclipse cycle on this moon, and the shadow already suggested it wouldn't be many. The frown on the face of one statue now made perfect sense to Ross, as it represented the end of sunny days. In contrast, the smiling one represented the triumphant return of the sun, and that planting day would be the following day.

Understanding that the scouting party should not begin their return journey at this late hour, Ross asked Gabriela to translate one final question to the King.

She complied as the King heard the request of, "Can we watch the shadow until it points to a specific stone and then sleep here for one night before returning to our own village?"

The King nodded in agreement once again, and sent a worker to prepare guest accommodations. Soon the arrowhead of the shadow revealed that only four more days of sunlight would occur before the eclipse. This civilization had one more day of regular activity before a harvest day, but the group of humans who had recently arrived on this moon had much more to prepare for.

In keeping up with appearances as husband and wife, Ross and Gabriela shared a bed of straw that night in a private room. It was the first bed that he had ever shared with anyone other than Patty, but that would be as far as it went. It wasn't that Gabriela was unattractive, and her intelligence made her even more appealing to Ross. He just didn't feel comfortable taking advantage of the situation. After all, their arrangement was just a ruse to help insure positive relations with the King. What Ross didn't realize, was that Gabriela was more than willing to fulfill whatever measures were necessary in order to maintain the facade of marriage. If he had advanced upon her, she would not have resisted.

Before falling asleep, Ross whispered, "These people are the descendants of the lost Mayan civilization aren't they?"

"They are indeed sir, and that certainly helps to answer the question of why their civilization on Earth had seemed to literally disappear overnight!"

CHAPTER FIFTEEN

ENLIGHTENMENT

Ross moved stealthily toward the door, and looked outside to see the beauty of another sunrise. As difficult and challenging as the conditions of this moon could be, he still had to give credit where it was due. Every day seemed to bring amazing, yet brief, sunrises and sunsets.

Glancing over toward Gabriela, Ross noticed that she was still sleeping soundly. He couldn't blame her, as it was probably the most comfortable place she had slept since leaving Earth. It certainly had been for him, and he hoped that she hadn't been offended by his lack of sexual advancement. She had given some subtle signals, and the opportunity was obvious, but such action may not have been prudent in the long term.

Moving outside, he could see several of the Mayan citizens beginning another busy day. They all seemed quite content with their lives, and Ross hoped better days were ahead for the pilgrims that had come with him from Earth. There were many things to accomplish in order to achieve the same level of tranquility that the Mayans enjoyed, and the next eight days would be tremendously important as a first step toward that goal. That meant that a quick return to the colony in order to begin preparations for the coming eclipse was vital.

A moment later, Ross' thoughts were interrupted by a worker who had brought the scouting party a large plate of food. The young man gave a gentle bow to Ross as he set the plate down on the nearby table, and Ross smiled at him while returning the gesture. If further contact beyond this visit was going to take place, Ross knew that he would need to learn at least part of the Mayan language from Gabriela. Colt, and a few of the others, had apparently heard the young man moving about, and were beginning to rise from their restful slumber.

Pointing toward the plate of food, Ross said, "Courtesy of our host. Help yourself."

Returning with two slices of something that resembled bread, Colt said, "Good morning sir, do you want me to wake the rest of our people up?"

Ross shook his head as he accepted a slice, then replied, "Thanks, but let them sleep a few more minutes."

As quietly as possible Ross and Colt then began to discuss their groups next course of action. An early start was in order so that they could cover as much of the distance back to the colony as possible, but they didn't want to insult the Kings hospitality. The scouting party had discovered the path to the Mayan city on the morning of their third day of exploration. Much of the previous two days had been spent searching for food and usable natural resources, so the return would not take as long. Luckily the twelve of them could cover lots of ground fairly quickly, but it would still be more than a full day's walk back to the colony even if they left immediately.

Ross looked at Colt and stated, "We should not, and will not, leave without first thanking the King for his hospitality. Our departure time will therefore be solely dependent on when he is ready to meet with us again."

As Ross went over to get another piece of bread from the plate, Colt nodded and responded, "I understand sir."

Ross reentered the room where he and Gabriela had slept, as it was now time to wake her. The increasing morning light coming through the window hit her just the right way, and he wondered if he had made a terrible mistake the previous night. Ross knew that mistakes had been made throughout his entire life, as working in politics had been inherently wrought with them. This situation however, was very different.

First in a low whisper, and then with ever increasing volume, Ross repeated, "Gabriela, wake up!"

She was either exceptionally tired, or a sound sleeper, because he called out her name nearly a dozen times before receiving any hint of a response. When Gabriela finally opened her eyes, she saw Ross standing several feet away from her.

Reaching toward her with the piece of bread, he said, "Good morning. Are you hungry?"

Rubbing the sleep from her eyes while sitting upright, she responded, "Yes I am, thank you."

The morning light from the window behind her lit up her hair as she stretched, and Ross' thoughts of having made the wrong decision were further solidified.

Handing Gabriela the bread, he said, "You seem as if you could sleep through almost anything."

As she munched away on her snack, Ross had no idea that Gabriela had been awake most of the night in the hope that he would change his mind and make love to her. She thought several times about waking him to initiate the action, but something had held her back. Eventually she fell asleep after surrendering to the fact that Ross was either afraid, or not interested. Perhaps there would be another chance for them in the future, and she would embrace such an opportunity if it arose. She understood the reality, at least for the present time, that she was much more valuable to him as his interpreter than as a lover. Realizing that value would keep her close by his side, Gabriela decided she would make full use of that opportunity to hopefully break down his defenses.

A moment later they emerged from the room to find the other ten members of the scouting party enjoying the food that had been provided for them.

Ross said, "Good morning everyone, can I talk to you for a minute?"

Returning the well wishes, the group gathered around to hear what Ross had to say.

He was brief, but to the point when he said, "I'm sure you may all have your own thoughts on the matter, but the two of us believe that the people in this city are descendants of the Mayan civilization!"

While some within the group looked surprised, others nodded in agreement at having reached the same conclusion.

Ross continued, "I have asked Gabriela to teach me some of the basics of their language when we return to the colony. I want to wait until then so that others, including all of you, who desire the same instruction can share in the benefit of her expertise. It would be foolish to believe that we will never encounter a Mayan citizen again, so we should be prepared for the eventuality of when we do. There are many things that we can learn from them that could make our future easier, and improving our verbal communication is the key to accessing that knowledge."

Once the entire group digested the concept of their hosts being direct descendants of the Mayan civilization, they began to bounce ideas off of one another. There was spirited discussion of how the infrastructure of the colony could best be improved, and an enthusiasm among the group became plainly visible. Ross hoped that mindset would also become infectious back at the colony. One idea that could be implemented was to copy the Mayan example of using small sticks, dry grasses, and mud to construct more complete and stable structures.

Ross hated to interrupt the collective creative flow, but added, "There is much that we can do for the colony in the long term, but our first most pressing concern must be to prepare our people for the upcoming eclipse."

The quiet murmurs of agreement were then interrupted when the second Mayan escort of the previous day announced the arrival of the King.

Ross, with Gabriela by his side, greeted the King with a slight bow of respect. Per previous instructions from Ross, she said good morning to their host and thanked him again for his gracious hospitality.

The King responded with a slight bow of his own, then spoke frankly to Gabriela for several minutes.

She listened intently, and then began her translation of his warning to Ross by saying, "The King wants you to know that there are conditions to our two civilizations living in peace, but if we can meet those conditions you are welcome to visit his city whenever you desire."

Ross replied, "Please tell the King that I understand, and that we will do our best to meet his expectations."

"Sir, I think it only fair to warn you that his conditions may not be easy for our colony to live by."

"That sounds serious, what exactly are the conditions?"

"First, he demands that our people be careful with our use of the natural resources. He has been informed by his own hunting parties that we have already destroyed an entire section of forested land with no regard to what effect that might have on the surrounding area."

"We had to do that in order to provide ourselves with shelter and protection from the wild animals."

"He knows that sir, but he is also aware that we can't continue to take anything that we need from the land without thoughtful consideration."

"The King makes a fair point on that topic, and is correct that we should be more cautious. What else did he say?"

"Our multiple fires have been too large. At our current rate of consumption we will burn through all the trees before others can grow to take their place."

"If that is true, then we will need to monitor how much wood everyone receives for their campfires. The colony will not be pleased with such a restriction, especially when they learn there will be four days of total darkness occurring every month. Is that all the King requires?"

"Not quite sir. There is one more condition, but as I said, it will be a challenge to enforce upon our people."

"What could be more challenging than depriving them of a much needed light and heat source?"

"Sir, the King wants us to also be mindful of our future population growth. It all ties in with the limited supply of food and natural resources.

"Are you serious? How in the world are we supposed to regulate that?"

"I don't know sir, but yes, the King is serious. He told me that during their time on this moon, his people have found it necessary to regulate their numbers. Only a certain amount of babies are born each year as replacements for the elderly who can no longer work, or have passed on. They have maintained a fairly stable number of citizens of differing ages for all job classifications, but there is a minimal surplus."

"That's a very interesting strategy from a management perspective, but I have no idea how I, or anyone else for that matter, could promise the King that we will keep our population from expanding."

"Sir, he's not asking for zero population growth. He is requesting slow growth to help preserve the food and natural resources on this moon that his civilization, and ours, must now share. When you look at it from that angle, it becomes a very reasonable condition for a lasting peace!"

Ross looked at the King for a long moment, and could see in his expression that he was deadly serious about what had just been discussed. Then he turned back to Gabriela, and said, "Please tell the King I will do my best to meet his conditions."

With a polite bow from both leaders, followed by a firm hand shake, the meeting was concluded. Ross then instructed the scouting party to gather their few belongings, as it was now time to depart. After leading the small group out of the Mayan city and along the path toward the water's edge, Ross became lost in personal thought.

CHAPTER SIXTEEN

FAITH IN THE PAST

By setting a brisk pace at the instruction of Ross, the scouting party covered a significant percentage of the distance back to the colony before nightfall. A first light departure the following morning enabled them to be within sight of the colony well before the peak of the midday sun. Rounding a rocky point along the shoreline of the massive lake, the peninsula housing hundreds of the population had become the scouting party's first glimpse of home. A short time later, they reached the area that had been designated as crop fields.

Megan Crenshaw, along with many of her hand-picked staff, listened intently as Ross and the others explained what they had seen and heard during their visit to the Mayan city. She was thankful for the valuable information pertaining to how the Mayans rotated their various crop fields, the growth period before a yield could be harvested, and the duration of each eclipse cycle. Those factors would each play a major role in her ability to provide the maximum amount of food possible for the colony. Ross also found it interesting that Megan didn't seem to care that the information had come from a supposedly lost civilization of Earth. To her it was simply helpful agricultural information from the next farm over, and that was all there was to it. He admired her for that, and hoped the entire population would receive the upcoming news with similar grace.

Upon reaching the plateau, Ross and the scouting party were greeted by a large group that included Janet, Jessica, and Aurora. Ross asked, "Did anything of major importance such as wild animal attacks, or fighting within the population, take place during our absence?"

Jessica stepped forward to hug her brother and said, "No threats or problems, but a significant event did take place."

"What do you mean?"

Colt's earlier bold prediction had become reality, as Jessica said, "The representative council has been informed by their constituents, and has concurred with the decision, that you should become the official leader of the colony. In short, the population has just elected you as their President."

Janet then came forth to give her son a hug, and said, "Congratulations Ross. I'm so happy for you, and that I could witness your second ascension to President of the people."

With an expression of disbelief on his face, Ross looked around at the many faces present and said, "Thank you all very much for your belief in my abilities, and I shall do my best to help our colony survive and move forward. As long as we work together, we can accomplish anything we put our minds to."

Colt stepped forward with a congratulatory handshake and said, "Should I start calling you Mr. President again?"

"That will not be necessary my friend."

"Very well sir."

Janet released her son from the embrace, and asked, "Do any of you in the scouting party need medical attention?"

Colt quickly responded, "Could you please take a look at my shoulder? It's pretty sore."

"I'd be happy to, come with me to the medical facility."

As Janet led Colt away, Ross said to Gabriela, "That's curious. Colt never mentioned that his shoulder was hurting at any point during the journey."

Gabriela stared back at him in disbelief, and said, "Sir, I hope I don't need to translate that for you too."

Turning to Jessica and Aurora, he said, "Do either of you think that mom and Colt are possibly interested in each other?"

"Well, my big brother just had a light bulb moment. It has been obvious to most everyone else for a few weeks that the two of them like each other, where have you been?"

"I guess I just wasn't paying attention to that sort of thing, and never gave it much thought until this moment."

Aurora added, "Dad, it is truly amazing what a man of your intelligence can miss sometimes."

Gabriela couldn't stop her verbal reply quickly enough, and softly uttered, "I hear that!"

Ross turned to her and said, "You knew Colt and my mother liked each other too?"

Knowing she had been given an opportunity to escape from the self-created potentially embarrassing moment, she replied, "Yes sir, it has been obvious to me as well."

Turning back to Jessica and Aurora, Ross asked, "Could you please get word out to the members of the representative council, the astronomers, and all the translators, that I would like to meet with them later this afternoon."

Before leaving, Jessica looked beyond Ross to Gabriela. Due to the woman's previous comment, Jessica had a suspicion that she was perhaps interested in Ross. That suspicion was confirmed, and the message conveyed, when Gabriela smiled toward her with a slight shrug of the shoulders.

Returning the smile, Jessica said, "I understand."

Gabriela knew the message was intended for her, but it had been delivered in a way so that Ross would believe she was responding to his request. Now knowing that Jessica seemed supportive of her interest, Gabriela suddenly felt more at ease around her than at any time previously.

A few hours later, Ross stood at the opening to one of the small caves about ten feet above the group of roughly two hundred. They had gathered on the plateau so that he could address them. He began with, "Please move in as close as possible so that you can clearly hear everything I have to say. I have some important and startling information to share with all of you that our scouting party has learned, and it will be up to all of you to pass that information on to the general public."

Jessica and Aurora, who had not yet been privy to the information looked at each other with puzzlement, then turned to ask Janet if she had any insight as to what was happening.

Janet, who was standing at Colt's side, nudged his ribs and asked, "Will you tell us what is going on?"

"Please be quiet. Ross has some important information to pass along, and you will want to hear every word of it."

With a communal look of disgust at their inability to unlock the secret, the three ladies returned their attention to what Ross had to say.

Ross continued, "First, please pass along my thanks to everyone. It means a great deal to me that they, and you, have faith in what we have all come here to accomplish. Your hard work and dedication since we arrived on this moon has not gone unnoticed. There have been many difficult challenges for all of us, but we can persevere as long as we remain strong. Second, my condolences also go out to those families who have lost a friend or loved one due to some of those challenges along the way."

Janet applied a little additional pressure, "Colt, please tell us what is going on."

"If the three of you will just be patient, Ross will tell you everything you need to know."

Throughout the next hour, Ross told of how he and the rest of the scouting party had discovered, and been hosted by, descendants of the Mayan civilization. He spoke of the pending eclipse that would need to be prepared for, and the conditions set forth by the Mayan King so that peaceful relations between the two civilizations could exist.

One member of the representative council created a murmuring buzz when he stated, "The Mayans were incorrect about the destruction of Earth when their calendar claimed the end of days would occur in December of 2012. How can we be sure that they are correct, or telling us the truth, about when an eclipse might occur?"

Fearing that question would arise, Ross was ready for it. He asked, "Would the individual who asked that question please step forward so that I may address you directly?"

A hand shot into the air as the young man shouted out, "It was me sir, and I'll be right there."

Arriving at the spot just below Ross' perch, the young man may have wished he had never asked the question. With a stern tone, Ross began to shut down his counterparts' narrow minded and extremely arrogant response to the knowledge that the Mayans had passed on. He inquired, "Sir. With everything that you, and the rest of the colony, have experienced within the last year, you pick this critical time to question the validity or intent of another civilization."

"Yes sir, I do."

"Alright, let's discuss a few of the facts. An extremely advanced alien civilization that has been studying Earth at various intervals for perhaps thousands of years comes forth with information that could lead to the extinction of the human race. That same alien species then offers a solution to a very small percentage of us that could save the human race from that terrible fate. You, along with most everyone else in this colony, take advantage of that opportunity, and climb on board one of their deep space transport vessels. We travel for the equivalent of six weeks of our own internal body clocks across a vast unknown amount of space to a solar system containing this moon, while understanding that thirty-five years have passed on what might remain of Earth. You must have had some level of faith in their good intentions throughout that entire process, or you wouldn't have made the journey."

"That's true sir."

"Well I'm glad to hear that, because that faith must have continued until this very day. Remember when we were all informed by our transportation hosts that our species could survive on this particular marble. Thankfully the atmospheric conditions here are similar to those of the world that we left behind, so adaptation in that respect was minimal. We then learned very quickly due to animal attacks, lack of food, water, and adequate shelter, that our survival wouldn't be easy. You know it has been a struggle from the first night. Our death count from the various challenges has reached four hundred and forty-two souls, unless a few more passed away during my absence. There will undoubtedly be more to come, but we can't give up. As a colony of pilgrims, we have begun to carve out an existence that can, and will, become more stable. An abundant source of water sits at the edge of our colony, and rudimentary shelters, including a medical facility, have been constructed. We have located additional food sources within the surrounding terrain, and crops will eventually be harvested. Do you see where I'm going with all this?"

"Yes sir, I think I understand."

"Sir, I'm not sure that you do. Now we have discovered that a civilization representing another segment of time in the human evolution of Earth has also been brought to this moon. They have obviously been here for an extended period, learned what needed to be done in order to survive, and are willing to pass some of that information along to us. Now you stand in front of this quorum willing to question not only their extensive intelligence, but the peaceful intent with which they wish to share it. This is not the time for anyone, let alone a member of the representative council, to be casting negativity throughout the colony. Now I must ask you sir. Please tell me just exactly when did your faith in this entire endeavor vanish?"

Ross had driven home his point quite concisely, and the young man gulped in shame for casting a negative impression. He replied, "Sir. It appears that I owe you and the Mayans an apology. I simply haven't given your passion for this new found information, or their civilization, the credit they were due."

"I thank you for that sentiment sir, and I apologize as well if I was too vehement in my response to your query."

"No problem from my end sir. I fully understand that I was in need of a reality check."

With a nod of understanding, Ross calmed himself and continued by adding, "We can only assume that they are correct about the regular occurrence, and duration of the eclipse. As stated, their civilization has obviously been living on this moon significantly longer than we have. I don't believe they would have built a massive sundial in the center of their city unless it served them a purpose. As to the 2012 prediction of their calendar back on Earth, that specific date of 12-21-12 was determined based on how our modern scientists interpreted the writings of the Mayan civilization. I intend no disrespect to the members of the scientific community who translated that information, but it is possible that they were the ones who were incorrect. We must all admit that modern human arrogance can sometimes get in the way of truthful knowledge."

A different voice from the crowd could then be heard asking, "What do you mean by that remark?"

"Only that we have a tendency to assume that all of our computations are correct without question. Please remember, that is the type of thinking that created problems for NASA with regard to the Challenger disaster. Everyone assumed that the work done by themselves, or by the person next to them, was beyond reproach, but that collective arrogance helped to cause a catastrophic tragedy. In the case of the Mayan calendar, our people may have simply calculated the message or the math incorrectly. We don't know if any people or other life on Earth survived the impacts created by the collision of the asteroid into the Moon, but it may have been the end of days as the Mayan calendar predicted. Just think about it. In the really big picture of space and time, the difference between 2012 and 2022 is the blink of an eye. It could be as simple as someone forgetting to carry the one during their computations."

Most within the assembled crowd acknowledged that Ross was correct in his assessment of the modern human flaw of arrogance, and they could self-reflect on that subject when each felt the desire to do so. As for the current moment, thoughts of how to prepare for the coming eclipse became the number one priority for the colony.

Feeling as if he might have gone a little too far with his attempt to inform those around him, Ross took a deep breath before concluding his remarks. He said, "All of you share the most difficult task of informing the remainder of the colony about the contents of my current message. Many of them will be scared at the thought of four days of complete darkness, and the rationing of their firewood will not help the situation. It is extremely important that all of you set a positive example for them. As always, I will be available to help with whatever you may need so that the colony can make it through this new challenge. Everything that we learn from this eclipse cycle will help us to be better prepared for the next one. I thank you for your time and attentiveness, now let's all get to work."

After Ross climbed down to the plateau, Jessica was the first to greet him. She asked quite candidly, "How are we going to ration the firewood?"

"I haven't worked that out yet, and am completely open to any suggestions that you, or anyone else, might have."

Janet chimed in and said, "Ross, this is unrelated to the firewood situation, but I have some information for you that you may find disturbing."

"This seems like the perfect time for it, so tell me what's on your mind mom."

"It's a medical concern more than anything else."

"Is someone injured or sick beyond the doctors' ability to treat them?"

"No, we know how to treat this particular epidemic."

"Did you say epidemic? That sounds rather serious."

"Poor choice of words on my part, but there has been over two dozen confirmed cases so far."

"Get on with it mom, cases of what?"

"Our medical staff has recently confirmed that twenty-seven women within the colony are pregnant."

"Twenty-seven, how did that happen?"

"The usual way I suppose, wouldn't you?"

"Yes, of course, but the opportunity of privacy for such an activity has not exactly been easy to come by."

"That's true, but where there's a will, there's a way, if you get my meaning. Besides, most are far enough along that conception took place sometime during the six week voyage on the transport vessels.

There are even a handful of the ladies that must have been pregnant before we left Earth."

"Although I'm very happy for the expectant parents, the peaceful future of the colony depends partly on our minimal population growth."

Aurora broke into the conversation by pointing out, "There is a good chance that many more will become pregnant in the near future."

"Ross spun around to ask, "What makes you think so?"

"Come on dad, be realistic. What else are some of the people going to do with four days of complete darkness?"

CHAPTER SEVENTEEN

THE BLACK VOID

When the final hint of twilight faded from view, the noises from the surrounding terrain suddenly stopped. From nature's perspective, the previous few hours had been quite chaotic. Loud howling, and other less familiar audible sounds, could be easily heard from the nearby animal life. The surface of the massive lake appeared to be boiling as it teemed with activity. Thousands of fish, and other strange aquatic species of life that had not previously been witnessed, had been jumping high into the air. Now, as the eclipse cycle officially began, all was eerily still and absent of any sound.

Preparations over the previous few days had gone as well as could be expected, but it was still unknown how the colony would handle four days of complete darkness. Among other concessions, firewood had been rationed. Consequently, the majority of the individual campfires were noticeably smaller than during previous weeks. If not within fifteen feet of one, it was difficult for Ross to see well enough to walk. After speaking with a huddled family or small group, Ross would seek out another dimly lit fire and proceed in the hope of not stumbling over something along the way. In that regard it became somewhat like connecting the dots as he made his way along a portion of the plateau. Before long a helpless feeling swept over him at the thought of rendering minimal assistance, so he returned to the family camp for some much needed sleep.

In what, under normal conditions, would have been yet another typically bright morning, Ross awoke to discover that the surrounding area was darker than during the previous night. At that moment, the true magnitude of what the astronomers had been warning him about became crystal clear. The eclipse was even more complete and awe inspiring than what he had ever expected or imagined.

Cautiously, Ross stood in a futile attempt to survey his surroundings. Nothing could be seen other than a few stubborn embers casting a minimal glow from the dying remains of the family campfire. Fearing that he could trip over a sleeping body if he moved toward the lone source of light, he softly asked the surrounding darkness, "Is anyone else awake?"

The male voice of Colt replied, "I am sir."

"Good morning Colt. It sounds as if you are somewhere to my left, but I can't see you."

Jessica then responded, "We don't know where either of you are, but Aurora and I are sitting about ten feet away from what's left of the fire."

Attempted stealthy footsteps could then be heard from Colt's general direction, and several seconds later Janet said, "Could somebody please try to get the fire going again? With the added light, we could all safely make our way toward it."

Jessica offered assistance by saying, "We can probably crawl over there in a few seconds. I don't think there is anything between our current position and the fire."

While waiting patiently for the rebirth of the fire, Ross pondered the origin of the footsteps they had all just heard. To him it seemed rather obvious that Janet had been the culprit. She had attempted to fool everyone in the group by moving away from Colt before she spoke, but Ross felt fairly confident that her actions had been in vain. When a dim light was cast upon them all by the ever increasing intensity of the campfire, Ross could see that Aurora was the one who had revived it. He caught the attention of Jessica, and then nodded in the general direction of their mother. Jessica returned the nod, and both of them set a course toward Janet's position. The time had come to have a little chat with her.

Jessica began by saying, "Good morning mom, did you sleep well?"

Ross found it to be rather puzzling, but the normally confident and intelligent woman was having a difficult time responding to the question. Finally he said, "It's alright mom, we know you are interested in Colt."

With a degree of shock upon her face, Janet stammered out a simple response of, "You do?"

"Yes mom. Apparently I was the last of our immediate group to realize it, but that was my shortcoming."

"I have no idea what you are talking about!"

"Don't be silly, there's no need for you to hide your feelings from us or anybody else. If you and Colt enjoy each other's company, then by all means spend time with him."

"I see. Well, just for the sake of conversation, are the two of you giving me permission to see more of Colt?"

"We have no right to grant or deny you permission to do anything along those lines. The choice is up to the two of you if you desire to see more of each other."

"Well, that is a very open minded approach."

Jessica jumped in, "It's not just our approach mom, but thank you just the same. You see, one of the many aspects of American culture that was improved upon since your memory of 1957 was more of an equality between men and women. In our generation, and the ones that have followed, women have attained more of a voice pertaining to their individual rights or actions. That includes their role in a relationship, as women no longer have to play the role of the subservient unless they desire to do so. Not all cultures of Earth have moved forward in such a manner, but that is irrelevant in this particular case."

"You make it sound as if it's the woman's responsibility to make the first move."

"Not exactly mom. I'm saying that Colt is a gentleman, and he seems like the kind of man who would respect your wishes. In the time on Earth that Colt was raised, it was not considered taboo for a woman to make the first move."

"I'm not sure I can do that."

Ross was then quick to point out, "It seems to me as if you already have mom."

"What do you mean by that?"

"I'm saying that you didn't need to skulk through the darkness a few minutes ago in order to make us believe you had slept in a different location last night."

With a sigh of relief, Janet confessed, "I feel like such a fool. I have been trying to hide my feelings as if I was still an adolescent school girl. It is true that I slept by Colt's side last night, but I can assure you that we did not have relations."

"We never said you did mom, and Jessica's point is that in the modern time you have more of a choice as to when, and if, that might happen."

With a nod of acknowledgement, Janet moved toward the group that had gathered around the small campfire. Ross and Jessica stayed behind for a private conversation, centered mainly on what might happen within the colony over the next several days. Although it was true that some people of Earth living in the extreme northern or southern latitudes had learned how to adjust to prolonged periods of darkness and cold, Ross and Jessica were not among them. Having a number of those individuals within the population could have been beneficial in providing comfort and guidance, but it was unknown if any such people were members of the colony.

Pointing toward the sky above, Ross asked, "Have you had a chance to look at that yet?"

Jessica gazed overhead for a long moment, and then replied, "That is truly amazing, and I never imagined that our host planet could block out almost the entire sky."

"I would like to speak with the group of astronomers if I can locate them in the darkness. Would you like to join me on a little adventure?"

"Yes, of course, but can't it wait? I thought the plan was to minimize movement and activity by staying close to our campsite for the duration of the eclipse."

"It was, but now I have some immediate concerns as to the magnitude of this eclipse."

Returning to the fire, Ross voiced his intent to locate the astronomers with Jessica. Although Colt volunteered to go with them, Ross requested that he stay and help protect those in the immediate area. Colt agreed to do so, but insisted on providing both Ross and Jessica with some sort of defense for their journey. A short time later, he had made each of them a rudimentary torch from two of the longer and stouter pieces of firewood. Using torn bits of tattered clothing, and some of the previously collected tree sap, he had tightly wrapped something around the branches that would burn slowly and provide a light source. If the need arose as they made their way across the plateau toward the peninsula, each branch could also be used to help keep unruly people at bay.

In what took several hours to accomplish, the two torch bearing travelers eventually located the astronomers. Although several other campsites along the way had rekindled their small fires, the group of stargazing scientists had not. They wanted to view and study the eclipse with as little disruptive surrounding light as possible.

Once he had managed to convince the group to gather around, Ross looked upon their torch lit faces. He began with, "Good day to you gentlemen, are you enjoying the most recent phenomenon?"

The outspoken Australian from previous meetings was once again the first to weigh in, "Very much sir, isn't that a most magnificent sight?"

"I'm not sure I would describe it that way, but it is quite humbling."

"That's true sir, but awe inspiring just the same."

"Agreed, and I must admit that you were all correct when you informed me that an eclipse caused by our host planet would be this consuming."

"We have been tracking the path of the huge black void. You may not have noticed yet sir, but a few stars have become visible over the far end of the lake."

"No I hadn't noticed, but I didn't realize that it was that close to normal nightfall yet."

"It isn't sir. In fact, it's only about high noon. The stars have become visible much sooner due to the eclipse blocking out all the light from the sun."

"That's interesting, but why is that important?"

The American astronomer intervened, "Sir, by tracking the path of the black void, anyone within the colony will be able to know exactly when the sun will return by simply counting how many times they see it. Throughout the entirety of the eclipse, the best way for most people to know when it should be daylight will be when there is an absence of stars. As you are well aware, literally millions of stars become visible when our position on the moon rotates away from the sun into what would normally be nighttime hours. In contrast, the host planet now temporarily blocks out most of the sky when our position rotates toward the sun."

"I agree that most everyone will be able to follow that simple logic, but I have a larger concern than the darkness."

"What's that sir?"

"What is going to happen to the surface temperature of this moon with no radiant light from the sun to warm it?"

"I think you already know the answer to that question sir, or you would have picked an easier time to visit with us."

"So how far do you think the temperature will drop?"

Another astronomer chimed in, "That's impossible for us to know at the present time sir, but we are confident that the temperature will continue to drop with each passing day."

"That's what I was afraid of. Can you please measure and chart the daily drop? The data could be most helpful as we prepare for future eclipses."

CHAPTER EIGHTEEN

DAYLIGHT

Shouts of joy could be heard from the far reaches of the colony, as the first trace of daylight cast by the post-eclipse dawn intensified. There were also multiple cries of mourning. It would be unknown for perhaps several hours how many more pilgrims had died from exposure during the eclipse, but a plan to count them was already in place. Per Ross' request, Gabriela had translated his intent to the group of strong young Peruvian runners many hours before. Their task, as it had been during previous head counts, was to move throughout the population as quickly as possible at first light. Then, via the translators if necessary, they would report the count of those who had died at each campsite to others maintaining tally sheets at various points throughout the colony. That count would be added to the four hundred and forty-two who had already been lost to various challenges during previous weeks. The system wasn't perfect, with the potential human error of double counting as a factor, but Ross felt confident that an accurate count could be obtained with cooperation and focus.

Meanwhile, events that had been witnessed during the final hours of the pre-eclipse dusk were repeating themselves. Strange wild animal noises could be heard, and the surface of the massive lake once again boiled with activity. That included multiple sightings of a life form that was thought to be myth, but Ross had learned that anything was possible on this moon. A buzz of curious fascination, mixed with pure disbelief, could be heard throughout the colony. Many had claimed to have seen more than one of the mythical creatures during the time just prior to and after the eclipse, but the vast majority of the population held fast to their feelings of denial.

When asked by a group of colonists if Ross believed the rumor, he responded with, "There was a time on Earth when billions of people thought I was insane for believing in an alien species that ultimately brought us to this moon. That was not a very comfortable feeling, and I vowed to never be that narrow minded when it came to discussing the possibility of other life forms. Although I did not see one of the mythical creatures in question, I cannot dismiss the possibility of their existence."

Having been previously unaware of the topic at hand, Jessica asked, "What type of life form are you discussing?"

"At least one hundred people have reported spotting creatures that they believe are Mermaids."

"Did you say Mermaids?"

"Yes I did, and those who witnessed them are quite emphatic about their observations."

"Do you believe them?"

"With everything that has happened during the last two years, and what we have encountered on this moon, it would be foolish to simply dismiss the thought."

"Yes, but Mermaids?"

"All I know is that anything has proved to be possible here, so I plan on watching the lake very closely just prior to the next eclipse in the hope of verifying their claims."

Several hours later, Ross met once again with members of the representative council. The counts had been tallied from each camp and sector of the colony, and the total number of dead was alarming. The first eclipse experienced by the colony had claimed the lives of four hundred and seventeen people. Most of them had been elderly and poorly nourished, but there were exceptions. Janet, and other trained medical personnel, had already begun an investigation into the cause of death, but it would take time to examine each of the bodies. The initial wave of examinations had revealed the obvious, as prolonged exposure to the extreme cold without adequate clothing or shelter had done them in. Ross couldn't help but take the news personally. In spite of his best efforts with the short notice, the colony had obviously been ill prepared.

Turning to Jessica he said, "This is just terrible. We have now lost a total of eight hundred and fifty-nine members of the colony. We now number slightly less than nine thousand. If our collective gene pool is to survive, we must minimize the decline of our population."

"That's true, but at least most of those who have died were probably well beyond their reproductive years."

"Speaking of that, the twenty-seven pregnant women should probably be examined immediately. We need to have them all report to the medical clinic as soon as possible."

"Slow down a minute Ross. For many centuries women have been enduring a pregnancy in extreme conditions, and I'm sure that our expectant mothers are just fine for the moment. Besides, the medical team is rather busy right now."

"Good point and they probably will be for some time."

"Thank you. Now, perhaps we should discuss a few of the more immediate priorities."

"That's a good idea. First, after the bodies have all been identified and examined by the medical staff, we need to gather and move them to where the others are buried. In that respect, we need to dig graves as was done for many of those who died before the eclipse."

"Alright, should I begin looking for volunteers?"

"Yes please, and let it be known that I will be the first of that volunteer group."

"Consider it done Ross. What next?"

"It's going to sound horrible, but it must be done."

"Go ahead."

"The clothing that belonged to the dead will need to be salvaged. If family members or friends can't use them, then others will. We can't afford to bury our dead in clothing that could help someone else survive the cold."

"I agree. Is there anything else?"

"Yes. We will need to build some type of memorial on or near the gravesite to honor all those that have died during the early days of our life on this new world."

"That's a great idea. I'll see if the engineers who built the perimeter fence have any suggestions."

"Excellent, and thanks in advance for all your help with everything Jessica. We will have multiple projects to work on in the near future, with precious little time to complete them."

"Just like our days in Washington then?"

"Yes, but without all the support staff."

In the days that followed, the colony worked feverishly to complete many tasks. Hundreds took part in the digging of the mass grave site for the dead, and a subsequent service was held for those who wished to attend. Using the model provided by the Mayans, colonists began to construct small shelters from sunbaked bricks of small sticks and dry grasses mixed with lakeshore mud. Once completed, the materials from a lean-to would then be used for a crude roof. That would provide a nearly fully enclosed area to theoretically hold in the heat of a small fire during the cold nights and future eclipses.

As had been the case since the day of arrival on the moon, the majority of the long term abductees from the deep water vessel were the hardest workers. For the most part, they had also adapted to the current living conditions much quicker than other colonists. For Ross, and anyone who cared enough to notice, the reasoning was obvious. Many, like Janet, had come from a time on Earth that was void of the sometimes overly pampered modern conveniences. They were therefore somewhat accustomed to a more difficult or challenging way of life. In that regard, the abductees became most helpful. They taught those in the general population how to grasp the idea of coexisting with the natural surroundings.

In the midst of all the other work, Megan Crenshaw and the accompanying agricultural brain trust had also been busy. They had planted a variety of seeds in one-third of the irrigated rows within the crop fields just two days after the eclipse had ended. It had not been the most glorious of tasks for her team to perform, but per her belief, the soil had been enriched with a measure of human waste in the hope of creating additional yield.

CHAPTER NINETEEN

THE NEIGHBORS

With each passing eclipse, the number of colonists to perish continued to decline. On the morning of the fourth, and most recent, post-eclipse dawn, the results of the count had revealed that only six people had died during the event. Ross flashed back over the previous one hundred and thirty-two moon days since the first of such dawns, and smiled. The total of the dead within that time frame was only seventy-three, and most of those had died during the second and third time of the black void.

Including the nearly complete cycle of thirty-eight days leading up to and through the first eclipse, one hundred and seventy moon days had passed since their landing. During that time, the colony had come a long way. As a whole, it had grown stronger, and developed into a much more cohesive population. Most had fit into a working niche that they enjoyed, so everyday activities had inherently become more streamlined with less wasted effort. Improved, yet cautiously tempered, hunting, fishing, and foraging techniques, helped provide a greater supply of food for the general population. That, along with

Megan Crenshaw's delivery of the first full yield of rotational crops, had lifted the spirits of most everyone.

On the day of the harvest, Ross had publicly credited Megan and the rest of her team for the outstanding work that they had done with the crops. Using the Mayan example, she managed to harvest those crops three days before the most recent eclipse, and had two other yields in various stages of growth. As has been the case previously, Megan planned on planting one-third of the irrigated land during the second post-eclipse day. That would help to insure a perpetual cycle. Ross knew that would be a long and busy day for all those involved, but was completely comfortable with how Megan had handled the task on previous occasions.

A few days later, Janet was providing Ross and Jessica with a tour of the four newly completed shelters that housed the medical clinic. The invitation to view the facility had come with a request however, as the entire medical team wanted to have a discussion with Ross. Prior to the first eclipse, Aurora made a prediction that had proved to be correct. The number of confirmed pregnancies was escalating, and the medical team was concerned about their collective health and welfare. That discussion would need to be postponed however, as Ross spotted one of the Peruvian runners sprinting toward him.

Gabriela had sent word via the young woman that Ross was needed immediately. A group of visitors, that included the Mayan King, could be seen approaching from just beyond the irrigated fields. Ross sent a return message with the runner that he and Jessica would be there in a few minutes. Then he turned his attention back toward the medical team and said, "Sorry everyone, but we need to go welcome the Mayan King. Can we talk about your concerns at a later time?"

Janet responded, "Of course, but I'm coming with you. I have never met a Mayan before, let alone the King."

"That fact holds true for nearly everyone in our colony mom, so others will undoubtedly wish to do the same."

Having already ascended the embankment leading up from the crop fields, the Mayan entourage crossed over the stream and moved onto the plateau. Gabriela greeted the King and his group of twenty or so, and then motioned toward a large stump so the King could sit while they waited for Ross and Jessica to arrive. Megan, having been witness to the procession moving through the fields and past her shelter, crept closer in order to view the upcoming meeting.

A gentle respectful bow by each of the two leaders was followed by a handshake, and then in his practiced, yet broken Mayan, Ross said to the King, "Hello my friend. Welcome to our colony."

The Mayan King seemed surprised to hear the words spoken by his counterpart, but nodded with understanding. Having previously used Gabriela as a translator, the King glared in her direction with an expression of irritation on his face. He then bluntly asked in the only language he knew, "Did your husband know how to speak my language at the time of your visit to our city? If so, then why did he disrespect me and my people by having one of his wives speak to me on his behalf?"

It was quite obvious to Gabriela that the King had been offended, and she knew her response to his inquiry could be vital in the history of how these two civilizations co-existed. If she admitted to the King that Ross had been ignorant to the Mayan language at the time of the previous encounter, it could, and probably would, be interpreted as a sign of weakness. On the other hand, his new found grasp of a few bits of their language could earn Ross some respect from the Mayan people. That scenario was better than having the King believe Ross had intentionally disrespected him, so she took a leap of faith. In Mayan, she responded, "No, my husband had no understanding of your language when we visited your city. It has been his wish since that time that many of his people learn your language in order for our two civilizations to communicate with each other. He did this as a show of respect toward you and your people, and has ordered me to teach the people who want to learn."

With the tension now easing in his face, the King looked back toward Ross. Then he asked Gabriela, "How much of my language has he learned?"

"He has learned several words and a few basic phrases, but is working hard to learn more when he has the time."

"If he has ordered you to teach his people my language, then you must be his most trusted and intelligent wife. Do any of his other wives shoulder the burden of important tasks, or are they simply used for breeding purposes?"

Now it was Gabriela's turn to be offended. Although accurate, the King's statement implied that she was no longer of use for child bearing. Fighting back the inner rage caused by his presumption, Gabriela breathed deeply, slapped a smile on her face, and responded, "That's a very good question; let me ask Ross what he thinks."

Before she could muster the words, Ross interrupted them, "Some bits and pieces of your conversation with the King came through, but it was very fast. I definitely recognized the word for wife. What did he want to know about that?"

"The King wants to know if any of your other wives are as trustworthy and intelligent as me."

"What other wives?"

"The King believes that you, like him, have many wives, but that I may be the most trusted. He's insightful, but I think we should inform him that you don't have multiple wives."

"What about you?"

"What about me?"

"Do you wish to continue in the role of my wife?"

"Well this is all rather sudden sir, and I'm not quite sure how to respond to such a question. Are you asking me to be your wife for the sake of continuing our previous façade, or is this a legitimate and formal proposal?"

"This is not the time to joke around Gabriela. I'm asking you how we should handle his belief that you are my wife."

"Who says I'm joking?"

"Gabriela, please!"

"Alright sir, try to relax. For the sake of harmony, I will continue the façade. It' probably best for all of us if the King believes you have at least one wife."

"Thank you. Now please inform the King that you are my only wife. Then present an offer of rest, food, and water before I show him and his party the grounds of the colony."

In the hours that followed, the Mayan King and his entourage learned much about their counterparts and the host colony through quiet observation. There were introductions to several hundred people who had differing shades of skin color, and like those few who had visited the city, wore clothing that was unfamiliar to the Mayans. The two women directly behind Ross, who the King initially believed to be other wives, were the first to be introduced by Gabriella. The older one, Jessica, was said to be Ross' sister, but the attractive and much younger Janet was supposedly his mother. To the King, that seemed confusing and utterly impossible, and the expression on his face showed it. Blended with a reintroduction to Colt and those who had visited his city, the King met Megan, Aurora, Amelia, and the crews of Flight 19. Certain members of the representative council, and all six astronomers had also been introduced as Ross took the King and his group on a walking tour of the colony. That was when the King discovered that as a ruler, Ross did not maintain absolute power over the people. He learned there was a council that represented the will of the citizens, and Ross met with them often to discuss issues involving the colony. Not once throughout the tour had anyone bowed when Ross walked past, and the shelters that the average citizen lived in were of seemingly equal quality to the one that Ross and his family occupied. The King also noticed that in spite of those limitations, Ross had heeded his warning at the conclusion of their first encounter. The citizens of his colony had indeed been convinced to become more harmonious with nature. The King realized that Ross must be well liked and respected by his people, but he doubted leadership could be maintained through a method void of force. And if such tactics did work, that in itself was a puzzling thought. Such an example of leadership could become a threat in the future to the King or his heirs, which meant cautionary measures must be taken.

Throughout a long and nearly sleepless night, the King contemplated over what his next move would be. Continued peaceful relations between the two civilizations seemed to be the prudent course of action at the present time, although the contact would need to be somewhat limited. Further study of Ross and his people would be wise, and any potential weakness would be exploited if the need arose. His counterpart possessed superior numbers, but most of those that the King had seen or met while in the colony would not be considered members of a fighting force. In that regard the King believed that his citizens were better equipped for survival in a conflict. Personally, after all that he had seen of the colony, the King knew he had total superiority over Ross.

After a hearty breakfast meal provided by their hosts, the King and his entourage bid a respectful farewell.

Ross again offered his best attempt at Mayan when he said, "Goodbye my friend. Have a safe journey, and please visit us again soon."

The King looked at Gabriela, and she urged him on by nodding and saying, "Go ahead."

Turning to Ross, he said in broken English, "Thank you."

Ross smiled in the belief that another breakthrough in their relationship had been achieved, and shook the Kings hand. Jessica smiled inwardly; as she knew that Gabriela was again proving her love for Ross. It was apparent that she was a strong willed and highly intelligent woman, and would do whatever she deemed as appropriate and effective. In this case, she took the initiative, and helped bridge the language gap between the neighboring civilizations.

To emphasize his supposed strength, the King set a brisk pace as his entourage headed off in the direction of their city. He never looked back, but felt confident that his powerful stride had not gone unnoticed by Ross and the others. Once beyond the rocky shoreline point and out of view of the colony, the King, sweating profusely, stopped to rest his tired legs. His thoughts then began to center on a specific thought. Would he absorb Ross' colony into the control of his domain by taking offensive action, or leave them be?

CHAPTER TWENTY

THE INTERNAL CLOCK

Having watched the Mayan entourage until they were clear of the irrigated crop fields, Ross could waste no more time waiting for the King to look back over his shoulder. Turning to Megan he asked, "Can you please have a few members of your team keep an eye on the King and his party until they have rounded the rocky point. They don't need to follow, but I would like to know if the King is returning for some reason."

"No problem. I'll send word when he is safely away."

"Thanks Megan."

"It may be a few hours though, as I doubt anyone of his age could keep up the pace he set for very long."

"Perhaps, but please don't underestimate the King. His entire life has been spent living in these atmospheric conditions, so he may have incredible lung capacity and stamina."

Knowing there was some unfinished business from the previous day; Jessica said, "Ross, unless there is something else more pressing, we should probably have that discussion with the medical team."

"You're right; let's head for the clinic right now."

Janet and several other members of the medical team were deep in conversation when Ross and Jessica arrived. They didn't even notice they had company until Jessica said, "Good morning everyone. Is this a bad time for a visit?"

Janet turned and replied, "Not at all. We were hoping that you would stop by. Now that the neighboring dignitaries have departed, can we return to yesterday's conversation?"

Jessica returned, "That's the general idea, and speaking for Ross, the medical team now has our undivided attention."

"That's good to know, because we have something very important to discuss with you."

Ross replied, "As Jessica said mom, we are all ears."

Maintaining her role as the lead spokesperson, Janet proclaimed, "The obvious lack of medical equipment that had been in use on Earth in my time, or advancements developed during subsequent years, will undoubtedly hinder our efforts."

Ross then asked, "Hinder your efforts to do what?"

"Deliver healthy newborns of course."

"What are you talking about?"

"It has become somewhat of a guessing game for us to identify when each woman will reach full term, and the birthing process itself could also be impacted. Many of the mothers and newborns could face challenges if there are complications."

"Your point of the potential danger is understood mom, but what do you mean by a guessing game?"

"Ross, you know that the gestation period of a human fetus is roughly forty weeks of Earth time."

"Yes. I believe that most people, especially parents, are aware of that, but what is your point?"

"I mean that physiologically, at least with regard to the duration, these women all appear to be going through a normal pregnancy. We don't believe that the travel through space, or the time on this moon, has altered that internal clock."

"So what's the problem?"

"The problem is that a day on this moon is different in terms of hours on Earth, so we have to guess at how many days or weeks it will be until they reach full term. Of course we are not totally in the dark. Certain physical symptoms can provide us with a rough estimate as to how far along each woman is."

"Well, that's a relief. I thought you were building up to a significant problem with their collective health, but you're really talking about a fairly simple math calculation. As to the possibility of difficult deliveries, it seems to me that some of the other abductees might be helpful."

"What do you mean?"

"Think about the women you met on the deep water vessel. You told us that some of them had been in captivity longer than you."

"What about them?"

"Well, maybe one or more of them have delivered a baby in more primitive conditions than you or other members of the medical team are accustomed to. If so, their experience as either the mother or as a midwife could provide insight."

A male doctor intervened by saying, "That's a wonderful suggestion sir, if such a person exists."

Looking in his direction, Ross said, "I don't believe we have been formally introduced sir."

"No sir, we haven't. I'm Dr. Hans Schmidt."

"It's a pleasure to meet you Dr. Schmidt. I admit that such a woman may not exist within our population, but we should find out. Of course there may be other options available to us. Perhaps a Mayan woman could help. After all, they have no knowledge of the modern medical technology that you all currently crave. No drugs for the pain, no sanitized hospital, no post-birth health care system for the baby other than breast feeding and a blanket. In short, they know of only one way to deliver a newborn, the way it had been done for centuries."

Dr. Schmidt's response revealed an air of superiority when he said, "But there is a language barrier, and they don't possess any medical expertise or training."

"That is a poor excuse for not enlisting their help in this instance doctor. A person may not need to have been formally trained in the field of medicine to be of assistance."

"That may be correct, but it's difficult for someone like me who is accustomed to a sterile environment with modern equipment and technology to simply ignore it."

"Please excuse me doctor, but the advanced medical minds of this team need to get over that belief right now. It's true that our so called modern civilization of Earth benefited from technology that was way beyond that of the Mayan civilization. In fact, there was probably too much of it. We had become so reliant on having the knowledge of the planet at the blink of an eye in the palm of our hands, that we stopped working for said knowledge. Anything we wanted to learn or discover could be done so by looking it up on our electronic devices. In some parts of the world we reached the point of not being able to think for ourselves, or drive our cars anywhere, without relying on our intelligent built-in gadgets. Although ridiculously easy for everyone, it was actually quite pathetic."

"We have the brain power and ability to develop such a civilization again if we so desire."

"That's not entirely true doctor. While I will agree that we possess the collective intellect, an important piece to the puzzle is missing. If the last several months have taught us anything at all, it's that none of that technology exists on this moon. We can reinvent the proverbial wheel, but can we locate or develop the natural resources needed to build it?"

Janet stepped back into the conversation and said, "This is a wonderful topic for further discussion gentlemen, but I suggest we get back to the original problem."

Ross replied, "That's a good point mom. So the task at hand is to do a little math. We need to establish an estimate of moon time with relation to a full term human pregnancy."

She replied, "That is correct. The first step will be to multiply two hundred-eighty Earth days by twenty-four."

"Great. Does anyone have a cell phone or a calculator that I can borrow for a minute? Oh wait, I almost forgot. We don't have any of those things do we?"

"That is quite enough Ross. You made your point."

"Sorry, but I couldn't resist. How about some paper and pencil? That will be quicker than calculating it my head."

"Each of us ran the numbers, and concur that it equals six thousand, seven hundred, and twenty Earth hours."

"All right, so we need to divide that into moon days. The astronomers informed me that one full day here is equal to seventeen hours and eighteen minutes of Earth time. Shortly after our arrival, I attempted to initiate an easier method of time keeping, but was met with overwhelming resistance."

Jessica added, "Ross, that's not important right now."

"Good point Jessica. Everybody, divide the total Earth hours by seventeen point three, and that will give us the amount of moon days of a full term pregnancy."

A figure of 388.44 days was confirmed by all those in attendance, then that was divided by the 44 day moon month to reveal a total of 8.828 months.

Ross said, "Alright. Point eight-two-eight is very close to five-sixths in fraction form. Since one-sixth of forty-four days is equal to seven and one-third, a full term human pregnancy should be roughly seven days less than nine months."

Dr. Schmidt stated bluntly, "That is nearly the same as the duration of a pregnancy back on Earth?"

Ross replied, "That is interesting, and while we're at it, let's see how a month here compares to one on Earth."

Everyone multiplied 17.3 hours by 44 days, and then divided that total by 24 hours. The figure came to 31.7 days, so Janet said, "That implies that a month here, in terms of total hours, exceeds the average Earth month by slightly more than one day."

Nodding in agreement, Ross added, "That should be fairly easy to keep track of as we move forward. Now all that you on the medical team, and the pregnant women, have to do is count how many eclipse cycles have occurred since the time of their respective conceptions. That, when combined with the physiological symptoms previously mentioned, should eliminate much of the guessing game."

Janet jumped back in, "That's a relief."

"Why do you say that mom?"

"Because now I can more accurately gauge when each of the women, including myself, will deliver their babies."

"Yes and. . . Wait a minute. What did you just say?"

"You heard me. Now I can more accurately gauge when my baby will be born."

Jessica jumped in again, "Mom, are you pregnant?"

"Yes I am. The doctor confirmed it a few days ago."

"Does Colt know?"

"Yes he does, but I asked him not to tell either of you, or anyone else, until I could speak with you about it first."

Ross came back in, "This is absolutely mind blowing."

"Aren't you happy for us Ross?"

"Well of course I am mom, if that's what the two of you want. It is, however, rather difficult to grasp."

"It is what we want, but why is this difficult for you?"

"Because, I'm a man who became seventy-two years old shortly before we all left Earth, and Jessica recently became sixty-eight. Hell. Aurora is forty-five, and Rachel would be over one hundred and fifty back on Earth. Now you tell me that you and Colt are going to provide Jessica and me with a little baby brother or sister. I don't intend to be rude, so please accept my apology for the obvious yet completely understandable shock. This is just a concept that I had never imagined, and it's going to take me a little while to get used to the idea."

"That's understandable Ross, and I accept your apology. How about you Jessica, what do you think of my news?"

"Ross is correct. It's a shock to say the least, but I have no problem with it."

"Well at least one of you is supportive."

"Ross never said that he wasn't supportive of you and Colt, he's just trying to wrap his head around the idea."

"That's right mom. I think it's wonderful that the two of you have come together. I have known Colt for several years, and he is a good man who is dependable and loyal to the end. It has been my honor to benefit from his steadfast protection, and to count him as one of my friends."

"I'm glad you feel that way Ross. I hope to spend many years with him."

Dr. Schmidt intervened once again, "Do you feel better now that you have told them Janet."

"Yes I do Dr. Schmidt, and thanks for your help."

"It was my pleasure Janet."

Ross moved to shake the doctor's hand and asked, "Will you be her primary physician?"

"If that is what Janet wants, then consider it done."

Having then heard Janet's verbal acknowledgement, Ross added, "Thank you sir, and please take good care of her."

Bracketed by her two children, Janet walked toward the family compound. Speaking plainly, she softly explained, "I want the two of you to fully understand my feelings on this matter. I'm your mother, and you therefore think of me as a much older woman. It must be difficult for you, because both of you are well beyond your child bearing years, yet here I am pregnant. The weird twist is that my internal body clock is still young. I was only thirty-four years old when I was abducted in 1957, and with all the time in captivity and on this moon, I have aged less than an additional year. Physiologically speaking, I gave birth to Jessica less than four years ago. I missed almost all of your respective lives, and I want to have another chance at raising a child into adulthood. My body is healthy and fertile. I am in love with a man that we all respect and admire, and his feelings for me are the same."

Jessica spoke for them both, "I guess we never really looked at it that way mom. Of course you're right, and those feelings are totally justified. As a still young and vibrant woman, you shouldn't be hindered by the fact that your two previous children are now senior citizens."

"Ross, is that how you feel as well?"

"Yes it is mom. Now that you have explained it to both of us, and I've had a few minutes to digest the information, I agree with Jessica.

I also understand why you were so adamant about discussing potential challenges with the birthing process in this environment, or how this moon had not seemed to affect an expectant mother's internal body clock."

"I'm learning that it's difficult to get anything past you Ross, and I thank you both for the support. I promise that I will never love either of you less once I have this child."

"I think Jessica and I are aware of that mom. I just wish I had known that you were pregnant before introducing you to the Mayan King."

"Why is that?"

"After the King learned that Gabriela was my only wife, he had his eye on you. I don't want to think of him back in the Mayan city believing that you could possibly be made available to his desires."

"I think you meant to say that Gabriela was your only supposed wife, but that's a topic for discussion at another time. As to the King's desires, Colt mentioned that he had noticed him looking in my direction several times. What can a girl do? I'm flattered that the King took a fancy to me, and that you and Colt are prepared to protect my somewhat less than virtuous soul, but you should actually be more concerned about Aurora."

"I didn't notice. Was the King eyeing her as well?"

"No. As strange as this may sound, my granddaughter was probably too old for his taste, but I was more to his liking. I'm referring to the strong interest that Aurora seemed to have with one of the men in the King's entourage."

ᎶᏃ

CHAPTER TWENTY-ONE
DAMSEL IN DISTRESS

Throughout the history of the human endeavor, and perhaps that of other species living in the vastness of the universe, love had surely triumphed over common sense or logic on countless occasions. In this particular instance, Aurora had provided Ross with the most clear cut case of that constant that he had ever been associated with. Flirtatious since the time shortly after her university years, Aurora had endured a series of gentlemen callers as a byproduct of that trait. None of them ever possessed that certain quality to fully capture her heart, but somehow, this man did. At the age of forty-five, she had finally met someone really special. Most of her days were now consumed by thoughts of how to see him more often. That process became the driving force behind her uncharacteristic misjudgment, and the most recent predicament for Ross.

Three more eclipse cycles had come and gone since the Mayan King and his entourage had first visited Ross and the colony. Hunting and foraging groups from both civilizations had run into each other on several occasions, and had even teamed up to kill a few of the wolf like creatures. Citizen groups had visited the population center of the opposite civilization for purposes that ranged from educational or medical to simple curiosity. The connecting trail had become more pronounced, and a small shelter had been constructed as an overnight rest area near the midway point.

Aurora had become quite familiar with the path as a consequence of traveling to and from the Mayan city on several occasions. She gladly volunteered her services as a guide for those making their initial trek, and met with her favorite Mayan hunter during the course of each excursion. That familiarity and comfort is what led Aurora to the unwise belief that she could make the journey from the colony solo. Anxious to see her hunter again, she could wait no longer for a group of travelers to form. At first light four days after the return of the sun from the most recent eclipse cycle, she set off.

Moving quickly, Aurora headed beyond the irrigated fields and toward the rocky point. Once out of sight from the colony, and knowing that the trail would eventually turn away from the shoreline, she decided to cut off a large corner and blaze a new trail. Her thought was to shorten the distance and travel time to the Mayan city by moving through a saddle in the nearby mountains, but her road would soon be lined with peril.

Hearing the beast well before getting a visual fix, Aurora froze in her tracks. Scanning the area, she noticed that a wolf creature was pursuing a smaller animal and had apparently not spotted her yet. As stealthily as possible, she began to move in the opposite direction. Seconds later, a low growl to her left revealed a second huge wolf, and unfortunately, this one was staring right at her. Remembering what her father had said about their pack like mentality, Aurora knew that running from the wolf could lead her into the clutches of others. At her feet were several sharp edged rocks not much larger than her fists, and much to her dismay, they were her best hope of defense. After retrieving one for each hand, she took a deep breath and said, "It's your move wolf!"

With the creature unmoving, yet poised for an attack, Aurora spun around to see if the first wolf, or others, were sneaking up behind her. There was nothing in sight, but by the time she reversed her pivot, the one that had spotted her was advancing. She had no choice but to counter the advance, and began to close the gap between them. With clenching fists and outstretched arms she yelled at the wolf in the hope it would be scared away. Feeling surprise might be her best weapon, she ran straight at the beast when she felt the time was right. The plan worked for a brief moment, and in the instant that the wolf took a startled step back, she made a break for it. The cover of the nearby trees could at least give her a chance at survival, but she would need to get there very quickly. Sprinting for her life, Aurora yelled out to no one other than herself, "Keep running, it's only about fifty yards to the trees."

While stalking smaller prey nearby, a Mayan hunter snapped his head quickly to the left. Then he asked the others with him in their native tongue, "Did any of you hear that?"

"Hear what?"

"I thought I heard a voice from somewhere on the other side of those trees."

Having reached the thicket of trees, Aurora began to weave her way through them. It was her hope that the close quarters might slow down the advance of the rhinoceros sized wolf. Now running short of breath, she loudly screamed out for the entire moon to hear, "Somebody please help me!"

This time all six of the hunters heard the voice, as the first man said, "It's coming from over that way."

Stopping within a dense area of the thicket, Aurora prepared herself for battle. She knew that her current position offered her a better chance against the animal than trying to outrun it for several miles. The odds were still against her. Superior size and strength eventually prevailed in most cases, but she was determined to make the wolf work for his kill. Her plan was simple. Beat the attacking creature in the head and neck area with her pointed rocks until the bitter end. Luckily, just as the huge creature began to crash wildly into the trees surrounding her, the group of Mayan hunters had closed in on her screams for help.

From roughly one hundred yards away, the hunter who initially heard the strange voice exclaimed, "Look. Over there!"

A second replied, "The animal has someone trapped within that tight grouping of trees."

Now looking more closely at the person under attack, one of the other hunters said, "That is the woman from the newcomers' colony that I have been telling you about."

With lightning quick efficiency, the six hunters moved in. They circled the wolf creature and relentlessly stabbed away at it with their spears. Once the animal had been subdued, the hunters turned their attention to the woman still tucked into the small pocket of trees.

Aurora, with fists still tightly clenched, was trembling. A small amount of blood dripped from the sharp rocks and her fingertips, but its color did not match that of the wolf creature. Throughout her attempts to stab at the lunging animal, she had not been able to inflict any damage. In contrast, adrenaline during the moments of the attack had caused her to squeeze the rocks to the point of creating several cuts in her palms. Staring at the hunter directly in front of her, she attempted her best Mayan and said, "Thank you all for saving my life."

A hand from another hunter shot through the trees to grab her wrist, as he stated, "I claim this woman as mine. I was the one who heard her cry for help, and identified where she was so that we could save her."

Another said, "That is true, but you have no specific claim to her. We all attacked and brought down the creature in a coordinated effort to save her life."

"I tell you this woman is mine."

"We all have equal claim to her."

The lead hunter quickly intervened. Looking at each of the other five men in the group, he said, "Who has claim to this woman is not for any of us to decide."

The hunter who knew Aurora more intimately than the others chimed in, "She is free to decide who has claim to her, and it may not be any of you."

Having recognized his voice, Aurora snapped her head in his direction and her broad smile revealed instant relief. She said, "I'm glad you came to my rescue."

The lead hunter spoke again in response to the question of claim. "Only the King can decide who shall have claim of this woman or if she has the right to choose. For now, our task is to clean this kill and prepare the meat for transport. After that is done, we can begin the journey back home. We will take the woman with us, and when we arrive tomorrow, we will present her to the king. If he does not want her, then any of you who wish to stake a claim can present their case. Until then, no one touches her. Is that understood?"

With an affirmative nod from each of them, the lead man then reached between the trees and carefully removed the hand of his subordinate from Aurora's wrist.

Earlier that day, Ross had sent out an inquiry to discover if anyone had seen Aurora. Eventually, word came back from Megan Crenshaw that a few members of the agricultural team had seen her jogging solo along the path leading to the rocky point. They had not been witness to her possible return, as they had been occupied with their respective tasks. Ross knew that Aurora hadn't returned, and it was obvious as to exactly where she was headed. He quickly assembled a group of twelve that included Colt, Gabriela, and four of the young Peruvian runners. Leaving Jessica in charge of any colony matters that might occur in his absence, he then headed off toward the Mayan city.

At first light the following morning, Ross sent the four runners ahead from the shelter at the midway rest stop. He had asked them to scout ahead and speak with any Mayan citizens they encountered to ask if Aurora had been seen. When they had tangible information, they were to come back along the main trail to reunite with the group and report their findings. Several hours later, as Ross and the remaining seven closed on the Mayan city, he spotted the runners heading toward him. They had good news to report, as they had been informed that Aurora was safe in the residence of the King.

Following their customary bow and handshake, Ross greeted the Mayan King by saying, "Hello my friend. It's good to see you again."

"Thank you, and welcome back to my city."

Although in less need of Gabriela's translation skills with each passing month, Ross still preferred to have her by his side when conversing with the King. In simple terms, she helped to avoid any possible misunderstandings as the two leaders spoke with each other. With her help, he inquired, "I understand that a woman from our colony is safely in your care, and with your permission, I would like to see her."

The King nodded, and while motioning for one of his wives to retrieve Aurora stated, "The hunters who found her said she was far from the main trail that joins our two cities."

"Far from the trail? Was she lost?"

"She wouldn't say, but when they arrived with her this morning, they claimed to have saved her from certain death."

Entering the room with her escort, Aurora said, "Hello dad. How are you?"

"I'm fine thanks, but the more appropriate question is, what happened to you?"

"I had a close call, but thanks to the six men who saved me, I'm fine. My minor wounds have been tended to, and I have received food and water."

"Indeed. The King was just commenting on your rescue. Would you care to elaborate for me?"

After hearing the tale of the events that had transpired the previous day, Ross shook his head in disbelief. He knew that Aurora had been very lucky. Her actions during the most recent adventure were beyond foolish, but at least she had not been killed. It was bad enough that she had attempted to make the journey to the Mayan city on her own, but to then take on the additional risk of a theoretical shortcut was incomprehensible. If not for the group of Mayan hunters that just happened to be in the right place at the right time to hear her screams for help, the outcome would have been terrible. If that were the case, it was probable that no trace of her would have ever been found.

Turning to Gabriela, Ross said, "Could you please ask the King if I could meet with the six hunters as soon as possible. I would like to personally thank each one of them for saving my daughter's life."

She delivered the request, and then listened intently to a rather long winded reply before the King motioned for an aid to retrieve the men. Turning to Ross, Gabriela said, "Sir, it looks as if we might have a new problem."

"What do you mean?"

"The King has informed me that some of the hunters wish to claim Aurora as their own for saving her life."

"Claim her?"

"Yes sir, it's one of their traditional customs. After the hunters saved Aurora, they presented her as a gift to the King. He did not want her as a wife, so the right of claim fell to any of those who saved her."

"Wonderful! And you said that some of the hunters wish to claim Aurora."

"Yes sir. According to the King, three of them do."

Turning to Aurora with a measure of visible frustration on his face, Ross said, "You failed to mention during your recent explanation that three Mayan men want to claim you as a wife."

"That's news to me, but it is flattering."

Gabriela interrupted them by adding, "Although some would consider Aurora's predicament to be rather flattering, you have not heard the ramifications of a multiple claim."

Before Ross could obtain a more detailed account of the ramifications that Gabriela referred to, the group of hunters entered the room.

Aurora said, "Those are the men dad."

"Good. I want you to follow my lead as I thank each of them individually and shake their hands. Gabriela would you be kind enough to lead us along the line and translate our words toward, and the reply from, each of the hunters?"

"I will indeed sir. We should start at the left end of the line. The leader is the one wearing ceremonial attire."

"Are you sure?"

Aurora intervened, "I think she's right dad. He was the one in command while we were in the wilderness."

As he moved down the line, it became obvious to Ross that number three, five, and six were the men who wished to claim Aurora as their wife. The last of those three had rightfully received the most interest from Aurora. She informed Ross and Gabriela that he was the man she had been seeing so much of during the past three months. Her giddy smile and flirtation in his presence became the trigger for the ensuing altercation, as the previous man in line snatched her wrist as he had done in the wilderness.

His forceful Mayan words came too quickly for Ross to comprehend, but the intent was clearly understood. Ross asked Gabriela, "What exactly is this man trying to tell me?"

"That he maintains the first claim to Aurora, and he will fight any man to the death that stands in his way."

As Ross stepped back and around Aurora to a position directly in front of the man, he said, "Is that so? Ask him if that includes her father."

Upon hearing the question, the hunter glared directly at Ross for a long moment to evaluate his resolve. Although at least twenty-five years his senior, Ross did not blink, so the man eased his grip on Aurora's wrist ever so slightly.

Seizing the moment to pull free from the hunters grasp, Aurora interjected, "I thank you again for helping to save my life, but you have no right to claim me as your prize. Only I will decide if any one of you can have me as their wife."

Gabriela responded, "It may not be quite that easy. Sir, I think our best move would be to ease the tension by thanking the King once again for his hospitality toward Aurora. Then we should be on our way as soon as possible."

"That's an excellent idea. Aurora, you should take the lead on Gabriela's suggestion."

As she led their approach to the King, he motioned for the three suitors to advance. Colt then spoke loudly enough so that Ross could hear, "Three hunters moving on your six sir."

Turning to confirm, he responded, "Thank you Colt."

Gabriela helped translate Aurora's thankful message to the King, then listened to his lengthy reply. Turning to Ross she said, "Sir, the King wants you to know that he was impressed with your bravery. You showed strength of will by staring down a man who is much younger and stronger than you in order to protect your daughter. Because of that, he has made a special consideration in how to handle this case."

"I'm glad to hear that everything has been cleared up. Thank him for the kind treatment of Aurora and his words for me. Apologize for any misunderstanding there may have been, and that we look forward to his next visit to our colony."

"That may be sooner than you think sir."

"What do you mean?"

"The King intends to visit our colony in ten days."

"That's good news, but why?"

"As part of the special consideration, and he will bring a larger than normal entourage for the occasion."

"What occasion?"

"Please be cautious of how you physically or verbally respond to this sir. Remember, this is not the most favorable arena to disagree with the King or attempt to undermine his authority. If you resist his will, you should wait until you have a more substantial supporting cast to stand your ground."

"Understood, now please tell me what we can expect from the King and his entourage during the upcoming visit."

"It will be a first ever event outside the confines of the Mayan domain. Their traditional customs require that the three hunters standing behind us will fight each other to the death for Aurora, and the survivor will take her as his wife. If she refuses to do so, then a male member of her family must fight the victor to the death for her honor. If it comes to that sir, the King is granting you the privilege of fighting his victorious hunter in the presence of your people."

Aurora stated bluntly, "This is absolutely insane. Who gave the Mayans the right to decide what I do with my life?"

Feeling thoroughly frustrated at the unforeseen turn of events that now confronted him, Ross replied, "Apparently you did Aurora. From the moment they had to save you from your own foolish and short-sighted arrogance."

Gabriela pressed, "Sir, your response to the King?"

"Please tell him that I understand the significance of the event, and all that will transpire."

"Is that all?"

"As you said, this is not the place to contradict his will."

ꝑ

CHAPTER TWENTY-TWO
THE SACRIFICE

Aurora had kept to herself during the journey home, and the days that followed. Throughout that time she had done some deep soul searching, and had arrived at the realization that the needs of the colony far outweighed her own personal desires. She, nor any other individual within the colony, was important enough to risk possible war with the nearby Mayan civilization. In spite of being in love with only one of the three men who would fight to the death for her hand, she would take her place as the wife of whichever hunter emerged victorious. Of course the choice of Aurora's sacrifice to maintain the peace as opposed to war could potentially be avoided. First, there was the possibility that the man she loved would be triumphant during the upcoming battle. That outcome offered the best case scenario. If one of the other hunters emerged victorious, then a less likely scenario could also become reality. Ross might be able to defeat a man who would probably be somewhat weakened by the effort needed to slay two other men.

While on the journey back from the Mayan city, Ross had already been mulling over that possibility. At the midpoint overnight rest stop, he asked Colt, "When we get back to the colony, can you help prepare me to fight a Mayan hunter?"

"Absolutely sir, and it would be my pleasure to do so. Did you have anything specific in mind?"

"Some hand to hand combat techniques with a knife or spear would be a good place to start. Then compliment that by teaching me some moves to use his weight against him."

"That sounds like a good strategy sir. We can begin the training soon after we arrive at the colony if you like."

"Thanks Colt. I think we should."

Several days later Colt and a few members of the Flight 19 crews were training with Ross. Stopping to check on their progress, Gabriela said, "You look as if you are having fun sir, but I didn't realize you needed so many instructors."

Ross replied, "All of these men have been very helpful in preparing me for hand to hand combat, and I think I'm nearly ready to do battle if it comes to that."

"That's good to know sir, but hopefully you won't need to go through with it."

"Believe me Gabriela, fighting against one of the Mayan hunters wouldn't be my first choice."

"Mine either sir."

From not far behind them they heard Aurora say, "You don't need to fight anyone dad."

Turning to see her walking toward them, Ross replied, "What do you mean?"

"I think it's a wonderful gesture that you are training to fight for my honor dad, but it won't be necessary. I will not be responsible for risking the future of this colony by having you killed by a Mayan hunter. Along those same lines, I do not wish to provoke a possible war between our two civilizations. I have therefore decided to become the wife of whichever hunter wins the battle."

Ross was proud of his daughter for arriving at such a noble decision on her own, but hoped her intent would not be necessary. There had to be some way of maintaining the peace with the Mayans without an unwanted marriage, or the loss of life. Stepping toward her, Ross said, "Aurora, I'm very proud of you for putting the needs of the many before the needs of the one. You should know that your mother would also be proud of you for offering to make such a sacrifice. That being said, I believe that war can always be avoided if those with opposing views work together in an effort to arrive at an alternative solution."

"What do you intend to do?"

"I haven't fully worked that out yet. The King and I may be able to agree that our respective citizens should no longer comingle. That would be unfortunate though, because I believe that both of our civilizations would suffer from that course of action."

Gabriela interjected, "What about the small groups of hunters or gatherers that would inevitably cross paths?"

"That could be a challenge, but only if those involved in such interactions were not honorable."

"Please forgive me for saying this sir, but I think you are being overly optimistic about our alternatives."

"Perhaps you're right, but optimism has nearly always worked for me. Besides, we still have a little time to come up with other possible solutions. We have two more days before the King and his entourage are scheduled to arrive."

ℇ

CHAPTER TWENTY-THREE

THE THRESHOLD

Ross stood, with Gabriela and others, next to the Mayan King to view the spectacle. They were positioned at the same slightly elevated location above the plateau where Ross had first informed the representative council and the astronomers about the existence of the Mayan descendants. The key players in the upcoming show of force were firm in their respective resolve. Each Mayan hunter was determined to kill the other two men during combat and win the hand of Aurora. Ross was mentally and physically prepared to fight for the honor of his oldest daughter if the hunter of her choice did not win. Aurora had vowed that she would not allow her father to do so. She would become the wife of whichever man survived. And the King, he was ready to prove his superiority over Ross as a leader of people by forcing his hand. The King believed that Ross would never defeat one of his brave hunters in a fight to the death. There would be a marriage, or war would ensue.

Although that part of the day's activity appeared to be a logical assumption, another aspect of the Kings overall agenda had been derailed. Soon after his arrival, the King spotted Janet and left his entourage to move in her direction. His interest in her had not faded, but he now realized that she would never become one of his wives. After a subtle respectful bow, Janet rubbed her visibly pregnant belly while grasping Colt's hand and said to the King, "I believe you already know my husband."

The King nodded in acknowledgment at having met the man on several occasions, but said nothing. It was an unfamiliar experience for him, and he was not happy about it. Janet had chosen another man, as opposed to becoming one of the Kings wives. He believed that her actions were impudent, and was once again puzzled by the thought process of the newcomers.

Turning from them in disgust, the King returned to his awaiting entourage. A moment later he stood face to face with Ross, and accepted his outstretched hand of friendship. The grip of his counterpart seemed significantly firmer than the King had remembered, but the customary pleasantries associated with the greeting remained unchanged. With Gabriela's help, the King said, "Thank you for inviting me back to your colony."

She translated Ross' reply of, "My friend, you know that you are welcome to visit our colony anytime you wish, but you and your entourage invited yourself for this occasion."

Surprised by the bold statement of his counterpart, the King replied, "I thought you would be pleased to have the battle fought within your domain."

"There shouldn't even be a battle."

"According to our customs, a battle for the woman in question must be fought."

"The woman that you speak of is my daughter, and our custom is that she doesn't have to marry any of your hunters."

Gabriela interrupted Ross by adding, "Sir, please be careful how much you push the King on this matter. It could lead to a larger problem."

"Back at the Mayan city you advised me to wait for such a conversation until my supporting cast was more substantial. Well, that cast will never be more substantial than it is right now, so we are going to have this conversation!"

"Perhaps you are correct sir, but please tread lightly."

"I understand what you are saying Gabriela, and thank you for the concern. Now please ask the King if there is an alternative to resolving this issue without the bloodshed of at least two of his hunters being killed."

Ross focused on the King's facial expression as Gabriela presented the question, and knew instantly that the answer was no. After another of the King's lengthy responses, she said, "Please excuse me for this sir, and remember these are the Kings words. In order to maintain the peace, he would have accepted Janet to be one of his wives. That would have been the case only if Aurora refused the victorious hunter, and you were not man enough to fight for her honor. He regrets to inform you, but that option is no longer available. The King has no desire to have a woman who has been impregnated by a man that he believes to be of inferior stock."

"Is that so? Did he have anything else to say?"

"Yes sir, he asked how soon we could get started."

Ross fought back the anger within created by the King's insults. Feeling as if there was nothing else that could be done to avoid the spectacle, he then replied, "As soon as the hunters are prepared for battle, we can begin."

The King nodded and asked, "Where should my people prepare an arena for the upcoming battle?"

After pointing toward a clear area near the base of the steep hillside, Ross said, "If you follow me, I know a good spot where we can watch your hunters do battle."

Several minutes later the three hunters, armed with nothing other than spears, emerged from the crowd to stand alone in the center of the circular clearing. In turn, they each stepped forward and bowed to their King before taking up a position along the defined perimeter. Before the King could signal for them to begin, a large shadow suddenly moved across the plateau and stopped directly over the field of battle.

Shielding his eyes from the midday sun, Ross looked up and quickly realized that the shadow had been cast by a familiar object. It was a three seated scout vessel that belonged to the alien species who had brought the pilgrims from Earth to the new world, and eight more completed the hovering "V" shaped formation. All eyes of both human civilizations began looking skyward within seconds, but the Mayan reaction to the ships was one of fear. As one ship lowered itself from the formation, the spectators created an opening for the craft to land.

Turning to the King, Ross said, "Please excuse me for a moment, as I would like to go welcome our guests."

The King said nothing, but cautiously followed roughly twenty paces behind with Gabriela close on his heels. When the hatch of the alien vessel hissed opened, the King was absolutely astonished at what happened next. With his own eyes, he witnessed Ross greet the three creatures with the same outstretched hand of friendship that he had used during all of their meetings. What was amazing to the King was how they had responded to Ross. It was unbelievable, because Ross had not kneeled at the feet of the Sky God or his two companions. Ross was also speaking freely with the Sky God and even laughed out loud a few times. To the King, that behavior was either completely foolish or incredibly brave. The even more puzzling aspect to him was that the Sky God showed no signs of anger toward Ross for any of his actions.

A few moments later, when Ross and the alien began moving toward the King, he gulped in fear. What had Ross told the Sky God about him and his intended actions? Not knowing what else to do, he motioned for all those in his entourage to kneel and bow their heads with him until informed to rise.

Gabriela, sensing a moment of weakness in the Kings position, took it upon herself to speak with Ross. She said, "I'm sorry to interrupt you sir, but I believe this unexpected visit has created a wonderful opportunity for you."

Turning his attention from his old alien friend, Ross noticed that all of the currently present Mayans, including the King and the three battle ready hunters, were in a position of complete submission. He replied, "It looks as if you are correct, and I have my new supporting cast to thank for it."

"Shall I use this opportunity to pry some information out of the King?"

"That's an excellent suggestion. Based on his behavior this morning, perhaps we should play a little poker with him. I don't want you to embarrass the man, but see if you can find out what is on his mind without giving away our position."

After lowering herself to the ground in order to hear what the King had to say, Gabriela informed Ross, "Sir, the King recognizes the alien scout ships based on stories from the elders and previous visitations that he has witnessed. The alien ships have not been seen by any of his people for dozens of eclipses, but he and the Mayan people believe that your old friend is their 'Sky God'. They will not rise from their current positions until they are informed to do so."

"That's very interesting. Did he say anything else?"

"He did indeed, but I'm hesitant to disclose everything that he told me."

"Why is that?"

"Because what he believes may go to your head."

"I would hope that you know me well enough by now to take that risk. Besides, how will we know if you don't tell me?"

Not being able to resist the moment, she then playfully added, "You make a good point Mr. Demigod. Having seen your interactions with the so called 'Sky God' and his companions, the King now believes that you are here as a representative to enforce their will. Accordingly, the King wishes to apologize. He realizes that any perceived weaknesses that he had in your leadership abilities must be completely false."

"I can see why you thought that information could go straight to my head, especially when you call me Mr. Demigod. Please don't address me that way ever again, or even sir for that matter. I know you meant for the first to be humorous in the moment, and the latter has always been as a show of respect. I appreciate that, but I would prefer it if you just called me Ross."

Smiling at his show of humility, and the perception of having just broken down another one of his walls, Gabriela replied, "Alright Ross. Do you have any specific instructions as to how we should proceed with the King?"

"Give me a moment to speak with my alien friend. I'm interested in what he thinks about this recent development."

"Yes sir. I mean, alright Ross."

After a brief exchange with the alien, Ross turned and said, "We should probably make him believe that he needs to remain submissive while we gather more information. Please thank him for the apology, but ask the King why he wishes to anger me by insisting that his hunters do battle for Aurora."

Rising from the ground once again, she said, "Ross, the King says he has no desire to anger you with any of his decisions or actions, because that will also anger the Sky God. He asks for your guidance in how he should proceed."

Without hesitation Ross scanned the area, but could not locate his daughter. He called out, "Has anyone seen Aurora?"

From behind a wall of spectators he heard, "I'm over here dad. Give me a minute to get through all these people."

When she arrived at his side, Ross asked, "Which one of the Mayan hunters is the one you're in love with?"

Pointing to Ross' left, she replied, "That one."

"Gabriela, could you please have the King raise his head so that he can see which hunter Aurora is pointing at. I want him to instruct that man to get over here right away."

Within seconds the hunter sprang to his feet and ran toward his awaiting King. Then he dropped to the ground again at Ross' feet as a submissive gesture. Ross pulled the man to a standing position, lifted his chin to look him in the eye, and then moved him next to Aurora's side. Turning back to Gabriela, he said, "Can you please inform the King that if he wishes to make me happy, then there will be no fight to the death on this day. This is the man that my daughter will marry, and the other two hunters will just have to accept that as her decision."

"To use an old cliché, that was nicely played Ross. Is there anything else you want me to tell him?"

"Yes there is. Please ask the King if he would like to make the Sky God happy by maintaining the peace between our two civilizations, or would he prefer the opposite? After that, tell him that he and his entourage should rise to their feet and be comfortable. The wedding will begin within the hour."

ƒ

CHAPTER TWENTY-FOUR

PROGRESS REPORT

Early the following morning, after the Mayan entourage had begun their journey home, Ross finally had a chance to sit quietly with his old friend. The purpose of the alien visit had been made quite clear just moments after their arrival. They had returned to the moon known as ₹-593-ૐπ-2-2 to check on the progress of those from ₹-829-ૐπ-3 who were most recently transplanted. That action would include a detailed discussion with Ross, but before they could do so, Ross requested that his alien friend field some questions from the general population. Unfortunately, that created a seemingly endless procession of inquiries that lasted throughout the night. The lengthy process was hampered by the fact that most of the questions had been presented by people who were unable to hear the answers in their own mind. Ross, with assistance from Gabriela and others, needed to translate the alien thought projection for them.

As to the Mayan situation, peace would prevail. True to the Mayan custom, Aurora had kept her word and became the wife of a hunter that had saved her life. The entourage had seen the King preside over a wedding as he had done countless times before, only this time; the ceremony was in the presence of the Sky God. He was also comforted by the knowledge that when he returned to the Mayan city, word would spread quickly among the people. The Sky God had been kept happy when the King had decided to maintain peace with the newcomers.

From Ross' point of view, it was spectacular that the Mayan King and his people chose to believe that the alien species were Gods. His only desire was an insured long lasting peace between the two civilizations of Earth, and that belief could help to make his wish reality. Gabriela cautioned him to not abuse his status within the Mayan belief structure, but Ross knew that the leverage it provided could be useful. If a conflict should occur, he would remind the King that war between their two civilizations could anger the Sky God.

When Gabriela excused herself from Ross and the alien so they could commence with their private discussion, she saw that Jessica was waiting for her not far away. Once face to face, Jessica asked, "Gabriela, can I speak with you for a moment?"

"I'm sorry Jessica, but it has been a very long night with all the translation that needed to be done. When you add that to the events and festivities of yesterday afternoon, you can just imagine how tired I am right now. Can we talk after I get a few hours of sleep?"

"Of course we can. I just wanted to quickly convey my thanks for all your recent help. You have provided a wonderful service for Ross and the colony, and have helped us all to avoid what could have been very difficult times."

"Thanks Jessica. I hope Ross feels the same way."

"I'm quite sure that he does, and I know that he will tell you how he feels when he has an opportunity."

"That would be nice."

"Don't worry, he will. Now go get some sleep."

Meanwhile, the communication between Ross and his alien friend had begun in earnest. Centering on the progress of the pilgrims, Ross answered several thought questions of the alien as to how difficult the early days on the moon had been. He explained how their overall numbers of population had suffered drastically due to animal attacks and fatigue during the relocation process. Then reported how awful it was that the number had been nearly duplicated when the colony faced the extreme cold of their first eclipse cycle. Ross did present some good news though. The rapid population decline had slowed considerably since those early days, and just recently began a reversal. Aurora, and a small group of pilgrims with accounting backgrounds such as hers, had been keeping meticulous notes. Those notes included the names of each respective colonist that died, and when the death occurred. Now the records included a few births. The most recent post eclipse population count had confirmed that there had been more births than deaths during the last forty-four day cycle. It was the first month on the new world that the colony had experienced population expansion as opposed to contraction, and Ross gained a measure of optimism from the count. He was well aware that a significant amount of time would be needed for the population to increase up to and beyond their original numbers, but it was a start.

In that regard, Ross felt it was important to establish a moon calendar so everyone born after the establishment of the colony would have an actual birthday to celebrate if they were so inclined. Thanks largely to the information provided by the Mayan sundial, and having now lived through several of them, the duration of each cycle, or month, was well known. There was however, one factor of time that remained a mystery.

That unknown element was only one aspect within a list of topics that Ross wished to discuss with his old friend. For some strange reason, none of his upcoming questions had been brought up by anyone during the all-night session, so Ross felt this was a good time to do so. He began by saying, "I would like to be able to inform our astronomers how to properly measure a complete year on this moon. A record of how long we have been here has been maintained by them, but it is incomplete as far as I'm concerned. The duration has been calculated in both days and cycles on this moon, as well as the length of each day using the time measurement system of Earth. Can you tell me how many eclipse cycles are needed in order for this moon's host planet to complete a full revolution around the host star?"

In an instant the answer of sixteen popped into his head via thought projection from the alien.

Ross said, "Well, that was easy enough. Thank you." He then brought up a topic that many felt was of no consequence, but Ross for one was curious. While pointing directly toward the massive lake, he stated, "Some people in our colony have reported seeing, on multiple occasions, a strange life form that lives in the water. It is supposedly half human, and half fish. Even though a creature of that makeup was always thought to be myth, on Earth we called them Mermaids. Can you tell me if our people are just imagining them, or are they real?"

As quickly as the previous answer had popped into his head, Ross heard that the life forms he referred to as Mermaids were in fact real. Yes they did indeed live in the waters of this moon, but that was not the only place they could be found within the cosmos.

The next question had not been on his original list, but Ross proceeded with the obvious follow-up. "Did the Mermaids live on Earth as well?"

Although Ross had never cared one way or the other about their existence during his entire life on Earth, it came as no real surprise to him that the answer was yes.

Now thoroughly intrigued, Ross then asked, "Did you bring these mermaids from Earth on the deep water vessel with the long term abductees?"

He learned that a few of what now lived in the nearby lake had indeed been saved from Earth, but most were already thriving on this moon. Ross was also informed that the so called Mermaid species living in the deep waters of ₹-829-ꝛⅉπ-3 had been transplanted there countless centuries before. As stated, Earth had been one of many worlds to receive them in an effort to avoid their extinction.

Before moving on to his next intended topic, Ross had to know one more thing about the Mermaids. He asked, "Why were they in danger of becoming extinct?"

The answer further solidified his already intense belief that his alien friend was a member of a truly noble species. The planet of origin for the Mermaid species had been destroyed thousands of Earth years before when the host star had gone super nova. The entire solar system had been vaporized in a matter of seconds, and all life forms that had not already been relocated to other worlds were lost to the galaxy forever.

Nodding with understanding, Ross pressed on. Next on his mind was the thought of other people from Earth. He asked quite plainly, "Other than our colony, or the Mayan civilization, did your species transplant any other humans from Earth to this moon? If so, then please tell me exactly which civilizations."

Even after all that Ross had seen transpire over the previous few years, what he heard in his mind was shocking. His alien friend informed him that a small segment of two other ancient Earth civilizations had been transplanted to this moon long ago. In fact, some of their descendants still lived on the surface. Additionally, it was highly doubtful they would ever encounter either one of those civilizations unless Ross took on the almost impossible task of initiating the contact. The two ancient Earth civilizations were separated from each other by a vast distance, and each of their locations was nearly on the exact opposite side of the moon from where Ross' colony resided. The alien thought projection revealed that he would not provide Ross, or anyone else, with the location of either civilization. Without that vital information, several months of exploration through some very hostile terrain would be needed to find them.

Although disappointed to learn of the near impossibility of contact, Ross again nodded with understanding. If he had learned nothing else in all his years of both military and political service, it was that some things were just not meant to be. Even so, he yearned to know who the other people of Earth were. With that he bluntly asked, "Can I at least know which civilizations you brought here?"

A segment of both the ancient Egyptians and the Incas of Peru had been transplanted, and a few things suddenly made more sense to Ross. With the presence of pyramids and other structures of engineering marvel, the locations of each of those civilizations had been a source of inquiry for many years. They were also two of the locations where modern day pilgrims had boarded the transport vessels to this moon. Now

Ross had confirmation to his belief that previous landing sites had been used for the effort. As a pilot, he also understood this approach as being more favorable than using an unknown site.

The recent communication with the alien had also made Ross ponder something else. Perhaps the Mayans were correct to a certain extent with their assessment. Maybe his old friend was a member of a species that was somewhat Godlike. The thought of various life forms suddenly appearing on one world or another as a direct link to alien transport could easily be interpreted as Godlike behavior. If not already known, Ross had just learned another lesson in how truly limited his supposed power was when compared to the alien species. With that thought, he prepared to delve into the final topic on his list. Staring directly into the eyes of his alien friend, Ross asked the all-important question of, "Can you please tell me what became of Earth?"

CHAPTER TWENTY-FIVE

EVOLUTION

Ross paced nervously just outside the medical shelter, while Gabriela sat patiently nearby. He was pleased to have her by his side, because she provided a desperately needed calming influence for the moment at hand.

Perhaps it was due to the realization that he now had more time to devote toward an individual, as opposed to the constant effort needed to insure the survival of the colony. Or perhaps the knowledge of his mother Janet falling in love with Colt, becoming his wife, and now expecting their first child had been the cause. For that matter, the overly dramatic adventure of Aurora falling in love with and becoming the wife of a Mayan hunter may have been what brought forth his most recent enlightenment. Ross had been unable to pinpoint exactly what had been the trigger, but he was glad that it happened. After inwardly denying his feelings for several months, he realized that he could no longer squelch them. Ross was in love with Gabriela, and thankfully, she felt the same way about him.

Ross flashed back to the memory of when he first spoke to her about his feelings. Gabriela had made the moment much easier than he had believed it would be, because she instantly responded that she had been in love with him for a long time. They had now been married for a few months, and no longer needed to pretend when in the presence of the Mayan King.

Hearing a shout of pain from within the medical shelter, Ross snapped back into the present moment. Gabriela briefly halted his pacing, and attempted to calm him with a gentle kiss. Holding his face between her hands, she said, "I'm sure the doctor has things under control."

Inside the medical shelter, Colt wondered if any of his bones would break under the pressure. His facial expression showed minimal signs of distress, but it was becoming more difficult for him to control. Colt knew enough to be aware that his pain paled in comparison to what Janet was going through, so he did not dare ask her to ease up. Janet was squeezing his hand tightly with relentless intent, but fortunately for both of them, the current ordeal would soon be over.

Along with Ross and Gabriela, Jessica and Aurora had been hearing the sounds of Janet's discomfort and pain for a few hours. The most difficult aspect for all of them was that there was nothing that they could do about it. As her brother continued to pace nervously about, Jessica said, "She's going to be alright Ross. Try to relax."

He responded, "I can't Jessica. It sounds as if she is having a really tough time of it. We lost her once many years ago, and I for one don't want to lose her again."

"Well neither do I, but this situation is vastly different from when we supposedly lost her before."

"True, but this result would be irreversible."

Aurora, sensing that her father was becoming overly worked up about the current situation, stated, "Dad. Gabriela and Jessica are right. You need to relax. The people with Janet know what they are doing. They will see her through this."

Just then, they all heard a horrific scream from inside the medical shelter. Surprisingly, Colt had also let out a yelp as the bones in two fingers of his left hand had finally succumbed to the pressure. The few ever so brief seconds of silence that followed seemed to last forever, and they were agonizing. Finally broken by the sound of a slap, and then the resulting cry of a newborn baby, a collective sigh of relief ensued. Janet had done it. For the third time in her life she had delivered a child, and as a result, Ross and Jessica now had a younger sibling.

Emerging from the shelter, a nurse announced, "It's a boy. Even though he's two weeks early, he looks healthy."

Jessica beat her brother to the punch and asked, "What about our mother, is she alright?"

"As expected, she's very tired, but she's doing well."

"Can we see them?"

"Give us a few minutes to get her and the baby cleaned up, and then all of you can come in and see them."

Janet had become the latest of those to deliver a baby on the new world, but her child was no more, or less, important to the colony than any of the others. Up to that point, most of the newborns had survived, with only a few succumbing to poor health and the misfortune of bad timing. In each case, those babies had been born a day or two before, or during, the long and bitterly cold environment of an eclipse cycle. In spite of the two weeks earlier than expected delivery, the upside for Janet was obvious. Her baby had been born five days after the most recent eclipse. The newborn would benefit from thirty-five days of warmth to gain much needed early strength before his first experience of the black void.

Relieved from the stress of the previous few hours, Ross smiled from ear to ear as Gabriela hugged him. While still in her embrace, he turned to Jessica and said, "Do you realize that we must be the only seventy-three and sixty-eight year old people in the history of mankind to have a newborn sibling?"

"I suppose that's one way of looking at it Ross, but he will probably treat us more like grandparents than as siblings."

Moments later, the same nurse who had announced the birth interrupted their discussion with, "Dr. Schmidt has said that you can come inside to see Janet and the baby now."

Once inside the medical shelter, the four of them could see Janet holding her newborn son. Jessica reached her side first, and after kissing Janet on the forehead said, "How are you doing mom?"

"I'm alright now, thanks."

Ross then moved in to provide comfort and express his congratulations by adding, "I'm very proud of you mom, you and Colt did great."

Dr. Schmidt, who was tending to Colts broken fingers, stated, "The labor probably sounded worse than it actually was for those of you who were outside. During the past few months I have had patients with much more difficult deliveries. Janet and the baby are going to be just fine."

Ross moved toward him and said, "Dr. Schmidt. I would like to thank you on behalf of the family for everything that you did for my mother and the baby. In addition, I thank you for all the positive work that you and the rest of the medical staff have provided for the colony."

"It was my pleasure sir, and if I may speak for the other doctors and nurses, thanks for the kind words."

Turning to Colt, Ross added, "Now, how are you doing?"

"Other than my fingers, I feel great!"

"That's good news. I'm sure that the doctor has already congratulated you, but I would like to be the first person not involved with the delivery to offer the same."

After a firm handshake, Ross and Colt made their way back across the room to Janet's side. A moment of collective admiration toward the baby by all those present was followed by Aurora removing a small notepad from her pocket. With regard to the recently developed moon calendar, an official record of the newest arrival needed to be noted. She scribbled in birth, followed by 05/12/01. As the baby had been born after the eleventh eclipse, those numbers signified the fifth day of the twelfth month during the pilgrims first year on the new world. Raising her gaze from the notepad, Aurora said, "For the record, have you decided on a name for the baby?"

Janet looked over at Colt and he nodded with approval. Then she turned to Aurora and replied, "Yes we have."

"That's great. What's his name going to be?"

Looking proudly down at the tiny face of her newborn son, she announced, "We would like to introduce all of you to Henry Travis Jensen. His middle name is for Colt's grandfather, as he taught Colt so many aspects of wilderness survival. Henry is of course for Ross and Jessica's grandfather. I'm sure that no explanation is needed as to why we wanted to name our baby after a man of such tremendous influence. Just like that man did, our son will go by the name of Hank."

CHAPTER TWENTY-SIX

MAGIC NUMBER

Walking into the shelter that most of the colonists now jokingly referred to as "The hall of records", Jessica spotted Aurora. As with every other month since their arrival, Aurora and a handful of others were busy with the figures of the post-eclipse population count. Looking directly at her niece, Jessica said, "How close are you to confirmation?"

"Well good morning to you too Jessica. What are you doing here?"

"Sorry about that. Good morning everyone. Ross asked if I could meet with you today to discuss the results of the count. His immediate attention was needed at the irrigation ditch leading to the crop fields, and he didn't know how long that would take."

"I hope everything is alright."

"I'm sure it is. You know your father. He thought that it would be rude to keep all of you waiting for him, so he asked me to help him out."

"Well in response to your question, we just completed our triple check of the figures. You should consider the number to be officially confirmed."

"Wonderful. Now could you please brief me, and I'll get the information to Ross as soon as possible."

"Tell dad that we expect to reach ten thousand before the next eclipse. The medical team has given us no indication of extreme illness or problems within the population that may lead to any deaths. There are also several women who are due to deliver very soon. Unless most of them experience severe complications, the newborns should more than compensate for any unforeseen loss of life."

"That's great news. Now what is the exact population of the colony as we speak?"

"As of this moment, our calculations have the number at nine thousand, nine hundred, and ninety-four. As usual, no Mayan citizens have been counted, but myself and the now two hundred and seventy-eight other pilgrims living with them in the midpoint village are included. Our village tally was easy to calculate, because one of our women gave birth, and there were no deaths. As for the original colony, the increase fits right in with the average range. There were fourteen newborns, and two deaths. All told, our population increased by thirteen at the two locations. That number was slightly lower than the average per month during the recovery period we needed to reach our original number. In contrast, you should know that the increase is higher than the average since that time."

"Please refresh my memory Aurora. Just how long did it take for the colony to fully recover from our lowest population count of less than eighty-nine hundred?"

"That took us more than four planetary years of sixteen eclipse cycles each. The official date of recovery to the level of nine thousand eight hundred and twelve was 28/13/05."

"I remember now, a little Japanese girl."

"I don't recall that specifically, but we could look the birth record up if you really want to know."

"No, it's not that vital. Thanks for the report, and to all of you for taking such good care of the population records. If you will excuse me, I need to go speak with Ross."

Throughout the coming days and weeks, it seemed the main topic of campfire conversation was who would be the mother of the baby that increased the colony population to the magic number of ten thousand. For Ross, the question was moot. His concern was more about when the event would take place. Although it was true that several women were in the late stages of pregnancy, Janet and the medical team had informed him that it would probably be near the time of the next eclipse before at least six of them gave birth.

Never known as someone who would just wait around for something to happen, Ross kept himself busy. He continued to monitor the progress of improving the overall infrastructure of the colony, and met with team leaders to discuss whatever concerns they might have. One such meeting was with Megan Crenshaw, and it was quite obvious from the start that she was less than happy.

Hank stood like a statue between Colt and Janet, and listened to everything that Ms. Crenshaw was saying to his big brother Ross. Looking up he said, "Am I in trouble dad?"

"It sure sounds that way doesn't it?"

"Yes sir, but I don't know why."

Crouching next to her younger son, Janet added, "I think you know exactly why you are in trouble, and it would be best if you owned up to what you did."

"Yes ma'am, if I have to."

Ross excused himself from Megan for a moment, and made his way over to young Hank. He said, "Hey buddy, how are you doing today?"

"I'm fine Ross, but I think I did something that got me into big trouble."

"I think you're right. I have listened to what Megan has to say about it, and I think the time has come for you and your parents to have a talk with her."

Janet looked at Ross and said, "What did Hank do?"

Before Ross could respond, Colt added, "It must have been something significant, because Megan looks really mad."

Ross attempted to prepare Colt and Janet for what was to come by saying, "Yes she is, and with good reason. You both know Megan well enough to understand that she is a woman who is very serious about agriculture. She is one of the reasons why the colony has enough food to survive each month. She means no real harm, but Megan doesn't always deal with the actions of children very well."

Colt responded, "Fair enough, but what did Hank do?"

"Let's just say that your upstart engineer of the future has creatively altered her precious irrigation system. She and Hank can fill you both in on the details. I'll just watch the show from here."

Now standing directly in front of her, Hank said, "I'm very sorry for what I did Ms. Crenshaw, but I just wanted to see how it worked. I didn't mean to break anything."

Megan, having calmed down considerably after meeting with Ross, responded, "You are growing up fast Hank, how old are you now?"

"I'm five years and three months old ma'am."

"Already? Well, thank you for apologizing. It takes a real man to admit when they have done something wrong."

Looking at his son, Colt prodded, "Hank, what else?"

"Ms. Crenshaw, I promise you that I won't play with the irrigation system anymore."

Looking up at Colt and Janet, Megan said, "He's very bright for someone his age, and that could be quite useful. I have an idea that might make everyone happy."

Janet replied, "Thank you, but what's your idea?"

"Well I feel that if Hank has the time to be destructive, then he also has the time to be productive."

"Fair enough, but what's your point?"

"Hank was caught red handed doing some damage to the irrigation system, and although I don't have proof, evidence would suggest that he has done so before. What I propose is that we correct the situation by having Hank work with my team to repair the damage that he caused. I have spoken with Ross about my thoughts of expanding the existing system into an adjacent area, so perhaps Hank could also help with that when the time comes. He is obviously intrigued by how the irrigation system operates, and this would be a good way to teach him a lesson. Hank would learn some valuable skills that could then be used to help the long term goals of the colony."

Before Janet could answer, Colt responded, "I think that is an excellent idea Megan. Hank needs to learn a lesson for his indiscretions, and helping to repair the damage seems only fair. When would you like him to report for duty?"

"Back on the farm in Blandinsville, my daddy used to say that there is no time like the present."

"I agree Megan. Hank is in your hands. I will come get him a few minutes before dark if that's alright with you."

"Well alright then."

Knowing that Megan only spoke those words when she felt a decision or situation had been fully resolved, Ross smiled as Colt and Janet moved in his direction.

Roughly two weeks later, Gabriela awakened Ross from his nap when Jessica had requested they both come to the medical shelter. Upon their arrival, they learned the birth had taken place just moments before. Aurora was already tending to the task at hand, and soon emerged from the shelter with a smiling face.

Ross asked, "Are the mother and baby both healthy?"

Aurora responded, "Yes they are, and even though the next eclipse will be upon us very soon, the doctor thinks the baby will survive."

"Then its official, we're at ten thousand."

"Yes, it's official. You can see the entry right here in the record book. It says girl named Samantha born on 37/15/06. Colony population now equals ten thousand souls."

CHAPTER TWENTY-SEVEN

LESSONS OF TRANSITION

Emerging from the family shelter, Gabriela noticed that Ross and Hank were approaching from roughly one hundred yards away. The boy seemed unharmed, but Ross was limping badly. After covering half the distance to greet the brothers, she asked Ross, "What in the world happened to you?"

"It was silly, and nobody's fault but my own. Hank was showing me an area inland from the perimeter of the newly expanded crop fields. During his free time from the duties of helping Megan expand the irrigation system, he had done some exploring. Hank discovered a group of small animals that were unfamiliar to him, and hoped that I could identify them."

"What does that have to do with the multiple cuts and scratches all over you, and your quite obvious limp?"

"Part of the terrain that we covered was difficult, and my feet slid out from underneath me."

Several seconds later, Gabriela urged, "Yes, and?"

"I tumbled down a hillside through some thorny bushes and came to rest in a stagnant puddle of liquid. Although clear like water, the consistency was more like syrup. The majority of my scratches, and a probable pulled muscle causing the limp, were due to the fall. Then the bushes caused more scratches on my hands and arms when I climbed back up the hillside."

"Do you think you have any serious injuries?"

"No. I'll be fine in a few days. Besides, Hank and I had a good time together this afternoon."

"How about you Hank, are you hurt?"

"No ma'am, I'm fine."

"All right, let's get you both cleaned up for dinner."

That evening by the campfire, Colt and Janet learned of the adventure that Hank and Ross had shared throughout the afternoon. Hank was a fearless and strong willed young man with an exceptionally inquisitive nature. Fortunately, he was also always mindful of his elders. Because of that, his parents felt he would heed their directive. Colt said, "Hank, you know that it's not a very good idea to go exploring by yourself."

"But sir, Ross was with me."

"I know that, but you had already explored that area of the wilderness on your own hadn't you?"

"Yes sir. I have been through that area a few times."

"Well it doesn't sound like a very hospitable place, so please don't go back until I can explore it myself."

The next morning Ross felt more aches and pains from the fall than during the previous evening, as his muscles had stiffened up throughout the night. Following a groan of agony as he slowly rose from the straw sleeping mat, he said, "I guess I'm not as young as I used to be. Every part of my body hurts."

Gabriela, although somewhat sympathetic to his pain, knew she more than deserved the right to speak her mind. Her verbal onslaught began with, "You're damn right you're not as young as you used to be. I held my feelings in check yesterday when you and Hank first told me about what had happened to you, but I won't hold back now. What were you thinking when you decided to blaze a new trail through the wilderness?"

"I was trying to help Hank. He wanted to learn more about the indigenous life on this moon, and I was curious about the small animals that he spoke of."

"Ross, we have been on this moon for six of its years, and I have been your wife for the majority of that time. From almost the moment we arrived, there have been various levels of danger due to the indigenous life. You have always insisted that exploration of new territory should be done in groups of no less than eight or ten, but for some reason you and Hank went off alone. It's going to be up to Janet and Colt as to how they want to handle this with Hank, but I will be the one responsible for chastising you."

"Alright Gabriela, you made your point."

"I have not begun to make my point Ross. You are one of the main reasons why many of us have survived. You would not allow people to give up hope during the early days of our life here on this moon. The leadership and numerous examples of clear thought that you demonstrated throughout the years have provided the colony with a constant source of comfort. In this case however, you made a serious misjudgment."

"Are you done?"

"No I'm not. This would have been bad enough in the earliest days of our life here, but to do it now is ridiculous. Your body is, at a minimum, eight years older than when we arrived because of the sixteen month year of this moon. Add that to the time we spent in space on the voyage from Earth, and you will soon be an eighty-one year old man."

"I'm aware of that Gabriela, please don't remind me."

"Apparently you need reminding. All you have to do is take one look at yourself. You look, and by the sound of your remark just a moment ago, probably feel like hell. You could have been more seriously injured during the fall, and Hank is not yet strong enough to drag you to safety if you had been."

"You're right, it was foolish. I now realize that if Hank had been the one to fall down that hill, I'm not sure I would have been strong enough to drag him to safety."

"I'm glad you understand. Now I'm aware that you and Hank want to have fun together, but as a favor to me, could you find an activity that is less life threatening?"

"That seems fair. Maybe we could try fishing. If Hank wants to learn, then I could teach him. After all, I learned from my grandfather back in Rumley when I was Hank's age."

Gabriela's forceful words had definitely hit Ross hard, and after several days of soul searching, he sent out a few of the young Peruvian runners with a message. He was requesting a special meeting of the representative council for the following morning, as there was an important topic he needed to discuss with them. That evening Jessica sat by his side and asked, "You seem lost in thought. What's on your mind?"

Jessica had always been his right arm during the difficult times of uniting the colony and the building of life sustaining infrastructure. Throughout the years Ross had freely delegated numerous responsibilities toward her, and had always been satisfied with the results. His response caught her off guard as he said, "I've been pondering over who will be my successor."

"Why would you do that? You were elected to an open ended term. The people love what you have done for them, so I don't believe that there is any thought of replacing you."

"Perhaps, but all good things must eventually end."

"That's ridiculous Ross, unless you're not feeling well. Do you need to tell me something about your health?"

"Not at all, I feel fine other than still being a little stiff after my recent tumble."

"That's a relief. Please don't scare me like that again."

The next morning, Ross, as usual, spoke of the collective effort by all those present. They, and others before them, had provided a stable form of leadership for the colony that didn't embrace the ugly aspects of a dictatorship. The current system seemed to pacify the vast majority, but Ross was aware that one aspect had never been addressed. He asked them, "Have any of you ever considered establishing a line of succession for the leadership of this colony?"

A questioning buzz could be heard among the collective, and then someone said, "I don't know about anyone else, but I haven't thought about it all. Do you have any suggestions?"

"I do indeed, but first I thank you for your honesty. My suggestion would be to establish a line of individuals who could become President if the need ever arose. That being said, I also believe that Jessica should be the first to follow in my footsteps. She has in reality acted as my Vice President since the time of our arrival on this moon. You all know that she is qualified for the position, and would serve the colony well. Therefore I ask that you please vote on that particular measure at this time."

Another buzz could be heard, and then someone asked, "Ross, you're not intending to resign from office are you?"

"Not today, but we all have to be realistic. The people elected me to an open ended term, but at some point I will step down. My desire is that decisions made by you presently, will make the inevitable transition smoother."

A robust English woman then spun around to face the majority of the representative council and proclaimed, "We have been asked to consider two questions. First, should we establish a formal line of succession for the Presidency? That question can wait for our next scheduled meeting to be deliberated upon. As for the present moment, there is the second question. A vote is required immediately with regard to Jessica Martin becoming our next President."

A moment later, Jessica leaned into Ross and asked, "Are you sure about this. What if they vote no?"

Before he could reply, the English woman turned back toward Ross and said, "We're ready to vote when you are sir."

"Thank you. Now by a show of hands please, all those in favor of proclaiming Jessica as my eventual successor."

The motion carried with ease, as nearly the entire mass of representatives raised their hands high into the air. Then, no more than a dozen could be seen when Ross called for all those opposed. Not far away Hank stood next to Ms. Crenshaw, and smiled as she uttered, "Well alright then."

Within moments after their return to the family shelter, Ross leaned into Jessica and said, "They must not know yet."

She replied, "How could they possibly know? After the adjournment of the meeting we came straight here."

"True, but you know how information can leak out."

"Yes, but I don't think that's very likely in this case."

Nodding in agreement, Ross then loudly asked, "Could I please have everyone's attention for a moment? Jessica has something to tell all of you."

With that Jessica informed the circle of family and close friends living in the surrounding shelters of her good news. She would, at some point in the undisclosed future, become the next President of the colony.

The soul searching for Ross continued throughout the next several days and nights that followed. Conversations with Gabriela about his intent were combined with extensive hours of consultation with Jessica. Wanting to fully prepare her, Ross toured the entire colony, and the midpoint village, with Jessica. She used the opportunity to become re-acquainted with various team leaders, and any issues she may have been unaware of.

One afternoon, while on a rest break near the water's edge, Ross scooped up a handful of course sand. Then he softly uttered, "There's just way too many to count!"

Jessica replied, "Excuse me."

"Huh? Oh, it's nothing. I was just thinking about a time long ago back on Earth."

"A pleasant memory I hope."

Ross had reached his decision several days before, but he hadn't told Jessica. The action would impact her the most, and the current moment provided a perfect opportunity. He said, "I'll wait until Megan completes the seed planting after the next eclipse, because I don't want to interrupt the routines of the colony. Then I will announce my resignation."

She replied, "I had the feeling that this moment was coming sooner than later. Thanks for providing such attention to detail while bringing me up to speed during the past several days. I won't insult you by asking if you have fully thought this through, but does Gabriela know yet?"

"Yes she does. We discussed the matter at great length before I broached the subject with the council, but I asked that she keep it to herself. Gabriela understands the need to keep the information between the three of us until the moment of the public announcement."

Two days after the newly expanded crop field had been planted for the first time, the representative council, and a few other interested souls, gathered around to hear what Ross had to say. Megan, her team, and Hank, were unable to attend. The task of constantly monitoring the irrigation system had kept them all very busy. As Hank inspected one of the trenches, Megan shouted, "Let me know if you see any problems. The first few days of water are vital for newly planted seeds."

"Alright Ms. Crenshaw, everything looks good so far."

Ross climbed up the lower reaches of the steep hillside to the spot he had nearly always used to communicate with the representative council. Glancing at Aurora, he flashed back to when he and the Mayan King briefly stood on the same spot. Aurora's freewill was in jeopardy that day, but fortunately, that potential crisis had been averted.

Gabriela snapped him back into the present moment when she said, "Ross, everyone is ready for you to begin."

Standing firm and tall, he began, "I would like to thank all of you for coming out this morning to hear what I must say. As we are now in the second month of our seventh year on this moon, the time has come for a transition. With sixteen months in each year, we have, in effect, been on this moon for slightly more than eight years as measured by our internal body clocks."

Turning to Aurora, Jessica said, "Could you please get your notepad out to write something down."

"Sure, but can you tell me what's going on?"

Before Jessica could respond to her niece, Ross began again with, "It has been my great honor and pleasure to serve as your President since the earliest days of our struggle on this moon. You have treated me, and my family, with kindness and respect, as many difficult decisions needed to be made in order to secure the survival of the colony."

Aurora noticed that Gabriela had a tear running down her cheek, and realized what was happening. In a moment of pure denial, she said aloud, "No dad. Please don't say it!"

Without breaking cadence, the bombshell was delivered when Ross stated, "Today, on this fourth day, of the second month, in our seventh year on this moon, I hereby formally announce my resignation as the first President of this colony. This resignation will be effective immediately."

The murmuring voices of the several hundred people in attendance began to build into a shockwave of emotion. Ross understood that he needed to complete his remarks quickly, so with arms raised high overhead, he quieted those assembled. Concluding his remarks, Ross added, "My successor, and those that will follow, must all be people of character. Each of them must also attempt whatever is deemed necessary to insure the continued prosperity of the colony. The council overwhelmingly confirmed my suggested successor, and many of you are well versed as to the capabilities and tireless dedication that she possesses. Ladies and gentlemen, please welcome the second President of our colony, Ms. Jessica Martin."

Before Jessica moved to accept her position as leader of the colony, she turned to Aurora and said, "You see, I told you that you were going to want to write this down."

Aurora gave her Aunt Jessica a hug, and then pulled out her notepad. The entry was simple enough. 04/02/07. Jessica becomes second colony President, as Ross resigns from office.

$$\text{\textsf{P}}$$

CHAPTER TWENTY-EIGHT

NEARLY RETIRED

The first few weeks of retirement from office had been enjoyable for Ross. Beyond the obvious benefits of sleeping in when the mood struck him, or not needing to keep abreast of the many projects and challenges facing the colony, there was the fishing. Blocks of relaxation time had not been available to Ross since during the six week voyage through space from Earth to this moon. That brief respite had been more than eight years of his internal body clock into the past, but it had been much longer since he had enjoyed the peace and solitude of fishing.

With help from Colt, Ross had created something from flexible saplings that could be used as a fishing pole. Although primitive when compared to the gear he had known back on Earth, at least it was something. True to his word, Ross taught Hank how to fish when the young boy could break away from his studies or work assignments. As a result, the two of them would often be found sitting along the shore of the vast lake.

As the brothers teamed up to land their most recent catch, Hank exclaimed, "Hey Ross, I think this is the biggest fish that we have ever caught!"

"I think you're right, this is a big fish."

While occupied with cleaning their latest prize so that it could become part of the evening meal, Ross and Hank didn't notice what was approaching. They were both caught off guard when a shadow suddenly engulfed them and the surrounding portion of the peninsula. Startled, they instinctively looked up. Although different in size to any they had seen during previous visits, the vessel casting the shadow had familiar markings to it. Without a doubt it belonged to the alien species they knew well, and those inside it had obviously returned to check on the progress of the colony. Their timing was off though. The alien visits had always occurred at regular intervals throughout the past six moon years, so Ross knew that something unusual must have transpired to make them deviate from that routine.

Jessica, while waiting for the hatch of the alien vessel to open, visually scanned the surrounding area for Ross. After locating him she asked, "Aren't you coming?"

"I will communicate with my old friend in due course, but the responsibility of discussing the progress of the colony now falls under your jurisdiction."

"I know that, but you can still attend the briefing."

"That's kind of you, but no thanks."

Several hours later, after Jessica had completed her lengthy conversation with the alien, Ross sat privately with his old friend. They discussed many topics as usual, but Ross was completely blindsided by one thought projected question from the alien. Was he still interested in the answer to a question he had asked during the first progress report visit? At that time, the question went unanswered by the alien. The topic had never been broached during any subsequent visit either, yet now, it was somehow open for discussion. After a few brief seconds of contemplation, Ross jumped at the chance to learn anything that he could. His response was quite emphatic as he said to his old friend, "Yes. I would very much like to know what became of Earth."

With intense focus, Ross soaked up all the information that the alien's thought projection presented. Although pleased to know that there had been small pockets of survivors, he was disappointed to learn of the most recent challenge facing their descendants. According to his alien friend, the small population of ₹-829-ঽπ-3 had worked very hard to overcome many levels of adversity throughout the centuries. They had prospered in a direction that was vastly different than what Ross remembered of his home world. It was painful to realize that the cruel fate of genetics could potentially hinder their continued progress.

Ross was then completely shocked by the content of his friend's next thought provoking question. Did he, along with a very small contingent, wish to return to their home world in a desperate attempt to salvage the situation? Although the offer presented a most intriguing opportunity for Ross to consider, his response could not be made with haste.

Ross presented the best poker face he could muster given his level of shock, but his insides were churning as he digested the possibility. Could returning to Earth really be an option for him? If so, then what was the alien's definition of a small contingent? Additional questions for the alien began to form in his mind, but they could wait. The first thing he needed to do was discuss the subject with Gabriela. Patty, who was Ross' lifelong soul mate and wife on Earth, had stayed behind. Even though that meant losing her husband and one of her daughters forever, she wanted nothing to do with hopping on a spaceship and traveling to God knows where. That separation had been extremely difficult for Ross, and he vowed to avoid such a painful scenario in his life ever again if possible. He knew that he had been incredibly fortunate to find love a second time with Gabriela, and he would not leave this moon unless she could, and would, come with him. Looking at his old friend, Ross said, "Your offer sounds both fantastic and challenging. I'm thankful for your ongoing concern with regard to mine, and other species within the limitless expanse of the cosmos. The opportunity for me to lead an attempt to insure the longevity of the people of Earth would be an incredible honor. Can I think it over, and discuss it with Gabriela and my family?"

The thought response was not exactly what Ross had hoped for. Although his request was granted, he would have a very limited amount of time to reach a decision. Rising from his seated position with a measure of apprehension, Ross shook the hand of his friend and excused himself.

After watching Ross pace nervously about for several minutes, Gabriela knew something major was on his mind. She asked briskly, "Alright Ross, what has your wheels turning?"

"Huh? Oh it's just something that my alien friend asked me during our conversation a little while ago."

"Well, it's quite obvious that you are deeply concerned about whatever it is. Do you want to talk about it?"

"Yes indeed, but we should both sit down first. I must pre-warn you, the topic is rather shocking and of tremendous significance. Once you have heard what I have to say, I hope we can arrive at a mutual decision as to our course of action."

"That sounds serious. Is everything alright?"

Once seated by her side on the ground within their shelter, Ross leaned in and whispered, "Gabriela, we are faced with a fantastic opportunity. My old alien friend has asked if we would like to return to Earth."

"What? Are you serious?"

"Yes I am. He informed me that although it seemed at the time to be a near impossibility, Earth actually survived the multiple impacts of massive asteroid and moon chunks that had rained down for several months. I also learned that a very small percentage of the human population survived those impacts, and several years later emerged from the caves to live on the surface once again."

"Well that's great news. Our species is alive and well in two different solar systems."

"Actually, we have been for centuries. Most of the population of Earth in the twenty-first century was simply too arrogant to believe there could be life other than our own in the universe. Even those of us who did believe in extraterrestrial life were unaware that small pockets of humans from three different ancient civilizations lived on a distant pale green moon. That is, until an advanced alien species brought our group here. Although those same aliens haven't informed us of any other locations, it's possible they transplanted humans to a variety of solar systems."

"That's an intriguing prospect to be sure, and perhaps we should ask them about it. As for those of us on this moon, when will the transport vessels be coming to pick us up?"

"They aren't coming to pick us up."

"They aren't? Then how is everyone going to make the long voyage back to Earth?"

"That's the rub Gabriela, because this opportunity has not been offered to the entire colony. Additionally, our alien friends have stipulated that I must be the one who leads this new endeavor. I have also been given the most unenviable task of deciding who among the inhabitants of this moon go with me. If I'm unwilling to do so, then there will be no flight. None of our people will have a chance of returning to Earth. At the risk of stating the obvious, my retirement would become a thing of the past if I were to take on such an endeavor."

"Well that presents several difficult decisions for you to be sure, and you're right, I for one don't envy your position. How many of the colonists can go on the voyage?"

"Before we get to that, we need to determine what the two of us intend to do. I will not, under any circumstances, leave this moon without you by my side. Please take your time to think it over, and be completely honest with me. Is it your intent to remain here for the rest of our lives, or should we, as a team, lead the return expedition to Earth?"

Ross barely had time to take a breath after finishing his question before Gabriela emphatically stated, "I don't need any time to think it over. We should return to Earth of course."

"I'm extremely happy to hear you say that Gabriela, as I believe this to be a noble quest that must be attempted."

"I understand Ross. Now tell me, do you already have a selection process in mind, or do we need to develop one?"

"The selection process is somewhat pre-determined. With the exception of those in our immediate family who wish to join us, we will be searching for young breeding stock."

"Breeding stock? What has happened back on Earth?"

"Keep in mind how our timeline was affected once we boarded the transport vessels to leave Earth. When you add up the time of the original voyage, all the moon months and years that we have been living here, and the upcoming voyage home, a great deal of time will have passed on Earth. The descendants of the original survivors are very small in number and scattered throughout various areas of the planet surface. Their collective gene pool is dying a slow death, and is in desperate need of an infusion of fresh human DNA. Otherwise, our species as we know it will perish from the Earth in little more than a century."

After the momentary shock of that message had been digested, Gabriela replied, "You're absolutely correct, that is a serious problem that must be addressed. I'm curious though; just how much time has passed since we left Earth?"

"Our alien friends have informed me that by the time we complete the six week voyage home, our small contingent will step onto the surface of Earth twenty-six hundred years after our departure."

Another shock wave hit Gabriela. As she attempted to digest the magnitude of that mind blowing information, she gulped and said, "That's absolutely amazing."

"Yes it is, and humbling as well."

Having once again gathered her composure, Gabriela pressed for one more bit of important information. She asked, "Ross, you still haven't answered my previous question. How many of the colonists will be involved in this new endeavor?"

While motioning over his right shoulder with his thumb, he replied, "There is room enough on that new alien vessel for only one hundred of us."

CHAPTER TWENTY-NINE

THE RECRUITS

With precious little time to work with, Ross emerged from the family shelter. Aurora's meticulous records could help with his present need, and for perhaps the first time, he was irritated that she no longer lived in a nearby shelter. Believing that Gabriela would respond positively, Ross had already set the wheels in motion through proactive thinking. Just moments after his conversation with the alien, he requested that four of the young Peruvian runners set a quick pace toward the midpoint village. Their task was twofold. First, they were to deliver his written note to Aurora. Ross hoped that she would understand the magnitude of his message, and take immediate action to recruit a few potential candidates.

Once adequately rested, the second aspect was for the runners to continue on to the Mayan city. Ross had always been careful to not abuse his position as a demigod within the Mayan belief structure, but this was an excellent opportunity to use that leverage. With an escort of Mayan citizens now living at the midpoint village, the runners were to relay a message to the Mayan King. The Sky God and Ross wanted him to choose ten men and ten women of strong young breeding stock who could be prepared to leave within the hour for the colony. They would not be sacrificed or harmed, but they would never return. Ross knew the request was huge in scope, but the King needed to know that by doing so, both Ross and the Sky God would be extremely grateful.

As for Aurora, the shelter that she currently occupied with her Mayan husband was several hours by foot from Ross and Gabriela's location. Add that to the time it would take for her and the recruits to get organized, and Ross knew that she probably wouldn't arrive until the following day.

As Ross spoke to the remainder of the family, and their immediate circle of friends, it became clear that some of them were interested in returning to Earth. Colt, Janet, and Hank led the procession, and that made Ross very happy. True to her ever present and steadfast dedication to duty, Jessica declined. Eloquent as always, she stated with conviction, "I have just begun what may be a lengthy term as President of this colony. The greater interest of the population would not be served by enduring another change so quickly after our first transition of leadership. I shall never express any regret in doing so, but the correct action is for me to remain on this moon."

Although saddened by the realization that her decision meant they would never see each other again, Ross nodded with obvious approval at her choice. He said, "Jessica, you have demonstrated an unselfish quality that proves why you were the correct person to be the new leader of this colony."

"Thank you Ross. I knew you would understand why I must stay. I wish you and those returning to Earth the best of luck with the hopeful restoration of a healthy gene pool. If I can help you prepare for the voyage, let me know."

A normally quiet and reserved member of the Flight 19 crews then asked, "Excuse me sir, but would it be reasonable to assume that you are looking for both men and women for this venture? If so, then what is the target age group?"

Turning to face the man, Ross replied, "Those are very good questions Lieutenant. Yes. Both men and women will be needed, and we should try to have them come from various cultures and backgrounds. I have initiated a plan of influence to recruit twenty youthful Mayans as part of the endeavor. As for the age group, we should attempt to establish a wide range. The top end would probably need to be cut off at about forty-five to insure both ability and fertility. The youthful end of the scale would have no set minimum age. I can remember several teenagers who endured the valley of fatigue with the rest of us when we first arrived. Based on how long we have been here, they are now in their early twenties. If we could entice some of them to be interested in looking at a broader picture than themselves, and it wouldn't create too much of a detriment to the future needs of reproduction for this colony, I would like for a few of them to come with us. For that matter, we could go even younger. Although it wouldn't be reasonable to think of them as viable candidates for several years, having a few of the youngsters like Hank would be a welcome addition to the mix."

"Well then sir, I meet your established criteria. If you have room for me, then count me in."

Another one of the pilots stepped forward to state his similar desire, and was followed by one more. Ross said, "Thank you gentlemen. My normal record keeper has not yet joined this conversation, but perhaps the three of you could give your names to Gabriela. Her memory is much better than mine, so that will insure that each of you will be placed on the list of potential candidates when Aurora does arrive."

Word spread like wildfire throughout the colony. For those who met the established criteria, they had a life changing decision to make. Janet had a perfect candidate in mind, but didn't know if she would be interested. With assistance from the pilots of Flight 19, she was able to locate the young woman quickly. After waiting for Ross to complete a private discussion with another young woman and her little girl, Janet moved forward with her first recruit. Standing before her oldest son, Janet said, "Ross, I would like you to meet Brittany Cooper of Helena, Montana. We first met on the alien deep water vessel, after she had been abducted in 2007. We have been discussing the desperate need for people in her age group back on Earth, and she is very interested in becoming one of the candidates for the special project."

Standing in response to the introduction, Ross replied, "Well, it's very nice to meet you Brittany. Thank you for your interest in helping our cause."

"It's nice to finally meet you as well sir. Throughout the years I have been hesitant to introduce myself, because I wasn't sure how I would be received by the first family."

"I don't think I fully understand. I mean, I would like to believe we were always informal and approachable. Why would you have been concerned about your acceptance?"

Janet intervened and said, "Perhaps I can shed a little light on the subject. That is, if Brittany doesn't mind."

Brittany replied, "Go ahead Janet, it's alright with me."

Janet informed Ross that Brittany was probably just embarrassed by her youthful exuberance. When Janet first met Brittany in 2007, she was a slender girl of seventeen. Janet told of how the young woman proudly displayed her bare midriff while wearing a short t-shirt and extremely low cut blue jeans. For young women of the time, it was a very popular fashion trend, but she, like most who became a slave to such things, had eventually grown out of the craze. Janet also pointed out that Brittany's internal body clock had advanced eight years. She was now a grown woman of twenty-five, and the curves of her body were evidence that she had filled out quite nicely.

Ross interrupted Janet's colorful rendition of the past, and said, "Mom, is it really necessary to embarrass Brittany, or me, by pointing out her supposed indiscretions and curves?"

Brittany was quick to jump back into the conversation by saying, "It's quite alright sir. I never considered them to be indiscretions. I also don't want to sound pretentious, but I was blessed with a nice body. I have absolutely no problem with Janet discussing the clothes I wore to showcase it."

Ross knew he had no chance of controlling the situation with either woman when Janet perceived Brittany's comment as a green light to continue. He hoped he didn't blush when Janet added, "Ross, you know that I'm a trained nurse and a realist with no prudish inhibitions or tendencies. I hope this doesn't embarrass you, but I'm open minded enough to know that Brittany will surely entice men of perhaps all ages. Just look at that body of hers. Please tell me you understand that it will only be a matter of time before she will assist with our attempt to enrich the depleted gene pool of Earth."

At that moment Ross realized that Janet might be taking this entire gene pool concept more seriously than anyone else. He decided to use that enthusiasm as a vehicle to provide all of the young women considering the endeavor with full disclosure. Looking at Janet and Brittany, Ross stated, "It would appear that debating either of you on this topic would be a waste of time. That being said, there is something that both of you should be aware of. Based on preferable ages for reproduction, this will not apply to Janet. However, all the younger women, including you Brittany, that are selected will need to be fully accepting of a vital concept. Before you fully commit, you must realize just what will be expected of you during the upcoming years. In order to enrich the dying gene pool of Earth, you will need to bare the children of, at a minimum, three or four different men. If you believe that you can fulfill that obligation, then consider yourself to be recruited for this endeavor."

Feeling somewhat like a lab rat, Brittany looked at Janet for verification. An affirming nod prompted her to ask, "Were you aware of that requirement before you spoke with me?"

Janet replied, "Although Ross had not spoken with me about that need directly, as a nurse I knew that somewhat drastic measures will be required to restore a healthy gene pool. If it helps to ease your mind, I accept the fact that my husband Colt will be involved as well. I would prefer that he doesn't do so with any women that I already know, but he will hopefully be able to father a child with a few other women."

Ross interjected and added, "Brittany, I know that the conditions we have discussed may be difficult to entertain for some people. Some with strong religious convictions may even find them to be repulsive, but it won't do us any good to bury our heads in the sand. Did you see the young woman and her little girl that I was speaking with before we were introduced?"

"Yes sir, I did."

"That was Natiya, originally from close to Kaputsin Yar, Russia, and her five year old daughter Kristyn. She has now fully committed both of them to this endeavor. Natiya's husband, Kristyn's father, was killed three years ago while hunting a wolf creature. The team of hunters had nearly subdued the animal, but he was trampled by the beast before it gave up all hope. Unfortunately, Natiya was then left alone with a two year old."

"That's a tragic story sir."

"Yes it is, but she is now ready to begin a new chapter in their lives. I have always believed that a person has the right to know exactly what they are getting into, so I was quite candid with her when she inquired about returning to Earth. Natiya is now aware of the requirement that you and I just discussed. Additionally, she understands that Kristyn will begin the same process in about fifteen years."

"That seems extreme. Is it really necessary?"

Janet beat Ross to the punch, and added, "Yes it is. This attempt at gene enrichment will not be easy. In order for the plan to be effective, the children of today, including my young son Hank, and the children you bare, will eventually need to carry on with the same requirement."

With that, Brittany was convinced. She said, "Very well. I accept the conditions and am willing to do my part, but only if I have a choice as to which men will eventually impregnate me?"

Janet replied, "Of course. No matter what the situation, a woman should always possess that right."

Ross added, "I agree whole heartedly. This should not be looked upon as random or non-emotional sex. The parental couples need to care for each other at some level, but they also need to accept that the relationships can't be monogamous."

"I understand, and that seems fair enough."

"Excellent. Will the two of you help Gabriela deliver the message of expectation to the female recruits?"

Janet asked, "What's the matter Ross, are you chicken?"

"Perhaps, but I'm also realistic. Although Brittany took this all in stride, most would probably handle the expectations better if they were presented by another woman."

Before noon the following day, Aurora, her husband, and two young women she had recruited from the midpoint village arrived. She reported that the four Peruvian runners and their escorts had gone onward to the Mayan city as planned, but didn't know how long their return to the colony would take. That would depend largely on how well the respective recruits could keep up with the always lively pace of the runners.

Ross was pleased to see Aurora, and immediately filled her in on more of the significant details of the overall plan. She was glad to see her father taking the lead with the endeavor. From her perspective, it was one more opportunity for him to showcase his leadership skills. After listening to the pertinent information, Aurora asked, "Now that I understand the true level of expectation for those involved, what can I do to help?"

With no hesitation at all, Ross replied, "Can you take over the official record keeping? We need a list of names for all those that are participating, along with a breakdown of male versus female and the respective ages. Janet can help you with the information of those who have already signed on, and in time, Gabriela will provide the same for the Mayan contingent. As for our extended family, we will be seven if you and your husband are both going."

"Of course we are going. He will probably enjoy the prospect of fathering another woman's child, but don't you mean eight of us?"

"No, it's just seven. Jessica has decided to stay here."

CHAPTER THIRTY

THE MANIFEST

Aurora stood at the top of the boarding ramp onto the new alien vessel. One by one she spoke with each recruit when they approached, and then checked them off the manifest once she had verified their information. Ross and Gabriela were the last to come aboard. They had walked up the ramp with Jessica by their side. It seemed the only way to insure a somewhat private goodbye, as several hundred colonists had come to bid farewell.

Looking at Aurora, Ross inquired, "Are we all set?"

"Yes dad. The other ninety-seven are all on board."

"Well then, I guess the time has come."

Jessica nodded and moved to give Aurora a hug. Then she said, "You have always been a wonderful aspect of my life. I love you dearly, and am very proud of everything that you have done throughout your life. Good luck with whatever the future may bring you."

"Thank you Jessica. You have been a fantastic aunt, and I love you too. There simply isn't enough time to express how much of a positive influence you have been, but you must know that I have always admired your guidance."

After hugging her niece once more, Jessica turned to Gabriela. She took her into an embrace and said, "I'm so happy that you and Ross found each other. You have taken good care of my brother, and I will always love you for that."

"Thank you Jessica. You are very sweet to say so. Like Aurora, I admire you for your positive influence. You also have an inner strength that may be unmatched by anyone I have ever known. As for Ross, I love your brother with all my heart, but I don't think it's possible for me to love him as much as you do."

"What an amazing thing to say. Thank you. I know Ross will always be in good hands with you Gabriela."

Ross broke in by saying, "Ladies, I hate to interrupt this overflow of sentiment, but three of us have a flight to catch."

Patting Gabriela on the shoulder, Jessica said, "Isn't it amazing how he can ruin a moment sometimes?"

"Yes, but as you know, some things never change."

With a nod of acknowledgement, Jessica turned to Ross. She said, "Well big brother, the moment I always feared is upon us. I hoped to be better prepared, but what do I say to the person who has meant more to me than anyone else in all of my life? Gabriela said that I possess an inner strength, but you gave me the incentive. From our youngest days back in Rumley, you were the one who taught me that most things are possible if I could develop an inner strength. Your dedication to the service of humanity has been prevalent since our youth, and it will continue beyond this day. I love you for everything you did as my big brother to help me find my path in life, and that life will be less complete when you depart."

Now fighting back his own tears, Ross hugged his sister and replied, "Well, it sure sounded as if you were well prepared for this moment. I doubt that I could say anything to top the touching sentiment you have expressed. You must know that I counted on your inner strength numerous times. Thank you for believing in me when Patty didn't, and for helping me to take on the many challenges that confronted me back on Earth as well as on this moon. I will miss you more than you know Jessica."

Jessica dried her eyes, smiled, and walked back down the ramp. A moment later, she along with hundreds of others, waved as the alien vessel began a slow rise from the surface. Having said their collective goodbye to Jessica sometime earlier, the Jensen trio of Colt, Janet, and Hank returned her wave from behind the large viewing window. As the vessel gained some altitude, Hank spotted Megan Crenshaw waving from near the waterfall. In spite of early difficulties, she had been a wonderful teacher and had become a good friend for Hank. He returned the wave, but couldn't be sure that she had seen him do so. It became difficult for him to contain his excitement, as the vessel was now high enough to view the entire colony. Although the majority of the recruits had experienced the sensation of flight, young Hank was not one of them. Looking up at his parents, he said, "This is really cool!"

Colt replied, "Yes it is, but just wait. The view gets even better as we go higher into the sky."

"It does? That sounds great!"

Janet then crouched beside her son and added, "In a few minutes we will be able to see more than you could have ever imagined."

As with Hank and Kristyn, there was a larger segment of recruits that had been born on this moon. They of course, were also experiencing flight for the first time. Gabriela had brought them all aboard before returning to the peninsula to fetch Ross. She believed that the Mayans would do well on the voyage, and like Janet, thought their genetic code would be of tremendous help once blended with that of some people living on modern day Earth. Gabriela wanted to check on how they were doing, so she asked Ross to join her as she did so. As they entered the compartment where all twenty of them had been temporarily placed, Ross greeted them in their native tongue. The men, as always, attempted to maintain their look of strength. As for the women, they presented no false bravado.

Wanting to show them all that could be seen from the viewing window before gaining too much altitude above their home world, Gabriela motioned for them to follow her. She suddenly realized that not only had the Mayan contingent never seen their world from above, but they were also unaware of what a window was. Back in their city, all the openings in the buildings for light and air were absent of glass. The substance was completely foreign to them. Turning back to face them all, she said, "You are about to see and feel a very strange thing, but there is no need to be frightened. Ross and I will show you a wall that is solid, but you can look straight through it. Even though we will be moving higher into the sky, you don't need to be afraid. The world will be getting further away, but you will not fall through the wall."

Ross looked at Gabriela and said, "I can't believe I never thought about how they would respond to glass."

"I could be wrong, but I don't think any of us from the colony who made the initial voyage thought about it either."

As the entire group approached the viewing window, Ross asked, "Excuse me folks, could we please create a space for our Mayan friends to look at their home world?"

Those near the window cleared a path, and the first Mayan to notice the see-through wall lost his composure. In spite of her proactive approach, Gabriela had been unable to prevent such a negative reaction. He, along with most of the Mayans, jumped back away from the glass. The next several moments were taxing for Gabriela, as her attempts to have them move forward didn't produce results.

After observing the futile action, Hank emerged from behind Janet in a completely unexpected move. Walking up to a trembling Mayan woman, he slowly reached for her hand. Then he asked, "Excuse me Gabriela, but can you please help me communicate with her?"

Although somewhat startled by his request, she replied, "Alright Hank, what would you like to say?"

Now softly holding the Mayans hand, Hank looked up at her and said, "It's alright. I was afraid too, but then my parents showed me that I couldn't fall through. You can see more than if you were on top of a mountain from over there. If I promise to not let go of your hand, will you come look with me?"

Staring down at his innocent face and eyes, the woman nodded and squeezed Hank's hand. Moving slowly at first so that he wouldn't frighten her, Hank edged the woman closer to the window. He stopped a few feet away, and pointed at the colony and large body of water below. A moment later he put his hand on the glass, and made sure that she noticed he was pushing on it.

Colt proudly whispered to Janet, "That's our boy, and I think he might just be a lady killer someday."

With a stern glare on her face, Janet turned and replied, "That may be true, but I for one hope that Hank can enjoy a lengthy childhood before he learns to exploit that trait."

Just then they heard Hank say to the woman, "You see. It's like I told you. This can't hurt you, and you won't fall."

Using a soft lilting tone to mimic Hank, Gabriela made sure all of the Mayans heard her translation. A moment later she smiled, as Hank's pupil reached out with her empty hand to touch the window.

Feeling both proud and satisfied with the effort and skill that his younger brother had displayed to ease the tension, Ross turned to Aurora. He said, "Now that Hank seems to have this situation in hand, no pun intended, can you and I have a few minutes to go over the specifications of the manifest?"

"Of course we can dad. Should we do that here, or in a more private location?"

"Let's step away without being too obvious. Then you can give me the breakdown."

Throughout the next hour, Ross was reminded of just how meticulous his oldest daughter was. She began with the obvious fact that she, along with Ross and Gabriela, were not going to be part of the process. Janet was listed as highly doubtful, because she was at the high end of the established age scale. Reproduction, although still possible in theory, was not a requirement for her. Aside from that, Aurora felt that the other ninety-six, including her husband, could be used to help the gene pool. Of the one hundred on board, fifty-four were male, with forty-six females. Including the Mayans, and those of ethnic backgrounds representing five continents, the belief was that forty-three of the females could eventually produce offspring. As for the fifty-four males, their higher numbers were equal with regard to diversity. All except Ross were believed to be viable candidates for the eventual fathering of children. Aurora then stated the obvious when she said, "We used basic math in our selection process. The reason more males were recruited was very simple. A male can impregnate a female more often than a female can become impregnated."

Ross couldn't help but laugh out loud at her statement, and he responded with, "So that's how it works huh? All these years, and I can't believe I never realized that."

Now smiling at her father's playful response, she added, "But of course you are well aware of how that works."

At the conclusion of Aurora's briefing, Ross returned to the viewing window. A pleasant surprise awaited him, as he witnessed several of the Mayans conquering their fear. With Hank as their guide, Ross watched as one by one they reached out and touched the glass.

Several moments later Ross stood by the window with members of his immediate family, and soaked in the view. They gazed with amazement as the outer most marble of the solar system slid past. The blue planet floated peacefully within the black vastness of space, and although much larger, the sight of it reminded Ross of how Earth had looked during the return trip from his moon mission aboard the Discovery. Unfortunately, the current view didn't last long, as the beautiful orb quickly shrank and faded from view when the alien vessel accelerated. As had been the case when they first entered the solar system tabbed by the aliens as ₹-593, Ross felt a blend of excitement and fear now that they had departed. During the upcoming six week voyage before Earth would appear in the window, there would be little else to do but get some much needed rest and think. Moving away from the window, his thoughts turned to Jessica. In many ways his sister was much stronger than he was, and there was no doubt in his mind that he had not yet begun to miss her.

ꝓ

CHAPTER THIRTY-ONE

RING AROUND THE MARBLE

Janet heard the compartment door behind her open, and the quiet footsteps that ensued. Turning to see that it was Colt who had entered, she asked him, "Is it time?"

"Yes. Our host has informed me that we should be able to see Earth in a few minutes."

Knowing that Ross had been emphatic in his desire to view their home world during final approach, Janet awakened him. Her oldest son had been sleeping peacefully for several hours, which was a welcome change. Due to a persistent high fever and bouts of coughing throughout the previous four days, sleep had not come easily for Ross. Janet had provided the best medical attention that she could muster, but had been unable to break the fever or determine the exact cause of his ailment.

As the three of them moved slowly toward the viewing window, Colt provided Ross with a stabilizing arm to hold. From a pace behind, Janet inquired, "How do you feel Ross?"

"Better, thank you, but I haven't fully recovered yet."

At the viewing window, they, along with several others that included Aurora, Gabriela and Hank, waited with nervous anticipation. A moment later Colt spotted a distant tiny blue marble and exclaimed, "Look. I think that's it over there."

Glancing in the direction that Colt was pointing, Ross smiled and said, "What a tremendous moment for all of us."

After finally locating the growing blue marble, Gabriela asked, "Why didn't we see either Saturn or Jupiter during our approach? Those two planets are massive compared to Earth."

Ross put his arm around her, and flashed back to when, as a boy, he had built a complex model of the solar system for a school project in Rumley. That memory served him well in the present moment, as he replied, "I remember that we couldn't see either of those planets when we left the solar system to begin this incredible adventure. Think of this system of planets as being positioned on a flat surface similar to an old fashioned DVD. I believe that the reason we couldn't see any of the larger planets in the outer reaches of the system then, or now, was because of our angle of orientation. We must have exited, and now re-entered, the solar system from either above or below that disk depending on how you want to look at it."

As the alien vessel closed on Earth, Janet was the first to speak of a potential anomaly. She inquired, "Can anyone else see what appears to be some faint rings around the planet?"

Having no idea that the new look of Earth was vastly different from when many of the other passengers had lived upon it, Hank innocently replied, "I see them too mom."

Once the alien vessel had settled into, and maintained, a gentle orbit high above the planet, Ross began a much closer visual inspection of what lay in front of him. There was no need to deny it; Janet and Hank were both correct. A few faint layers of rings could now easily be seen orbiting Earth. For anyone of old Earth who possessed even a mild interest in space, the rings of Saturn were a well-known fact. Ross theorized that like those rings, the ones now encircling his home world consisted of small rock debris. It was a reasonable assumption to believe that they numbered in the hundreds of thousands at a minimum, and were probably the byproduct of the asteroid impact into the former moon. What had not subsequently impacted Earth, or burned up entering the atmosphere, must have been captured into a lower orbital path. In so doing, the massive amount of debris would have assured the eventual and total destruction of Earth's former satellite communication system.

Now gazing upon the surface of the planet itself, Ross noticed there were a few subtle differences. Having spent a tremendous amount of time training for, and venturing into, space during his much younger years as an astronaut, Ross had a vivid memory of what Earth had looked like from orbit. Not surprisingly, it was now different. Throughout the course of what had been multiple and prolonged impacts on both land and water, some coastal areas had taken on a new shape. There were a few island groupings that Ross didn't recognize, and there seemed to be considerably less land mass to the known continents. In that regard, what had been known as Florida was gone. To the west, the lower part of Texas also had a completely different shape. It was obvious that Rumley was much closer to the beach than it used to be, as the land area of Houston, San Antonio, Laredo, Corpus Christi, and all points in between no longer existed. Although unsure as to the exact location of the new coastline, Ross believed the former state capitol city of Austin was now also covered with azure blue water. The vivid color when compared to turquoise implied greater depth, so perhaps that had been the impact site of a major chunk from the moon or asteroid. If so, then it was an interesting coincidence. Many scientists had long believed that a similar impact some sixty million years before had created the Gulf of Mexico, and caused the extinction of the dinosaurs.

With help from several orbital rotations by the alien vessel, Ross was able to identify where lit areas in the darkness revealed pockets of the surviving population. Not one of them was located far from the coastline of an ocean or sea, and that included what appeared to be a good sized settlement in what remained of Texas. Ross could have studied the intricacies of the planet surface and the new rings for hours as they spun slowly beneath his current position, but a telepathic question from his alien friend interrupted him.

Turning from the window, Ross spotted the alien and moved in his direction. After shaking hands, Ross said, "Unless you have already chosen a specific location to land, then yes, I do have a suggestion. Could you please drop our small group off on the North American continent? Near the site of the 1897 crash that involved your father to be more specific. I can't be sure if the area still goes by the same name, but when we departed twenty-six hundred years ago it was known as Texas. During a few of our multiple conversations throughout time, you expressed a desire to visit the site where your father crashed and died. Well my friend, by landing where I suggest, you could accomplish what had previously been denied by your superiors of the time."

For Ross, there was a separate motivation to select that particular location as opposed to any other. His proposed site would be close to his former home on Earth. More importantly however, was that there appeared to be a population center reasonably close to the site. That would be as good a place as any to meet with the citizens, and hopefully initiate the gene enrichment program. As the lone male recruit who would not be called upon to procreate, Ross figured there would be no need for him to venture to other population pockets of the planet. Without reservation, he could delegate some of the administrative duties of the program to Aurora and Janet. If all went well, those same duties could then be turned over to others living in the various population centers of Earth. Finally there was the thought of where he wished to reside during what remained of his twilight years, and his eventual final resting place. Based on his current less than perfect health at nearly eighty-one years of age, Ross knew that his time was limited. When the inevitable moment came, his desire, just like that of his father and grandfather, was to be buried in land that he had known as Texas.

ᛈ

CHAPTER THIRTY-TWO

NEW EARTH

For the small group of scientists and other citizens that had excitedly gathered as witnesses, it came as no real surprise that an alien vessel had landed. From their perspective, it was a matter of when, not if, such a historic event would transpire. To that end, they felt honored that the landing had taken place in very close proximity to their community.

The citizens of new Earth had benefited from the many writings and stories of the "before time" told by those who had entered the caves just prior to the apocalypse. The information provided those who survived with a blueprint of what not to do now that humanity had been given a second chance. According to all that had been passed down from one generation to the next throughout the centuries, the onslaught of asteroid and moon chunks that impacted the planet had simply expedited what some believed to be inevitable. Mankind had done a poor job of caring for their home world, and eventually, they would have perished as a consequence of that neglect. The natural resources of Earth, including the fresh water supply, were being abused without much regard, and the ever increasing toxic pollutants in the air were contributing to global warming. In time, such warming would lead to a dramatic shift in the atmospheric conditions, as ice covered regions of the planet had already begun to recede substantially. Instead of initiating a serious approach to rectifying the problems created by mankind's less than subtle footprint, much of the technology and finances of the time were still being used for antiquated purposes. Perhaps the most glaring example of such misguided endeavors was that of the catalytic converter, as many still held on to the preposterous notion that oil was the most precious liquid commodity on the planet. In addition, there was a belief among some that any advancement in technology should be focused solely on the development and further enhancement of weapons systems. It was insane conceptually. The world that people knew and loved was beginning to crumble around them, yet many could only focus on aspects that would multiply the problems they faced. With an underlying current of mistrust among many nations of the world, and in some cases within regions of a singular country, humanity was beginning to spiral out of control.

Armed with that basic knowledge, many who survived the apocalypse began to slowly rebuild the civilization of Earth using a different model. As one of the byproducts of that initial belief system, science and technology eventually found a way to explore space again. Using small unmanned machines equipped with wheels for mobility and sensors for gathering information, a vast amount of knowledge about the two closest neighboring planets of Mars and Venus had been processed. Much like the NASA probes during the half century before the apocalypse, these modern day devices had successfully landed and probed the surface of the respective planets. The advancement of the current probes was their ability to return to Earth with samples that could be further studied. Several smaller research probes had also been inserted into the orbital flow of the rock debris rings that encircled Earth. It was a few of those probes that had detected, and then alerted, the scientists to the approaching spacecraft. Consequently, the people standing just a few feet away from the now landed vessel had been tracking it since it first settled into orbit.

Their excitement heightened as a ramp slowly extended from the alien vessel. However, when the hatch hissed open a few seconds later, the collective excitement changed to shock. Silhouetted by the backlighting from within the spacecraft, two figures stood side by side. Although the shorter of the two was obviously some form of extraterrestrial life, the tall one next to it appeared as if it could be a male human. The surprise of the moment was intensified, when additional human forms began to muster behind them.

Descending the ramp with his old friend into the fresh and cool air of the night, Ross inhaled deeply a few times while looking over the crowd, and then said, "Good evening everyone. My name is Ross Martin."

A woman that looked to be in her early thirties moved forward, gulped with obvious trepidation, and then replied, "Hello Ross, my name is Tori Nobles. It's evident that you are familiar with our language, so you will understand when I ask a strange question. Are you human?"

"Very much so, and judging by the puzzled look on all of your faces, that must be rather unexpected."

"Well Ross, yes it is. In fact, that's an understatement if I've ever heard one. Perhaps you could help us all understand by providing an explanation?"

After shaking hands with the young woman, and then introducing her to his alien friend, Ross began to tell their tale. He briefly informed her, and the entire welcoming party, of why he and the human contingent were on board the alien vessel. While doing so, the recruits, and members of the alien crew, began to make their way down the boarding ramp. As citizens of new Earth embraced the reality of initial contact with an alien species, and the mysterious humans, Ross took a moment to look skyward. With a smiling face he said, "It feels great to be back on Earth, and to once again gaze upon the star groupings and constellations from a familiar vantage point."

His new hostess replied, "Well I can't speak for you Ross, but I have several questions about all that has transpired. Before we get to that though, can I offer you and your group some food and water?"

"Thank you Tori, that's very kind of you. And yes, I also have several questions."

After a hearty meal consisting of a seemingly endless supply of fresh vegetables, the question and answer session began. Many within the community gathered around for the exchange of information, and there was much that Ross, the recruits, and the small alien contingent learned. Among other things, they were informed that the modern humans were more scientifically advanced than those of the previous Earth. Each small pocket of humanity around the globe was interconnected in terms of communication via computer systems and powerful transmitting satellites in orbit. Although that aspect was similar to the past, the new global community took it further by freely sharing any advancement in technology. In simple terms, there were no secrets. There were also no national borders, as the global map was no longer comprised of individual countries. The entire population of the planet, now numbering less than twenty-thousand, lived under one unified flag of humanity. Also of note, was that everyone lived within fifteen kilometers of the globally altered coastline.

According to the historical discs and holograms that contained the ancient writings of the cave dwellers, and those who emerged from them several years after the apocalypse, people killed each other over fresh water. Then sometime later, pounding rain became overly abundant throughout the entirety of the planet surface. Mother Nature flexed her muscle and demonstrated superiority over her domain, as she literally flooded the planet for nearly a century. That attempt to self-cleanse was successful, as the engulfing massive dust clouds from the asteroid and moon impacts eventually settled from the sky. More recent historical writings and storytelling revealed how the level of the oceans slowly rose nearly two hundred feet because of that atmospheric cleansing.

Within a few centuries, the turbulent weather patterns of the planet had fully subsided. The fresh water supply from rain or snow became scarce again, and most of the land turned arid. With no other viable choice, the people moved close to the sea. Although the technology had not been widely used before the apocalypse, the knowledge of how to desalinate the ocean water existed. By consulting scientific journals from the past that had been preserved, a new wave of scientists and engineers were able to construct a workable desalinization plant. They shared the knowledge with others, as it obviously became a crucial aspect of continued survival. Eventually, each community could produce a virtually endless supply of fresh water via the process of transforming the nearby ocean salt water.

That created the blueprint for a new way of thinking about the environment. In spite of similar knowledge of the automobile and other gadgets from before the apocalypse, the modern scientific thought was to forgo such things. Instead, the focus centered more on intellectual pursuits, and in using technology as a means to produce abundant nourishment and shelter for the population. Hydroponics quickly moved to the forefront of scientific endeavors, and that, combined with the desalinization program, made everything else a distant memory. As a consequence, Earth never went through another industrial revolution, so the toxic and obviously noticeable air and water pollution problems of the past never redeveloped.

Ross was captivated by all that had been presented to him, and when he learned that a handful of museums existed at various locations around the planet, he asked, "Is one of them close to this community?"

Tori replied, "Unfortunately, no. I have never been to one, but our collection of historical disks and holograms contain samples of what can be learned at a museum. Every citizen has access to them, and they have been fascinating to study over the years. Sadly, the information from the pre-apocalyptic time is very minimal. I wonder if you could answer a question about your time that has puzzled me for years."

"I can't promise you anything Tori, but I'll certainly try. What would you like to know?"

"Was it common for people to own automobiles that could transport forty to fifty people?"

Realizing that she must be referring to an image of a bus that had probably been parked outside one of the survival caves, Ross replied, "No, the largest vehicles were not privately owned. Many people did own a car, truck, or van, but those models usually carried four or five people. Sadly, there was an excess of them in many parts of the world."

Tori nodded with understanding, then continued the history lesson of modern Earth. She told of the exploits of the scientific community, and how proud they were to have begun exploring space as in the time preceding the apocalypse. The historical records of the previous space program had been confirmed when one of the modern day probes returned from Mars with unquestionable proof. What had been the surprise was the content within the ancient probe. It provided detailed information about mankind and the civilization that inhabited Earth. One could theorize that such a probe was sent to provide a record of human existence, which could then be potentially discovered on Mars if Earth had been completely destroyed. Ross of course knew that such a probe existed, but that it also had not been public knowledge. He also didn't want anyone in his current surroundings to become aware that he was the one responsible for it. As President, Ross had signed the executive order insuring that NASA would send a few such probes to Mars. That action had occurred during the last hectic months before the asteroid impact, and Jessica was the only other person still alive who knew about it.

Before everyone called it a night, Ross answered many questions pertaining to the second moon and the pilgrimage that he had led. He spoke of how the colony had prospered, but only because of determination and perseverance. A strong community concept had eventually been developed, but only after convincing selfish individuals to search deep within for the broader picture. After his general overview, Ross seized the opportunity to ask his alien friend an important question. He wanted him to point out which of the thousands of stars in their current view was system ₹-593.

Although Ross shared the location of the star with all those present, he didn't reveal the entire thought message of his alien friend. What he had heard in his mind was, "Ross, look at the constellation that your species refers to as Orion. Below the three stars that make up the great hunters belt, there are three more that run nearly perpendicular to form his sword. Because you were one of the very few of your species who was involved with a cutting edge technology designed to discover what lay beyond your world, and then subsequently led the human endeavor to discover a new world, you could easily be described as the tip of the exploratory sword. Therefore it's quite appropriate that the moon you and your people all lived upon is in orbit around the faint star just off the tip of Orion's sword."

Early the following morning Gabriela and others were awakened by Ross, as he was suffering through a loud coughing spell. After checking to see that he was alright, Gabriela looked out the window and exclaimed, "Ross, come quick. You have got to see this!"

Groaning with obvious displeasure, Ross rubbed the small amount of blood from his previously clenched palm while Gabriela wasn't looking, and then slowly moved toward her. Once at the window, he replied, "Wow. You're absolutely right, that is a magnificent sunrise."

Aurora joined them a moment later, and was also struck by the beauty of the morning light. She then added, "Amazing. Do you think it's that beautiful every day?"

Ross responded, "I don't know, but the early morning light bouncing off the orbital rings like that sure does create a truly inspiring sight."

A moment later, as Ross dragged himself away from the captivating sunrise, Gabriela said, "That was a very nice thought projection last night from our friend about you being the tip of the sword. I agree with his belief of how important you were to our collective survival, and I'm surely not the only one among us who does. You should probably thank him for the sentiment."

Having now learned that he was not the only one to hear the previous night's telepathic message, he replied, "Yes it was nice of him, and I was planning on walking over to his vessel to speak with him about it momentarily."

Ross stepped outside, but was surprised to see that the alien vessel was no longer where it had landed the previous evening. Only time would tell if his old friend would return, but Ross hoped he hadn't left the planet before they had a chance to say goodbye to each other. Several hours later that question was answered, and Ross felt a sense of relief as he spotted the alien vessel floating quietly overhead.

While the alien moved down the ramp toward Ross and Gabriela, they both heard a thought projection of happy thanks. Their old friend had just returned from visiting his father's crash site of many Earth centuries before, and therefore felt an inner peacefulness at finally having the chance to do so. Then the alien approached Ross and did something that was completely unexpected. Reaching out with his open palm turned upward, he handed Ross the emblem and necklace that had represented so much of their collective past. Then both Ross and Gabriela received a sad thought, as their friend projected, "I must return to my home world now, and I don't know when I will be able to come back here for another visit. In the event that we never meet again, I wanted to return this to you. I hope all goes well for you in the future my friends. May your species survive and flourish as it aspires to become a member of the vast galactic community."

Knowing that a handshake simply wouldn't do, Gabriela stepped forward to hug the alien. It was the first time that the alien had experienced such a thing, so he fired off a thought projection intended only for Ross.

Nodding in the affirmative, Ross replied, "Yes, that is normal for our species to behave in such a manner, especially the females. It tends to occur most when we experience certain emotions such as joy or sadness, but it can also be a way of expressing extreme fondness toward an individual. In this case, Gabriela is hugging you because she is very fond of you and is saddened that she may never see you again. You may think this strange, but I would like to do the same if you don't object."

After having done so, Ross put on the necklace and said, "On behalf of my species, I thank you for everything my friend. Safe travels to wherever the stars may take you."

That night Ross sat with his immediate family and a few of the recruits on the nearby beach. He explained to Hank and Kristyn how this new world for them had only twelve months in a year as opposed to the sixteen months on their birth moon. Then he told them that they would never again need to endure an eclipse that lasted four days. He continued by adding that because of all the additional months on their former home world, six years back there were equal to just a little more than eight here on Earth. Accordingly, Hank was actually eight years old, and Kristyn was seven.

Nodding with comprehension, Hank then turned his gaze skyward. A moment later he bluntly stated, "Hey Ross. A few of the people living here told me that some of the star groupings have names. Was it like that when all of you lived here before?"

"Yes it was Hank. The stars can form many different shapes if you use your imagination, and we had names for lots of them. For example, those seven stars forming an almost square shape with a handle to the left are called the Big Dipper, and that small group of five shaped like the letter "W" is known as Cassiopeia. That really big formation over there with the long swooping curve is called Scorpio, and that large group is the great hunter Orion."

"Wow. That's cool."

"I think so too. Do you see those three bright stars in the middle of Orion that are almost in a straight line?"

"Yes."

"Those are called Orion's Belt, and the three stars just below them form his sword. Please try to always remember that, because you, Kristyn, and the twenty Mayans with us, were all born on a moon known as ₹-593-ʒπ-2-2 that circles around that faint star next to the tip of the sword."

Smiling with obvious delight, Hank nodded to confirm and said, "I'll remember, I promise." Then while pointing asked, "What is that thing around your neck Ross? I've never seen it before."

Looking at his young brother, named in honor of the man who inspired Ross to gaze upon the heavens, he reached to touch the symbol and said, "Well Hank, my grandfather gave me this and the necklace when I was a boy not much older than you. His father had given the symbol to him when he was a boy, and before that the symbol had belonged to the father of my alien friend. I kept them safe for many years, and then my alien friend did the same. Now he has given them back to me, and I hope that someday you and other members of our family will continue to keep them safe."

"That's cool, but what does the symbol mean?"

"To me the symbol represents limitless possibilities. It's a symbol of everything!"

Seated on the opposite side of Hank, Janet smiled while listening to the conversation between her two sons. Without warning, her peaceful moment was interrupted when she began to cough. Feeling her forehead, she looked over at both of her sons and said, "Well Ross, it looks like I'm paying the price for tending to your ailment so closely. My cough, and what feels like a slight fever, would imply that I have caught whatever bug has been making you feel so poorly."

SPECIAL PREVIEW

EVOLUTION SHIFT

BOOK THREE OF THE NEW WORLD SERIES

PREVIEW: EVOLUTION SHIFT

CHAPTER ONE
HALLUCINATIONS

His most recent battle had been extremely challenging for Ross, but Janet and Dr. Halley finally managed to break his stubborn high fever. There had been much concern for several hours, as throughout that time they had needed to pour nearly a dozen buckets of ice over Ross's body before his temperature and vital signs returned to normal levels. Once Ross had been stabilized, and then drifted off to sleep, Gabriela, Janet, Aurora, Hank, and even Tori Nobles, took turns watching over him.

Colt assumed the first watch after stating, "I swore a solemn oath many years ago to protect Ross, so respectfully, I will take on the majority of this task. I will not hinder any of you from providing comfort for him, but I must, as part of my own self-preservation, remain close by Ross's side."

The subject was never debated when Janet added, "You know it will be of little use to challenge my husband on this matter. His training as a secret service agent has made him fiercely loyal to the oath of protecting my son."

For the remainder of the day, and then throughout the entire night, Colt never left the side of his former boss. He slept on a few occasions when someone else had relieved him, but never for more than an hour. For those who knew him, Colt's actions came as no surprise. He had stood as a faithful sentinel for Ross throughout the years on ₹-593-ꝛ∪π-2-2, but the oath spoken of had occurred long before that on Earth. In all those countless times Colt had never showed any negative emotion, but this situation was different. When Janet came to relieve him for a break just after the first light of dawn, she reached up to wipe a tear from his cheek. Janet loved and admired the way Colt had always taken care of her eldest son, and knew that it was breaking his heart to see Ross in such a precarious state.

A few moments later, after Colt had fallen asleep, Janet heard Ross moan ever so slightly. She moved to his side with a wet towel for his forehead, and then smiled while breathing a sigh of relief when she saw his arm move a few inches under the covers. Privately, Janet had developed an ever growing concern that Ross might never awaken, but kept that horrific thought from Gabriela and everyone else. In spite of his favorable vital signs, Ross had remained motionless while sleeping for over eighteen hours since the fever had broken. Fortunately, Ross's slight arm movement had now made her concern moot.

Suddenly, and with relative ease, Ross rolled onto his side facing away from Janet. Then he unexpectedly uttered, "Jessica, it's time to wake up."

Janet was flabbergasted, and wondered if she had really heard Ross speak or was it simply a hallucination based on her own over exhaustion and wishful thinking.

The answer to her internal question came quickly, as Ross added, "Jessica, wake up! We need to hurry, or we won't have time for breakfast before Grandpa drives us to school."

Janet didn't quite know what to do, so she rubbed her eyes for clarity sake and began to lean in closer.

Then Ross, who was well accustomed to his little sister entering his room to wake him for school, became irritated. With no verbal response from her, Ross increased his tone and said, "Come on Jessica, quit fooling around and answer me. I want to tell you about a really weird dream I had last night."

Leaning back to her former position, Janet realized that she was not hallucinating. However, there was now a new cause for concern over Ross's condition. Although pleased that Ross had spoken three times, with words that had expressed coherent thought, it was disconcerting to her that none of his statements had any actual bearing on the present reality.

She sat motionless through several seconds of awkward silence, and then took a glance around the room to see if either Gabriela or Colt had been awakened by Ross. Neither showed any sign of consciousness, so Janet decided she would take a chance. Leaning forward once again, she whispered a response of, "Ross, Jessica can't hear you, because she isn't with us."

Ross rolled back over toward the soft voice, and then his eyes instantly grew larger. While shaking his head from side to side, Ross closed his eyes again in the hope of clearing away his vision of Janet. Unfortunately it didn't work, because when he re-opened his eyes, she was still there. Then Ross gulped and, much to Janet's surprise, asked, "Am I dead?"

Janet responded, "No you're not dead, although it was touch and go at times during the last few days to be sure."

"Well if I'm not dead, then this must be some sort of hallucination."

After placing her right index finger upon her lips so that Ross would respond more quietly, Janet asked, "A hallucination, why would you say that?"

"Because you can't possibly be here, you died almost four years ago!"

"Don't be ridiculous Ross, I'm very much alive."

"That's impossible. I remember the day in 1957 when dad told me about the car accident that took you from us."

Suddenly Janet realized that Ross was correct. Because he apparently believed that he and Jessica were still children living in central rural Texas, he really was having a hallucination. She once again glanced around to see if Gabriela or Colt had stirred, then tried to ascertain the depth of Ross's hallucination. Maintaining her soft tone, she asked, "You wanted to tell Jessica about a really weird dream you had last night, would you like me to go get her?"

Ross stared at his vision of Janet for a long moment, and then loudly asked, "Jessica, are you awake?"

Once again there was no response, but the increased volume of his question had been enough to wake Colt. Shifting himself from fully horizontal to a seated position, Colt then stretched and inquired, "What's going on?"

Janet turned toward her husband, and once again used her index finger to keep the room quiet. Then she repeated her question to Ross of, "Do you want me to go get Jessica?"

"I want to tell Jessica about my weird dream, but you can't possibly go get her because you are not real!"

While maintaining her best bedside manner, Janet said, "I understand Ross. If you believe that I'm a hallucination, then you should close your eyes until Jessica comes to wake you?"

With that Ross closed his eyes, and Janet could see his body relax. Colt, who was now standing, shrugged his shoulders and inquired, "What's going on with Ross?"

Janet moved toward him and replied, "This last bout of fever must have triggered something within him, because Ross is having a strange hallucination. I'll wake Gabriela and keep her out of his direct line of sight, but can you do me a favor?"

"Sure, what do you need?"

"We need a young girl who might pass for a childhood version of Jessica to determine the extent of this hallucination. Ross says he wants to tell Jessica about a weird dream he had last night, so Kristyn could really help us out. Could you please go get her and Natiya as quickly as possible, and explain what is going on?"

"Alright, I'll be back in a few minutes."

Upon their return Janet instructed Kristyn on exactly what she needed her to do, and then moved close enough to Ross so that she could hear everything that would be revealed about the dream. Kristyn then began her task by softly pushing on Ross's shoulder and continuously repeating the request of, "Wake up Ross, it's time to get ready for school."

Ross opened his eyes and smiled at the sight of the young girl. For the moment anyway, Janet's plan had worked. Ross immediately said, "Good morning Jessica, how are you?"

"I'm fine thanks, how did you sleep?"

"Great, but I had the weirdest dream."

"Was it scary?"

"Sometimes, but mostly it was just weird."

"Well what happened?"

"I dreamt that when we grew up, we were still best friends. I married Patty and then became an astronaut, and you were a lawyer. Then later on, when all three of us were much older, I became the President of the United States."

"You, the President?"

"Yep, but that's not the really weird part of the dream. When I was an astronaut on a moon mission I met an alien from outer space, and years later he helped some of us escape to another world when it looked like Earth might be destroyed."

"You're right, that is a weird dream."

"There's more. When we were old we got to see mom."

"What do you mean?"

"In my dream, mom didn't die in the car accident. The aliens I mentioned had abducted her and kept her in captivity for a long time."

"They didn't hurt her did they?"

"No she was fine, and she didn't get very much older while she was held captive either. She still looked as pretty as she does in that picture of the four of us next to dad's bed."

"Well that's good, what happened next?"

"The aliens took us to live on a moon in a faraway solar system, and she came with us."

"That sounds nice."

"It was great and I'll tell you more about it later, but for now we need to get ready for school."

Janet had heard enough, and dried the tears in her eyes before advancing to Kristyn's side. Then she softly said, "Ross, everything that you just told Kristyn is true. It wasn't a dream, all of that really happened."

Once again faced with an image of his mother Janet that he thought to be a hallucination, Ross became visibly rattled. Then he looked at the young girl posing as Jessica, and asked her, "Who is Kristyn?"

"I'm Kristyn!"

"No you're not, you're Jessica."

Janet moved closer to Ross, and said, "It's true Ross. This is not 1961, and you are not a boy any longer."

Now looking even more scared by the current moment, Ross stated, "This is not happening. None of this is real."

Janet's bedside manner was beginning to wear thin, so she took a deep breath to collect herself. Then she said, "Ross, if you don't believe us, then just pull one of your arms out from under the covers."

After a reluctant moment, Ross complied with the request of his hallucination. What he saw instantly shocked him back into the reality of the present moment, as he was staring at the frail and wrinkled arm of an old man. After briefly scanning his surroundings for familiar artifacts that could perhaps refute the obvious, Ross returned his gaze toward Kristyn and said, "You're not Jessica, who are you?"

"I'm Kristyn, don't you remember me?"

Then Ross glared at Janet and said, "I'm an old man!"

From her unseen position some fifteen feet behind him, Gabriela replied, "Oh my dear husband. You most certainly are an old man, and you have been acting as stubborn as always."

Janet breathed a sigh of relief when Ross exclaimed, "That sounded like Gabriela!"

Moving to his side, Gabriela replied, "Yes Ross, it's me."

The relief then took hold of Colt when Ross added, "We are all back on Earth, aren't we?"

Now firmly clasping his frail and exposed hand, Gabriela leaned toward her husband and kissed him. Then she replied, "Yes we are Ross, and it's because of you."

ABOUT THE AUTHOR

Kurt possesses a spirit of adventure, which drives his thirst for experiencing new places and activities. He maintains a love for the great outdoors, and enjoys traveling whenever his schedule permits. One of his favorite activities is hiking in the clean mountain air, where the tranquil locations provide him with an opportunity to develop characters and storylines for his books. Kurt currently resides in Northern Nevada, where he and his wife have lived for more than a decade.

CPSIA information can be obtained
at www.ICGtesting.com
Printed in the USA
FFOW02n1514080618
47049234-49374FF